TWO

STEVE SWARINGEN

Spears & Cornelius Publishing

ISBN: 0-9990958-0-3
ISBN-13: 978-0-9990958-0-5

Visit the author's website at SteveSwaringen.com

Second Edition

To you,
the ardent reader,
the inquisitive learner,
the introspective intellectual,
the passionate thinker.
That rare soul who actually bothers to read the dedication.
Enjoy.

ONE

Commander David Decker was in a hurry, but attention was something he didn't want to attract.

Several joggers wound their way down the path around the parade ground as he walked, the grass still wet from an early-morning spring shower. The clouds were quickly dissipating, promising a sunny day, and a flock of mockingbirds danced overhead, darting in and out of a grove of pecan trees in subtle bloom.

Decker ignored all this. He moved with a measured pace and tried to remain inconspicuous as he checked all the faces, looking for anyone he might recognize—anyone who might recognize him.

As he came around a grove of large trees, he saw Admiral Frasier sitting on a bench, reading from a tablet.

Decker approached casually and sat on the end opposite Frasier, his jaw clenched as he waited for the admiral to acknowledge his presence.

Without looking up, Frasier said, "On days like this it's good to find an excuse to get outside and enjoy nature."

Decker studiously looked at the trees. "Thank you for making time to see me on short notice, Admiral."

"What's on your mind, Commander?"

"I need to know what's going on."

The admiral looked askance at him. "I beg your pardon?"

"Sixteen hours ago I get orders to surface my boat in open waters under clear skies in broad daylight. Some lieutenant drops onto my deck from a helo and hands me sealed orders to turn the *Sam Houston* over to my XO and board the helo for immediate extraction. No explanation. They bring me here, tell me to get cleaned up and ready for a VIP meeting in two hours. What's going on?"

Frasier looked away from his tablet toward the trees. "I'd like to tell you that if I knew anything I'd tell you, but we both know that's not the way things work in the navy. Some things are 'need to know.'" He rubbed the back of his neck. "It appears some of us don't."

Frasier bit the inside of his cheek as a squirrel stopped its journey up the side of a tree and turned to look at them. "I was told …"

He broke off the sentence as a jogger approached their bench. After the man passed, he continued. "I was told they needed you temporarily for a special assignment. I asked why. They said the details were classified, and to go back to my desk and figure out how to backfill while you were away."

This wasn't helping. Decker's mind raced, trying to imagine what could be happening—and what he could do about it.

Frasier looked down at his tablet. "Do you have any concerns about leaving Sandoval in charge?"

"What?" Decker's head flinched back. "No, he's absolutely up to the task. You've seen my personnel reports. In my opinion, he's ready for a command of his own."

For the first time during their conversation, the admiral looked directly at him. "David, I think I understand what you're worried about. You've been passed over for promotion twice; you're up for consideration the third time. But this is not how that goes down. Whether the outcome is promotion or retirement, this is not how that happens. Something else is going on here."

Decker winced, but he knew the admiral was right. It probably wasn't his career on the line. But he still didn't know what was going on, and he didn't like being in the dark.

He glanced at his watch and realized he was out of time.

Both men stood and Decker saluted. Frasier returned the salute and extended his hand. Decker accepted the gesture. "If anything happens to me, sir, I'd appreciate it if you'd keep Sandoval in mind for command of the *Sam Houston*. He's earned it."

3

Frasier smiled. "A lot of men have earned it, but I'm holding that one for your imminent return. Fair winds and following seas, Commander."

Day -2, 0850 Hours

"Commander Decker. Petty Officer Weaver, sir," the young woman said as she saluted.

"I've been asked to escort you to your meeting, Commander. If you'll follow me."

Decker smiled and gestured for her to lead the way. He followed her across the lobby toward a security checkpoint, wishing he was fifteen years younger.

They entered an elevator, where she pressed the button for the top floor and presented her face to an iris scanner. The elevator started climbing.

"So, where are we going?"

He saw the hint of a smile on her face.

"A secure conference room on the fifteenth floor, Commander."

Not exactly a helpful answer, he thought.

"And what is your role here?"

She looked at him with that almost-smile again. He decided it was her nature to smile a lot, and it took all the discipline the navy could instill in her to restrain it.

"To get you to the conference room on the fifteenth floor, Commander."

Why is everything a riddle today?

A chime announced their arrival. The doors opened into a small reception area with a desk facing the elevator and a seating area off to the right. A man sat behind the desk, and armed MPs stood on either side of the only other door leading out of the reception area. Decker recognized two men in naval uniforms who were seated in a waiting area.

"Commander Steadman. Chief Petty Officer Guerrero. What brings you two troublemakers here?"

Both men rose from their seats and turned toward him. They smiled at each other and bumped fists. Turning back to face Decker, grins gone from their faces, they saluted. Steadman deadpanned, "That's classified, sir. Need-to-know."

Decker shook his head and returned the salute. He opened his mouth to speak when Weaver interrupted. "The secretary of defense is ready to see you now, Commander Decker."

Decker turned to follow Weaver. Three steps later he stopped mid-stride. "The who?"

She looked back over her shoulder at him with that almost-smile. "This way, Commander."

She led him to a corner office on the top floor. A secretary posted outside waved them in. Weaver opened the door and stood back for him to enter.

This can't be good.

Decker's career flashed through his mind. He was the lowly commander of an unremarkable reconnaissance submarine, twice passed over for promotion. He couldn't think of anything, good or bad, that he'd done that would warrant being called in for a personal meeting with the secretary of defense.

Once more into the breach.

He stepped forward into the office.

TWO

The room was a contradiction. The walls and furnishings were elegant: dark-stained raised wood paneling, built-in bookcases, a large oak desk and a credenza built to match the walls, a small conference table surrounded by plush leather chairs, and hardwood flooring with a couple of area rugs.

But decoration was nowhere to be seen. No pictures. No plaques. No trophies. Not even any books in the bookcases. Just a couple of folders stacked on one corner of the desk, as though the occupant had just moved in and expected to move out just as quickly.

Except that Decker had seen the man's name stenciled on the door.

A haggard-faced soldier stood from behind the desk and came around to greet him.

"Commander Decker. It's a pleasure to finally meet you." He extended his hand.

"Secretary Rutledge. It's an honor, sir."

7

Rutledge motioned Decker toward the conference table on the other side of the room. "I imagine you're wondering why you're here."

"That would be at the top of my list, sir."

Rutledge smiled and turned toward a large screen mounted on the wall behind the conference table. "I have a few satellite reconnaissance images I'd like you to take a look at." He activated the monitor and looked at Decker. "Tell me what you see."

Decker studied the image on the monitor. "I'm not an intelligence analyst, sir, but I see a computer-generated fake. And not a very good one."

Rutledge's smile morphed into a smirk. "Explain."

Decker motioned to the screen. "Here on the night side of the planet … there are no lights anywhere. There are certainly still some dark places on Earth at night, but nowhere is there an expanse that large without any lighting visible from space. And here, on the day side, the coastlines are all wrong."

Rutledge turned back toward the monitor. "No argument, on either count. Nevertheless, the images are real."

Decker's frustration was mounting. Nothing in the last twenty-four hours made any sense. Now, with his career already on the rocks, he was on the verge of getting into an argument with a man second only to the president in the chain of command—over some artist's rendering.

Rutledge pointed to the screen. "What you see was taken by a satellite we placed in orbit around a planet in a solar system approximately fifty-seven light-years from here."

Decker's mind jumped to the obvious conclusion. *Great. Now I have to tell the secretary he's an idiot who's been hoodwinked by a computer nerd with an overactive imagination.*

He decided to pursue a more diplomatic tack. "Sir, assuming we had the technology to send and receive signals over that distance, these images would have to have been sent fifty-seven years ago. We certainly didn't have the technology then. Beyond that, it would take thousands of years to get a satellite from Earth to this hypothetical planet, even if we knew how."

Rutledge cracked a wry smile. "That was yesterday."

He handed Decker a folder with classified markings. "Your orders are to have your team there the day after tomorrow."

Day -2, 0930 Hours

The lights were still up when Decker walked into the small briefing room. Four rows of theater seating faced the front where a large screen stood behind a small table. Steadman, Guerrero, and Weaver had taken seats in the front row, along with two civilians he didn't recognize.

Decker took an empty seat at one end.

An army general joined them. Decker, Steadman, Guerrero, and Weaver all snapped to attention and saluted.

The general returned the salute and then walked over to Decker, extending his hand. "Commander. General Fleming. I've been looking forward to meeting you."

Decker and the general shook hands, then Fleming motioned for everyone to sit.

"Everything you're about to hear is classified at the highest level. These things are not to be discussed outside a secure facility and not with anyone who is not now in this room or specifically authorized by me."

He turned and looked to one of the civilians sitting on the other end of the front row. "Dr. Kreitzman, if you please?"

Fleming took a seat behind Decker alone on the second row as Kreitzman moved to the front of the room.

Kreitzman was a gaunt man who appeared to be in his middle sixties. He didn't look ill so much as malnourished —like he had a hard time remembering to stop working and eat.

The old man stood at one end of the table to address the room. He tapped a button on the console set into the table, causing the room lighting to dim and an image to display on the monitor. The scene was a large lab with complex equipment strung all over the room in a jerry-rigged fashion.

"Gentlemen, and lady." Kreitzman smiled, nodding to Weaver. "Approximately six months ago we began testing a new technology that promised to allow instantaneous transport of objects across arbitrary distances. We began by transporting a block of wood across the room. It worked."

Kreitzman tapped another button. The image changed to a split-screen video of two rooms. Each room had a table in the foreground with a complex apparatus. The table on the left had a metal box in the middle of the equipment. "So we transported a computer to the next building." A moment later the box disappeared from the room on the left and simultaneously appeared in the room on the right.

The setting changed again. Two different rooms now, with two different tables. Instead of a metal box, there was now a small cage with a live mouse.

"Then a mouse to the next city."

The screen went blank. "Feeling adventurous, we borrowed a new military satellite that was scheduled for launch on a traditional booster and inserted it directly into orbit. That worked so well, we sent a similar satellite into orbit around Mars. After a week, we brought it back and downloaded the highest-resolution imaging of the surface of Mars ever recorded."

Kreitzman tapped again and a series of high-resolution images of various surface features of Mars flashed up.

"We felt the next logical step was to send a probe to Pluto, so we borrowed another satellite from the production pipeline, configured it to take high-resolution, multispectral images of anything it could see, and shipped it out. We pulled it back twenty-four hours later."

11

Kreitzman looked out at his audience. "That's when things became really interesting."

Dr. Kreitzman tapped another button. The screen changed, showing the sun from a great distance. There were a few other faint objects barely visible, highlighted by annotations added to the image. "The first thing we noticed was that Pluto was nowhere in sight. Then we noticed the sun was much closer to the satellite than expected. We assumed we'd made an error in targeting and just misplaced the satellite within the solar system. But then we noticed the spectrum of the star was wrong."

The image changed to a comparison of two spectrographs, highlighting differences.

"At this point, I asked Mr. Swenson"—Kreitzman nodded toward the other civilian in the front row—"who was responsible for configuring the transit portal, to double-check his calculations. He advised me that it was not necessary to recheck the calculations—the satellite had gone where it had been told to go. Mr. Swenson, it turns out, had gone rogue on us."

Everyone turned to look at Swenson, who shifted uncomfortably in his chair as he tried to suppress a smirk.

Nothing about the man was remotely military. He looked more like a thirty-year-old kid who still played video games in his mother's basement.

Kreitzman continued. "It seems that Mr. Swenson believed we lacked imagination, only shooting for Pluto. He searched through published astronomical studies to find what he considered the best candidate for an 'Earth-like' extra-solar planet. Keep in mind that these studies were based entirely on optical and radiological studies from Earth-based and near-Earth observatories. Being unable to predict the exact orbital location of said planet, he programmed the portal to place the probe above the orbital plane directly above the star, giving the best chance to observe whatever planets were present without *a priori* knowledge of their location.

"This revelation obviously led us to look at the collected data in a different way. For the first time, we had a close-up look at another star. And for the first time, we had a relatively close-up look at planets in another solar system. The distance of the probe from the planets it captured meant there was very little detail in the images collected, so we focused more closely on what we could observe of the star. After assessing its spectrum and size, we realized one planet was, indeed, in the habitable zone. We only had twenty-four hours of data, so we could only roughly estimate the shape and speed of the planet's orbit."

Dr. Kreitzman updated the image to zoom in on the planet with a time-lapse video. "When we focused our attention on this planet, we noticed patches of white visible on the planet. And we noticed they were shifting. Like clouds. That meant it had an atmosphere. And water vapor. And water."

Kreitzman paused as though that was a profound statement. No one in the room reacted, leading Decker to believe the others either already knew about this or, like himself, had no idea why that would be significant.

Kreitzman continued. "Now we had enough information to predict the location of the planet with sufficient accuracy to put the probe in orbit around it. We reconfigured the satellite to map the entire planet. We shipped it out and let it run for a full week."

The screen went dark again.

"That was a long week back here on Earth." Kreitzman scanned his audience again. "Gentlemen, this —" he tapped another button "—is Two."

The screen changed to a simulated time-lapse flyby of the planet constructed from the image data collected by the satellite. It began at a significant distance with the globe filling about half the screen, spinning on its axis. The similarities to Earth were uncanny. The surface was about two-thirds ocean with a few continents and some smaller islands. Visible ice caps exhibited on both poles. Variations in color were suggestive of deserts, forests, grasslands, mountains, streams, and lakes.

After a minute or so, the perspective shifted and zoomed in for a closer look. Decker felt like he was sitting in a space capsule, racing toward the planet. Seemingly just before crashing into the ocean, his imaginary spacecraft suddenly stopped falling and shot out across the water.

Decker judged the altitude to be about a mile. As he approached the coastline, he thought he might have seen creatures in the water but they flew by so fast he couldn't be sure. Sandy beaches leading into the foothills of a rocky mountain range. Tall, tall trees. Following a streambed up through mountain passes. Snowcaps melting, feeding the stream. Down the other side, over foothills, and onto an open plain covered in green grass and painted with a patchwork of colorful flowers.

Had he seen animals grazing back there?

The camera slowed to a stop and seemed to perch itself above a large grassy clearing. It began a slow spin, capturing the surrounding landscape.

The clearing appeared to be a relatively flat area nestled among a range of low hills. Alternating patches of grass, wildflowers, and small trees covered the hills.

Not far in the distance a river cut through the landscape, and beyond that a range of much taller mountains. Tall trees, broken in a few places by rocky patches, covered the slopes. A double waterfall broke over a high cliff as its waters rushed to join the river.

Kreitzman left this final image on the screen and paused for a full minute to let this all sink in. "Gentlemen, God has opened a door for us. We must decide whether we have the courage to walk through."

THREE

Kreitzman's eyes sparkled. "Questions?"

Guerrero piped up first. "What are *we* doing here?"

Never afraid to get to the point, thought Decker.

Alejandro "Alex" Guerrero always made Decker think of a mil-spec firecracker whose fuse had already been lit. Contrary to this image, and to Guerrero's credit, Decker had never seen him explode. He was glad to have him on the team.

"I'll take that one." General Fleming stood from his seat on the second row and came to the other end of the table. "You may have noticed that Dr. Kreitzman said he could transport 'objects' using this technology. So far he and his team have not worked out a way to send signals. Everything we've learned so far has been by sending an automated probe, letting it collect data, and then bringing it back for analysis. Then we send another probe configured to help answer the questions raised by the last. We need to accelerate that process dramatically. The only way to do that is to put people on the ground on the other side who can drive the process in real time."

"But why us?" Guerrero looked around the room. "I don't know Mr. Swenson here, but with all due respect to Commanders Decker and Steadman, Petty Officer Weaver, and myself, science is not exactly in our wheelhouse."

General Fleming smiled. "A very astute observation." He leaned against the edge of the table. "The first astronauts were chosen from elite military backgrounds. The one thing they knew about going into space was that they didn't know what they were doing. To deal with the inherent risks, they needed people who were fit, strong, disciplined, courageous, and intelligent. Still today, military special forces are the easiest places to find such people. You five are not here to study the planet. You're here to establish a base camp—a beachhead of sorts—for the second half of your team."

He nodded toward Guerrero. "You and Commander Steadman will provide force protection for the rest of your team. I should say that at present we're not aware of any specific threats you'll face, but right now what we don't know far exceeds what we do know. Petty Officer Weaver will be managing the collection of data and analysis for return to Earth, as well as requisitions for equipment and supplies should you find you need things we didn't anticipate. Mr. Swenson is your technical expert on the transit portal and other advanced technology you'll be using. Commander Decker will have operational command of the mission.

"The four of you"—Fleming gestured to indicate Decker, Steadman, Guerrero, and Swenson—"will be the first team. The current plan is for you to transit the day after tomorrow. You'll have three days to secure the area and establish your base camp. Then the rest of your team, five scientists and Petty Officer Weaver, will join you."

Guerrero shifted in his seat. "You said you've sent 'objects' through this thing. Dr. Kreitzman mentioned a mouse. Have you sent any people through it?"

Fleming opened his mouth to reply, but Swenson jumped in first. "Yes. Several. I've personally been through it five times. It's nothing to worry about."

Guerrero tilted his head and pursed his lips.

"Rules of Engagement?" Steadman asked.

Commander Christopher "Chris" Steadman was one of the best strategists and tacticians Decker had worked with. As commander of a reconnaissance submarine, Decker frequently participated in the insertion and extraction of special forces teams on clandestine missions. He had worked with Steadman and Guerrero before, and sometimes on missions that went south. Decker couldn't think of anyone he'd rather have on his side if a mission went sideways.

Fleming leaned back against the edge of the table as he looked at Steadman. "That, Commander Steadman, is a very complex question. The difficulty in answering it is the primary reason you're not leaving today. The six of us"—Fleming made a sweeping gesture that included everyone except Dr. Kreitzman—"will spend a good part of the rest of today and tomorrow exploring that question in great detail. For now, suffice it to say that we're not invaders or conquerors. We're explorers. If we find any indications of intelligent life, we're there to make friends, not take their stuff. So far we've seen no signs of intelligence, but that's part of why we're sending you and the scientific team that will follow."

Steadman nodded. "And how long will we be deployed?"

"Another good question without a clear answer. Our scientific advisers are asking for three months to complete an initial assessment. That's the plan of record. You've heard it said that no plan survives first contact with the enemy. You might be there three months. You might be there three minutes."

Decker felt his scalp prickle. "When will we meet the rest of our team?"

Fleming ducked his head before he looked back up at Decker. "That's a bit of a challenge. We're pulling this together double-quick. You five were relatively easy. We knew where to find you and had a significant degree of confidence in your capabilities and cooperation. The scientists we're recruiting are all civilian. They're spread all over the country. They have jobs and in some cases families. Most of them have no history of security clearance. We have a massive effort underway to vet and recruit each of them, but they won't be here until after you leave. You'll meet them when they arrive on the planet."

Decker's stomach churned.

Fleming continued. "In the meantime, Commander, Petty Officer Weaver will provide you whatever background information we have on each of them." Fleming looked at his watch. "We'll continue this discussion after lunch. Petty Officer Weaver will escort you all to the cafeteria. I remind you that you are not to discuss these matters outside a secure facility, which the cafeteria is not. After you finish there, Weaver will bring you to another secure conference room. Gentlemen."

Fleming gestured toward the briefing room door.

Everyone stood and began making their way out of the room. The general caught Decker's arm as he passed. "Commander, if I could keep you for a moment."

Decker held back and waited for the rest of the group to leave before closing the door. "Sir."

Fleming sat on the edge of the table and motioned Decker to a seat on the front row. "You appear to have concerns you haven't expressed."

Decker moved toward the seat but didn't take it. "Why the big hurry? This is the wrong way to put together an operation that requires a high-functioning team. We need people who know each other, understand each other's strengths and weaknesses, know how to work together. That planet's been there for billions of years. It isn't going anywhere."

The general moved from the table to another seat on the front row, resting his elbows on his knees and rubbing his eyes. He again motioned Decker to an empty chair. After Decker sat, Fleming said, "The problem isn't on that planet, it's on this one."

Fleming ran one hand over the stubble on his head. "This transport portal isn't the first revolutionary technology Dr. Kreitzman brought us. In the last ten years, he's made incredible strides in power generation, power distribution, and even propulsion. All still classified at the highest level. His power technology makes nuclear energy look like a beleaguered firefly."

Fleming looked at Decker. "We upgraded your submarine with a new power plant just last year. Zero maintenance. No detectable radiation signature. No intrinsic waste heat. Ignoring other concerns, you could stay submerged for decades. In the right hands, it provides safe, clean, cheap, and almost unlimited electricity. In the wrong hands ... well, we just can't let this technology get into the wrong hands. So we keep it secret and limit distribution of knowledge to only a handful of people. No one but Kreitzman himself knows the principles behind it."

Fleming pursed his lips and furrowed his brow. "But we have reason to believe we have a leak." His hands opened as he rested his forearms on his knees. "Nothing indicates that details have been exposed, but there's a lot of chatter suggesting more than one foreign government has gotten wind we have something new cooking in electrical power plants. It's creating a lot of stress in diplomatic circles, especially with our Middle Eastern friends who are still heavily invested in the world's continuing dependence on their petroleum reserves.

Fleming sat up straight and shook his head. "This secret, on the other hand, is too big to keep. There's just no way this doesn't eventually leak. Someone will confide in a spouse, a parent, a sibling, a girlfriend. Word will get out. And when it does, everyone will to want a piece of it."

Decker's posture stiffened. "How does sending this team on such short notice change that? The secret is still too big to keep. In fact, it only gets bigger."

Fleming pushed his shoulders back. "It doesn't change it. But at least we'll know what we have so we can come to the table with a considered strategy for how we share this new planet. It just might make the difference in whether we destroy our own planet fighting over who gets the new one or find a new reason to collaborate so we can all prosper together." He tapped the arms of his chair with his palms. "We need to know what we have before word gets out."

Decker rubbed his temple. "You said a minute ago that Kreitzman is the only one who knows how this stuff works. Where are we if something happens to him?"

Fleming looked Decker in the eye. "It's a concern. That one sits on the president's desk. The way it was explained to me, there's an inherent conflict between the national security interest of the state and the private property interest of Dr. Kreitzman. The state wants to possess the technology so it will be assured access in the event Kreitzman becomes unable, or unwilling, to provide it. But the notion of private property, in this case, private intellectual property, is one of the fundamental principles on which we founded our republic. He invented it. It's his idea. He has the right to decide who gets to use it and how. At least as long as he doesn't do anything that could be construed as a threat to others."

Decker took a deep breath and let it out slowly. "You said there might be leaks. Any chance that Kreitzman himself may be shopping this around?"

Fleming shook his head. "I can't rule it out, but I doubt it. I've been working closely with him for several months now. He's as solid as they come. He's already raking in more money than most national governments just selling electricity. According to him, a stable world is better for business than a world at war. Impoverished and decimated populations don't have money for electricity. Or high-tech weapons, for that matter. From my perspective, it's a sword that cuts both ways. It adds risk to the program that there's no backup if something happens to him. But backups would mean a much higher risk of leaks. I've met few people I would trust more with a secret like this than Dr. Kreitzman."

Decker looked down at his shoes. "Why me?"

The general looked sideways at him. "Why not some younger up-and-coming commander looking for a shortcut to make captain? You already put your finger on

23

it. This is not the right way to do this. Frankly, I worry less about the unknowns you'll face on a planet fifty-seven light-years from Earth, never touched by human hands, than I worry about the challenges I know you'll face trying to wrangle this herd of stray cats. The people in the room today are solid. You've worked with Steadman and Guerrero before. Weaver and Swenson have my confidence as well. The rest of the 'team' is almost by definition a collection of showboats all out to exceed the others in making a name for themselves."

Fleming turned to face Decker directly. "I need someone who can mold them into—as you called it—a high-functioning team, without having to resort to vain threats of military discipline. Convince them that there's more to be gained by fully investing themselves in the success of the team and the mission than by pursuing their own self-interest. Admiral Frasier's personnel reports say that's what you do best."

Frasier looked Decker in the eyes. "Now I need to know, Commander, are you the man?"

Decker didn't hesitate. "Yes sir."

FOUR

"Gentlemen, this is your last chance to back out. It's a big commitment."

Decker's words hung in the air in the small spherical chamber as the team ran through a final check of their equipment.

Guerrero rechecked the clip on his rifle for the third time. "No chance, Skipper. I joined the navy to see the world. True, it was *this* world I expected to see, but I'm not about to turn down the chance to be the first human to set foot on another planet."

Steadman laughed. "You won't be the first, Sherlock. We all four transfer together. At the same time. You'll just be one of the first four."

Guerrero chunked a cereal bar from his pack at Steadman, who deftly snatched it out of the air inches in front of his face. Steadman stuffed the snack into a pocket with a lighthearted "Thanks."

Guerrero sealed his pack. "The way I see it, no one will be able to prove that I didn't get there some infinitesimal fraction of an instant before either of you. I got there first. That's my story, and I'm stickin' to it."

Decker shook his head. "And you, Chris?"

"Same here, Skipper. I didn't sign up to read about it in *Star and Stripes*. Let's stop talking and push the button."

Decker turned his attention to the only civilian on his advance team. "Mr. Swenson?"

"Yes, sir." Rusty Swenson's head popped up, causing him to lose his balance as he struggled under the weight of his pack while trying to adjust the straps. "I'm in. I just hope I don't have to carry this pack very far."

Guerrero smirked as he hefted Swenson's pack higher onto his shoulders while Steadman tightened the straps.

"You'll do fine, Mr. Swenson," Steadman said.

Decker nodded as the others pulled on their packs and shouldered their rifles. They took one last look around the room at the crates of supplies and equipment around them. Everything seemed to be in order. "Control Room, we're good to go. Push the button."

A disembodied voice echoed through the room. "Roger that. All indicators are green. Remember to watch the writing on the wall. When you see it change, you'll know the transition is complete."

Three men in jungle camouflage turned toward the blank spot on the wall where someone had scrawled the word *ONE* with blue chalk. Swenson focused his attention on the other three.

"Ten seconds to transfer. Good luck, gentlemen. Five … four … three … two … one. Initiating tr—"

FIVE

Swenson stumbled as he felt the floor suddenly pushing up against him.

The military men fared better, maintaining their footing but reacting nonetheless. Steadman and Guerrero both pulled their rifles around to the ready. Decker braced himself against a stack of shipping crates.

Steadman spread his feet for more stable footing. "What's happening? Why are we climbing?"

Swenson tried hard not to laugh. "We're not. It's just the increased gravity. The sensation is the same as standing in an elevator car as it accelerates upward, but in this case it's due to gravity, not motion."

Steadman and Guerrero both glared at Swenson, who ducked his head. "What? Didn't we mention that gravity would be ten percent higher here?"

Decker pursed his lips and shook his head. Steadman and Guerrero stowed their rifles.

Guerrero read the word scrawled in green chalk. "Two. Is that the best they could do for a name for this place?"

Decker looked around the room. "I guess that's the best they could do on short notice. From what I gather, there are a lot of people arguing over who gets to pick the official name. I think anyone in a position of authority is worried about bigger issues right now."

"I think the idea was to think of this chamber like an elevator car," Swenson said. "Earth is the first floor. This planet is the second."

Guerrero lifted an eyebrow as he looked at Swenson. "Whose idea was that?"

Swenson shoved his hands in his pockets and shrugged.

Decker looked at the engineer. "Are we ready to take a peek outside?"

It took Swenson a moment to realize they were waiting for him.

He lurched toward a console set into the wall below the chalk sign, toppling over the chair as he tried to sit.

"Sorry, sir," Swenson said as he powered up the console.

Decker shook his head.

All four men watched as the monitor produced a panoramic view of the area surrounding the transport pod.

A brilliant green grass that appeared to be about ankle deep covered the area. Patches of flowers of various colors and varieties dotted the landscape. A river ran a quarter mile to the west. On the other side, the forested foothills of a mountain range pocked with rocky patches rose above the horizon.

Steadman gestured toward the monitor. "This looks exactly like the final scene from Dr. Kreitzman's simulation."

Swenson looked up from his console. "It is. This transit pod has been here for several weeks. The image data for the final scene of the flyby was collected here."

"But we just got here," Guerrero said. "In this pod. How can it have been here for several weeks?"

Swenson pointed to the sign on the wall. "This is not the chamber we were in a few minutes ago on Earth. That chamber is still on Earth. Only the contents moved. That's why the writing on the wall is different."

He returned his attention to the instrument readouts. "Looks like we're right on schedule. The sun is just above the horizon and rising. Clear skies. Light breeze. Cool, but not cold. Everything nearby looks just like the images collected by the surveys."

Decker placed a hand on Swenson's shoulder. "Launch the drones."

Swenson turned back to his console. "Before I open the door, I need to equalize air pressure. This will just take a few seconds, but you'll probably feel it in your ears. Something like what you experience during descent and final approach when you fly in an airplane."

29

He pressed a few buttons. A faint hiss of air faded away as Swenson's console beeped. "Pressure equalized. Cracking the hatch."

A round section of the wall of the spherical chamber cracked open, hinged at the bottom. A crescent of bright sunlight formed along the top edge and quickly grew. He opened the hatch until the crack was about two feet wide at the top.

"Launching the drones." A collection of eight dark spheres, each about eighteen inches in diameter, levitated out of cradles and flew out through the opening in the hatch.

As soon as the last drone left, Swenson closed and resealed the hatch.

Everyone turned their attention to a large side monitor on the console. Live video feeds from the eight drones reported their progress as they spread out and surveyed the area in a prearranged pattern.

Guerrero gestured at the screen. "How do those things fly?"

"Pixie dust," Swenson said.

Guerrero gave him a smoldering look.

Swenson met his gaze. "Sorry, sir, but that's classified."

Guerrero looked to Decker, who ignored him. "What are we learning, Mr. Swenson?"

"The computer is building up a more detailed map of our immediate area. Terrain, vegetation. Especially looking for animal life on the assumption that animals are more likely to be a threat to us than plants. It will take a few more minutes to complete the initial survey. Then we can review the results and decide how to proceed."

Swenson turned back to Guerrero. "If it's any consolation, he won't tell me how they work either."

Guerrero gave him a pat on the shoulder and went back to watching the monitors.

"Hey! Go back." Guerrero pointed to one of the video feeds. "This one here. I think I just saw a squirrel!"

Swenson followed Guerrero's finger. That particular drone was surveying one of the wooded areas in the foothills. "We need to let the drones finish their survey, but I can rewind that stream here on the main monitor."

The video in question popped up full screen on the center monitor and started rolling backward.

"There!" Guerrero saw it again. Swenson looped the short segment of video as the drone swept past the tree. A small furry animal, about the size of a squirrel, was climbing the tree. As the drone floated past, the creature turned its head and looked directly at the drone. Its puffy cheeks made it look like it had a mouthful of nuts.

"What's a squirrel doing here?" Guerrero asked.

"Well, it's premature to say that's a squirrel," Swenson said. "We'd need our zoologist to take a closer look at it. But there's no question it looks a whole lot like an Earth squirrel. That's why they wanted to get people on the ground here. The data coming back from the automated probes looked a lot more Earth-like than anyone expected."

TWO

Decker stepped back from the console. "How about this theory, Mr. Swenson? This is all a hoax. We're still on Earth."

SIX

Swenson turned to look at Decker. He'd expected this at some point—he'd considered that possibility many times himself.

"Based on the information currently available, that's a valid theory that deserves consideration. In fact, I would agree that the preponderance of evidence points exactly there. Ultimately, you'll have to draw your own conclusions, Commander."

Decker stared down at Swenson. "What do you believe?"

Swenson leaned back in his chair as he looked up at Decker's imposing figure. "When Dr. Kreitzman recounted the story of how we got to this point, he presented my motivations for retargeting the Pluto probe as he understood them—as I explained them to him. There was some truth in it. In effect, that I thought to go for Pluto lacked imagination. But the primary motivation for me was to test this theory that this might all be an elaborate hoax. Everything I'd seen seemed to be on the

33

up-and-up, and yet the claims were incredible. The evidence, especially when we started going off-planet with the experiments, could easily have been faked. So I devised a way to test that theory. The plan was to send the probe to Pluto, take pictures, and bring it back. If I shipped it somewhere else, without telling anyone, and it came back with Pluto pictures, I would have evidence of fraud. If it instead came back with data consistent with where I sent the probe, which no one else knew in advance, that would make a strong case the technology was real.

"To be fair, I didn't expect we'd actually find a habitable planet. I would have been happy just to see a different star and no Pluto. Also to be fair, I can't absolutely rule out the possibility that during the twenty-four hours while the first probe was collecting data, someone discovered the change in destination and acted quickly to construct a new data payload to support the hypothetical hoax. At the end of the day, almost everything we believe is a matter of faith, of believing something you can't prove. As soon as you think you have, you can always conceive a way to fabricate the results on which your belief is predicated. What you ultimately believe is some combination of wishful thinking—what you want to believe—and choosing the belief that explains the facts with the smallest appeal to faith. I believe we're on another planet, a real planet, fifty-seven light-years from Earth. A planet that is not Earth, but is remarkably similar. Having said that, I think you have to consider the possibility I may be in on this hypothetical conspiracy."

Decker nodded. "Fair enough, but if this is real, how did it come to be so similar to Earth?"

"That's the ultimate question. We may find an answer out there." Swenson motioned toward the hatch. "But my guess is we'll never know for sure. Without a testable theory, we have no strategy for finding an answer. That's why we've only been tasked with cataloging what's here, not determining how it came to be."

Swenson's console beeped.

He turned in his chair to see the results of the survey. "Most everything looks just like the earlier automated surveys on which we based our plan."

Steadman stepped forward to look at the console. "*Most* everything?"

Swenson scrolled through the data. "Yeah. We might have a problem here."

SEVEN

Swenson tapped a few buttons and a new video popped up on the monitor. "This was taken in the grove near where we saw Guerrero's squirrel. This animal wasn't seen in any of the earlier data."

What looked like an adult bear was visible under a fruit tree. It was standing on its hind legs and pulling down a sizable branch.

"The computer estimates it at about five foot six standing up, probably about five hundred and fifty pounds. That would make it slightly small for an adult Earth black bear, but keep in mind that it's acclimated to the increased gravity here. I would expect it to be every bit as strong as any bear on Earth."

Decker leaned in for a closer look. "Why did the earlier surveys miss it?"

"Unknown." Swenson ran his fingers through his hair. "If it were in this area, it would be hard to miss. Most likely that means it wasn't here during those surveys. It may just be foraging for food. Maybe the fruits have just begun to ripen."

Decker turned to look at Steadman and Guerrero. "Is it a threat?"

Steadman tilted his head. "It certainly has the means. We have the firepower to counteract, but that would be a last resort. The question is whether it would have motive to attack us. And whether there's anything less confrontational we could do to avoid conflict."

Decker put a hand on Swenson's shoulder. "Mr. Swenson, can you send one of the drones back to that area and see if you can find him again?"

"Sure." Swenson tapped a few buttons and a live feed came up on the monitor from one of the drones as it approached the grove. It found the tree, witnessed by one medium-sized low-hanging branch broken at the base and fallen to the ground, picked clean of fruit. The bear had moved on.

Swenson had the drone do a slow spin. As it turned toward the river, they saw the animal meandering on all fours toward the water. Swenson edged the drone forward, keeping a discreet distance as he followed.

After a couple of minutes, the bear looked back over its shoulder. It stopped and turned toward the drone, which hovered about six feet behind and about six feet off the ground. It stood up and faced the dark sphere, slowly tilting its head from side to side.

Finally it turned back toward the river, dropped back down onto all four paws, and lumbered away again.

"Stay with him," Decker said.

Swenson urged the drone forward until the bear looked back over its shoulder again. Seeing the drone following, it turned and let out a loud roar. After noting that the object had stopped, the bear turned back and lumbered on toward the water. But after a few steps, it looked again and saw the drone had once again resumed its pursuit.

The animal turned back toward the interloper, stood up to its full height, bared its teeth and let out a mighty roar.

Swenson held the drone in place.

When the trespasser didn't retreat, the bear dropped back down on all fours and in two powerful bounds covered the distance to the drone and leaped into the air.

The image of the massive beast flying directly at the camera with both forepaws extended froze on Swenson's console. He started pressing buttons. "Um. We seem to have a problem. I've lost communication with the drone."

"Bring another around to see what happened," Decker said. "But keep a safe distance."

Swenson started working. The image of the bear attacking the drone was pushed off to a side monitor, and live video from a second drone came up on the main screen as it approached the altercation. The bear held the defunct drone in its forepaws and repeatedly smashed it against the rocky ground. The central core of the sphere held up well, but the outer shell had been completely destroyed. Pieces of shrapnel were scattered around the area.

Finally the bear dropped what was left of the drone to the ground. It looked at it for a few seconds and then bent down to sniff at the remains. It licked at the surface, then tried to bite into it. Not being able to get a purchase with its teeth, the animal quickly gave up and turned back toward the stream, resuming its slow, lumbering pace.

"Do you still want me to follow?"

Decker stepped back from the console. "Yes, but keep a respectful distance. High enough that he can't reach it, and far enough away that he doesn't pay it any attention."

Decker turned to Steadman and Guerrero. "Thoughts?"

Guerrero didn't hesitate. "I wouldn't mind having him on my volleyball team."

Decker and Steadman both glared at him.

"What! He's got mad skills. Agility, strength, passion. He didn't attack until after we invaded his space, and even then he asked us nicely to leave. When we didn't, he gave us two clear warnings before he struck. In my book, we asked for it."

Decker looked at Steadman.

Steadman arched an eyebrow. "When you put it that way, I have to agree. Is he a threat to us? That's hard to say. He certainly has the potential, but as Guerrero points out, he didn't strike out at the drone without provocation —albeit slight. On the other hand, we probably smell a lot more like food than the drone. I wish I knew more about bears. This would be a good discussion to have with our zoologist."

"In the meantime?" Decker asked.

Steadman hefted his pack. "If there's just the one in the area and he doesn't live here, he might not hang around. I suggest we track him with a drone and just do our work somewhere else. We could also leverage additional drones to keep an eye on a perimeter around where we're working."

Decker turned back to Swenson. "Mr. Swenson, can we do that?"

Swenson scratched the back of his head. "It'll be easy enough to automate one drone to track the bear and let us know if he starts moving toward us. Using additional drones to keep an eye on a perimeter around a field team is a good idea, but we don't have an algorithm yet that I would trust to reliably detect threats in an unknown environment. It would be best if a live person kept watch on the drone feeds here at this console."

"That sounds like a plan. Mr. Swenson, configure the drones and let us know when you're ready. You'll be here monitoring. Commander Steadman, you and Guerrero will start deploying the sensor array per the original plan, adapting as necessary if he shows up again. I'll start unloading the pod. We've lost almost an hour against the schedule. Let's see if we can make some of that up. Just don't get sloppy."

Day 1, 1031 Hours

"Hey, guys, we may have another problem here."

Guerrero quickly crouched, setting the sensor pod he'd been configuring on the ground, grabbing his rifle, and looking into the forest. Steadman took a position behind him, back to back, scouting in the opposite direction.

Steadman activated his comm. "What do you have, Mr. Swenson?"

"Well, first, we're going to have to stop with the 'Mr. Swenson' bit. Mr. Swenson is my dad. My name is Rusty."

"The problem, Mr. Swenson."

Guerrero heard the edge in Steadman's voice as his own adrenaline spiked. *This is why you need a team that has trained together.*

"Sorry, sir," Swenson said. "I have another undocumented critter in the trees, just south of your position."

Guerrero turned to look south. "What are we looking for? Is Yogi back?"

"It doesn't look like a bear. Much smaller. It looks more like a chimpanzee. He was snacking on fruit a minute ago when I first saw him, but now he's watching you."

Steadman saw it first, pointing into the trees. The chimp was sitting still and watching them, holding a half-eaten fruit in its hand. The stare-off continued for about two minutes before the chimp casually took another bite of fruit, never taking its gaze off Steadman and Guerrero. It chewed slowly and swallowed, then took another bite.

Guerrero whispered, "What's the plan, boss?"

Steadman responded in a normal voice to be sure Decker and Swenson heard him too. "He just seems curious about the newcomers. And content with his fruit. Mr. Swenson, continue to monitor and let us know if his posture changes. We'll get back to work."

"Since Mr. Swenson isn't here, I'll take that task. Rusty out."

Guerrero hung his rifle on his back and picked up the sensor he had dropped. It looked similar to the drone, but only about six inches in diameter, and was mounted atop a two-foot shaft. Three hinged legs attached at the bottom of the shaft and folded down to form a tripod, supporting the probe about three and a half feet off the ground. After he set the sensor/tripod assembly on the ground, a hydraulic system extended shafts from each of the three legs, driving them into the soft ground to anchor the sensor.

Guerrero activated the unit.

Swenson's voice came over the radio. "Number twelve is confirmed online."

"Roger that," Guerrero said.

He picked up the bundle of sensors they still had with them and started walking. Steadman followed the map on his tablet as he led them to the location for the next installation.

Guerrero kept looking back over his shoulder to see if the chimp was following. Swenson must have been watching them, because about the fifth time he turned back to look, Swenson said, "He didn't follow. He lost interest after you moved on. I've brought in a fourth drone to track him so we can keep the other three watching for new threats around you."

"Roger that," Steadman said. "Keep us advised."

Day 1, 1910 Hours

"Not sure what it is?" Guerrero asked.

Swenson looked at the contents of the open package in his hands. "Not a clue. I know it's food, but I can't identify anything more specific. The one I had for lunch was much the same. Even after I ate it, I still didn't know what it was."

Swenson took a seat beside the others around the campfire Guerrero had built in the middle of their partially constructed base camp.

Guerrero looked at the empty wrapper of his own MRE. "Does anyone know when the microwave gets here?"

"It should be on the first shipment tomorrow," Decker said. "Along with a mini-kitchen and some real food. Then we can put the rest of these emergency rations back in the crate."

Decker looked at Swenson. "How's the perimeter sensor array doing?"

Swenson balanced what was left of his meal on his lap and picked up his tablet. "All sensors are operational and calibrated. We're picking up a wide variety of critters lurking about. Mostly small. They all seem to be hanging back away from the camp. I don't know whether it's the fire, the lights, or us. If they start encroaching we may need to think about a fence. I've activated the automatic monitoring algorithm, so we'll get a warning if anything starts moving toward us. The bigger it is, the earlier we'll hear about it."

Guerrero tossed the MRE wrapper into the fire. "What about Yogi?"

"The bear? He headed back into the mountains. The last the drone saw of him, he was entering a cave. Given what happened to the last drone that got too close, I made an executive decision to not follow him in."

Decker chuckled. "Good call, Mr. Swenson, but please let me make the executive decisions for now."

"Yes, sir." Swenson's ears may have reddened, but it was hard to be sure in the light of the fire.

Guerrero watched the glowing embers as it burned down to coals. The smell and the crackle of burning wood mixed with the distant croaking of frogs (or something like them) by the river reminded him of camping trips growing up.

Steadman finished off a bottle of water and said, "I can't get over how much this place looks like Earth. Even here in the dark, you can hear what sounds like crickets and frogs over by the river. Besides squirrels, chimps, and bears, we saw, and heard, several types of birds today. Grass, fruit and nut trees, cedars, flowers."

"Not what you expected?" Decker asked.

"No. I always thought life on other planets was supposed to be … strange … weird … different. This looks more like Earth than Earth. The only things missing are houses and roads."

Guerrero shook his head. "You got that right. There's something wrong here. It's like somebody fabricated this place, made it up to look like Earth."

Steadman did a double-take. "You're thinking like space aliens or something?"

Guerrero glared back at Steadman.

Steadman tilted his head. "Okay. I guess that's not so far-fetched now that I think about it. I still haven't fully recalibrated my worldview. So we may also have an alien threat."

The sudden beeping of everyone's tablets interrupted the conversation. Steadman and Guerrero took up positions on opposite sides, just outside the circle of chairs around the campfire. Rifles in hand, they slowly circled clockwise looking into the darkness outside the camp.

Swenson consulted his tablet. "It looks like your chimp came back. Can't say for sure if it's the same one. He's in the grass about fifty yards north-northwest, bearing three-four-eight."

Steadman and Guerrero converged on that side of the circle. With the lights on in the camp, they could only see a few feet into the darkness. Steadman said, "Lights out," as he pulled his night-vision gear into place.

Guerrero followed suit with his own, but Decker held up a hand before Swenson could implement the lights-out order. "Countermand. Mr. Swenson, what's he doing now?"

Swenson looked at his tablet. "As soon as everyone turned to look in his direction, he hunkered down. He's still looking this way but not moving."

Decker sat back down by the fire. "Mr. Swenson, keep a close eye on our friend. Gentlemen, stand down and take your seats. Let's see what we can learn about our host."

Day 1, 1921 Hours

"He's started moving again," Swenson said. "Tentatively. He moves forward a couple of feet at a time, then waits to see if we're reacting."

Decker, Steadman, and Guerrero were trying—unsuccessfully—to appear nonchalant. Decker looked at Guerrero, who was facing in the general direction of the chimp. "Do you still have any of those protein bars on you?"

"Sure." Guerrero pulled one out of a vest pocket and offered it to Decker.

Decker didn't take it. "Hold it out where the chimp can see it. Open it and start eating. Slowly. Do you have another?"

"Yeah," Guerrero said as he unwrapped the protein bar.

Steadman fidgeted in his chair as he had his back to the intruder. He pulled out his tablet and linked to the surveillance feed Swenson was monitoring.

"It's a pity we don't have our zoologist yet," Decker said. "Does anyone know anything about chimpanzee behavior?"

Guerrero and Steadman shook their heads. Swenson said, "Just what I've seen in movies, which is to say nothing I'd stake my life on."

"Mr. Guerrero, there's a crate about twenty yards behind Mr. Swenson. That looks to be about the same distance from us as our guest. Unwrap the second protein bar and place it there. Make a show of it. Let him know it's for him."

Guerrero unwrapped the second bar and stuffed both wrappers into a pocket. He held them up for the chimp to see, then took another bite of the first. He stood from his chair and walked slowly toward the crate, keeping the two snacks where their visitor could see them as he approached. When he got to the container, he took another bite of the first while gesturing toward the chimp with the second before putting it on top of the crate. Then he walked back to the campfire and sat down.

The chimp looked back and forth between the men at the campfire and the food on the crate. When he started moving again, he followed an arc, keeping his distance from the team as he made his way toward the box. He crept through the tall grass, stopping every few steps to make sure no one was moving.

When he got to the crate, he kept his eyes on the newcomers as he reached over to pick up the snack. He held it to his nose and sniffed it, then touched it to his tongue. He watched them a moment longer and then raced off into the darkness, prize in hand.

Day 1, 2300 Hours

The man sat alone in the office, the only light coming from a small desk lamp. He turned his computer off, finally ready to put an end to a long day.

One last task, he thought as he pulled out his phone. Checking an anonymous e-mail account, he ignored the inbox and went straight to the spam folder.

There. Finally an update.

He opened the e-mail, ostensibly offering free desktop background images. He clicked the link and waited patiently as the document downloaded. A scenic landscape appeared. A few more taps and the simple message was decrypted: "He's in."

Excellent. Maybe now we'll finally make some headway in learning what Kreitzman has been up to.

EIGHT

"Any chance of getting a weather forecast?" asked Decker as he sat down beside Swenson at the campfire.

Swenson dumped the rest of his unfinished emergency-ration breakfast into the fire. "Not really. In the run-up to this mission, we didn't see any significant weather events." He looked up at the dark clouds that had blown in overnight. "We have no local history to compare this to."

Steadman looked up at the fast-moving clouds. "It's going to rain. The wind will pick up, and we'll probably see lightning. Maybe hail. Maybe tornadoes."

Swenson grinned. "Maybe. Maybe not. The weather patterns and indicators may be different here than they are on Earth. We don't have enough data yet to say."

Steadman shook his head and went back to work on his breakfast.

Decker waved at the sky. "What about getting a satellite view of this?"

TWO

Swenson shook his head. "I checked that this morning already. The mapping satellite is over another part of the planet. It'll be a couple of days before it works its way back to our area."

Decker looked at Steadman and Guerrero. "Prioritize the storeroom first. Get it weather-tight and then move on to the science lab. If we can get those two finished before the rain hits, we can move indoors."

Day 2, 1115 Hours

The clouds grew thicker as Steadman and Guerrero worked to attach the doors to the almost-finished storeroom. Guerrero stood on a stepladder to align the door to its hinges as Steadman supported the weight of the door from below.

A flash of light caught Guerrero's attention, but before he could react to it, the sound of a massive explosion rolled through the hills. Both men dropped the door as Guerrero dove from the ladder. He landed in a shoulder roll and came up to one knee with his sidearm already out, scanning the horizon. Steadman had also drawn his weapon, his back to Guerrero and scanning in the opposite direction.

Steadman saw a second flash in the distance, followed briefly by a clap of thunder. Steadman holstered his pistol as he turned to see Guerrero with his still pointed into the hills. "You see giants, Mr. Quixote?"

Guerrero stood and holstered his sidearm. "*Someone* is hurling lightning bolts, Sancho, and I don't see any windmills."

Steadman laughed.

Swenson's voice broke in over the comm. "I'm reading atmospheric discharge of electrostatic energy. You guys may want to take cover."

Steadman keyed his mic. "Would that be the thunderstorm I warned you about?"

Decker came on the radio. "All right, Mr. Weatherman. Get inside."

Heavy rain fell as they made their way to the medical lab. The medical equipment hadn't come yet, but their only functional computer console was housed there, and they had already moved all their food and water supplies into the building to minimize the risk of attracting predators.

"How far did you get?" Decker asked as everyone gathered.

"Not far enough. The storeroom is finished except for the doors. So we'll have some cleanup to do inside after this is over. How far did you get with the science lab?"

"Not far enough." He'd been working on the science building by himself to try to speed things along. "The foundation is assembled, but not much else."

Decker turned to Swenson, who was still working at the computer console. "Can you deploy the drones to give us some idea of how long this will last or how severe it will get?"

Swenson smacked his forehead with his palm. "I should have thought of that earlier. I can spread the drones out radially around our location to find the perimeter of the storm cell. Along the way, we'll get a rough map of the intensity of the storm. Once we find the perimeter, we should also be able to determine what direction it's moving and how fast."

"Do it. What's the status of the perimeter sensor array?"

Swenson checked the console. "The sensor array is fine. It's designed to handle much worse than this. It looks like most of the wildlife that's being tracked has gone to ground, as you would expect."

"So we wait." Decker motioned Steadman and Guerrero to makeshift seating on a couple of crates. "Anyone up for an early lunch?"

Guerrero groaned. "Weren't we supposed to have real food for lunch?"

Steadman chuckled. "That was before the weather changed our priorities. The kitchen is out there in those crates that came this morning if you want to go get it."

Guerrero started walking toward the door when a loud clap of thunder signaled another nearby lightning strike. He grabbed an emergency ration packet from a crate by the door instead.

Steadman smiled and took another packet. "Live to fight another day."

Decker picked up two MREs and dropped one on the console beside Swenson. When the packet hit the console, an alarm went off and everyone's tablets started chirping.

Swenson studied the readouts. "Yogi's back. He's headed directly for our position. In a hurry."

Decker looked at Steadman. "Can he get to us in here?"

"Unknown, but unlikely," Steadman said. "These buildings are designed to handle hurricane-strength storms. But Yogi's strength and skill are unknown."

"How much damage can he do to what's out there?"

"Quite a lot. Everything is shipped waterproof. They'll stand up to this storm, at least as it stands right now. They're not designed to withstand assault by a bear."

"Mr. Swenson, what's he doing now?"

"Unknown. He's inside the perimeter where I can't get precise data."

"Pull back one of the drones."

"Already done … it's one minute thirty out. The bear will be on us before the drone gets back."

Steadman picked up his rifle and looked at Decker. "Arm up?"

Swenson interjected. "If I may?"

Decker looked at the engineer. "Go ahead."

"My bet is that he's looking for shelter from the thunderstorm. The sudden onset caught him by surprise and he couldn't get back to his cave in the mountains. He probably sheltered in the orchard, then got scared out of his spot by a nearby lightning strike. To him, our

53

buildings look like large boulders. He's probably planning to huddle down next to one and wait out the storm."

Decker looked at Steadman. "Stand down, for now."

Steadman stepped up beside Decker and lowered his voice. "Sir. That thing could be out there destroying the equipment we need to complete our mission. Standing by puts it in jeopardy."

Decker looked pointedly at Steadman. "Or, Commander, that thing could be scared for its life and be looking for a place to hide until the storm passes. Just like us. I can have everything out there replaced in less than forty-eight hours. Except for that bear. I can't replace that. Our orders are to tread lightly, Mr. Steadman. Until and unless he becomes a threat to my crew, we watch and learn. Am I clear?"

"Yes, sir." Steadman set his rifle back down.

Swenson looked up from his console. "The drone is coming on-station. Video up on the monitor."

The heavy rainfall dramatically reduced visibility. At first the screen was just gray, the camera unable to resolve anything further than fifty feet. Then the image of the camp began to resolve itself as the drone approached. Swenson took over direct navigation and circled the compound, looking for the bear.

"I don't see him anywhere," said Guerrero. "Did he just keep running?"

Swenson swept the drone around the campsite. "I don't think so. I should have picked that up on the perimeter sensor array, at least if he made it any distance from the camp."

Steadman gestured at the monitor. "Wait. Swing back … there. See if you can zoom in through the door."

There, huddled in the back corner of the storage building, sat the bear, hunkered down against the cold wind blowing in through the unfinished door.

Decker stood back from the console. "Looks like he found himself a cave after all."

NINE

Decker leaned back against one of the crates. "What are we going to do about this?"

Steadman continued watching the scene in the storage building. "We have some time. He's not likely to make any trouble until after this storm clears out."

Decker and Steadman shared a look. "Point taken," said Steadman.

Another loud thunderclap rattled the building. Decker shook his head. "Any updates on the weather forecast?"

Swenson had been focused on the bear. He switched back to looking at the data from the other drones. "Three of the drones have found the nearest edge. The others are still looking. It looks like it covers a pretty large area. Until we find the edges and get at least a few minutes of tracking data, I won't be able to predict when it might clear out."

Steadman shifted on his improvised seat. "The thunderstorm is no longer our biggest problem. It'll blow over, and once it does Yogi will come out of his new

56

cave. If he gets a whiff of food in the compound or decides he likes his new cave better than his old one, we could have an unwelcome new neighbor."

Another loud clap of thunder echoed through the surrounding hills. Decker watched Yogi try to scrunch farther into the corner of the storage building. "Any ideas about what we can do about that?"

Guerrero looked at the visage of Yogi's backside on the console. "Ideally, we need a strategy that makes him afraid of our compound without directly associating that fear with us."

Decker's ears perked up. "Why?"

"If he's afraid of us, he'll be more likely to regard us as a threat. It puts us at much greater risk when we're exploring outside the compound."

"That's sound reasoning," Steadman said, "but it severely limits our options."

Swenson turned from his console to face the others. "I may have an idea. I put a request in yesterday's return package for a zoological encyclopedia. It came in this morning's shipment. I've been reading up on bear behavior. Keep in mind this information is based on observations of Earth bears and may not apply to the bearlike animals we see here. With that said, in the biomes where they're found on Earth, they're usually at the top of the food chain and thus not given to fear of much. One thing we do know—he's afraid of lightning."

Decker shook his head. "And do you have a way to create lightning?"

57

"Well, no. At least not on an atmospheric scale. That would be a pretty tall order. But I think I can create a realistic thunderclap using the speakers on one of the drones. The hardware is not capable of creating anything with the same volume as those nearby hits we keep getting, but I think if I create the sound of distant thunder, we might motivate him to move away from it. Not so much in fear but in the spirit of self-preservation. We already know where his cave is in the mountains. If we use the drones to herd him in that direction, he's likely to be eager to go."

Guerrero nodded. "One potential problem. He's already had a bad experience with one of our drones. If he sees it when he hears the thunder, he'll couple the two threats in his mind. He won't fear the camp; he'll fear the drone. But that anxiety, combined with his victory in the last direct conflict, will motivate him to attack."

Swenson leaned forward in his chair, resting his elbows on his knees. "Good point. I'll have to keep the drones where he can't see them. But they have to be nearby to make the thunder realistic. I should be able to use the terrain to hide them. It will mean using at least two drones so we can keep the 'thunderstorm' going without having the motion of the drones catch his eye."

Another clap of thunder reminded them the storm hadn't left yet. Decker looked at Swenson. "Bring back another drone. A third if you think you need it. But keep the rest of them on weather duty."

Day 2, 1525 Hours

Still huddled inside the medical lab, Decker paced the floor. Swenson monitored the weather data from the drones and simultaneously kept an eye on Yogi to know when he woke up. Steadman and Guerrero had both tapped into Swenson's encyclopedia of zoology, Steadman reading up on bears and Guerrero reading up on chimpanzees.

"He's up," said Swenson.

Everyone quickly converged on the engineer's console. They saw Yogi peeking out of the storage building, looking around.

"Where are our lightning bolts?" asked Decker.

Swenson zoomed out with the camera watching Yogi so they could see the whole compound. "One is behind the storage building," Swenson said, pointing it out on the screen. "The other is behind the medical lab."

They watched as Yogi trudged out into the compound. He very quickly homed in on a particular crate and started sniffing around it.

Guerrero groaned. "Please, not that one. That's part of the kitchen."

Decker rested a hand on Swenson's shoulder. "Fire one."

Swenson tapped a control and a loud thunderclap sounded from behind the storage building. Yogi perked up and looked in the direction of the sound. After a brief

59

moment of surveying the horizon, he returned his attention to the crate.

"Fire two."

This time everyone in the medical lab flinched when the thunderclap came. It sounded like lightning had struck in the room with them. Yogi looked up again, and this time he decided to move on. He lumbered his way across the compound, then picked up his pace to a gallop as he crossed the plain toward the forest.

Decker tapped Swenson's shoulder again. "Task one of the drones to track him, at a discreet distance. Keep the other in reserve in case he comes back this way. We may need to remind him this is not a good place."

He looked at Steadman and Guerrero. "Gentlemen, we have work to do, and we're way behind schedule. Let's get to it."

They headed out into the compound, everyone with the same first stop in mind—the storage building. Had Yogi done any damage?

Steadman was the first to look through the door. "Oh, great. Guerrero, go get the shovel."

Decker came up next, looking inside. "Bag it and tag it. We'll gift that to our zoologist when he gets here. I'm sure he'll appreciate it."

Guerrero looked into the storage building and then at Steadman. "Who? Me?"

"Yes, you. And then see if you can find something to sanitize the floor."

Day 2, 2045 Hours

Just before sunset the intruder alarm went off again. The chimpanzee had come back. He lurked a safe distance from the camp and kept an eye on them.

And they kept an eye on him.

It was well past dark when they shut down for the night. They managed to get the remaining structures assembled before sunset and then spent the rest of the evening moving all the accumulated supplies and equipment into the various buildings—mostly the storage building—so it would be protected should they have further weather events. Or intruders.

They were behind schedule, but with careful prioritization they could still be ready for the arrival of the science team the following day.

Guerrero had built another campfire and they had gathered around it to eat dinner.

Guerrero looked at his packet of emergency rations. "The first thing I'm going to do tomorrow is to put the kitchen together. You've got your priorities; I've got mine. Real food is mine."

Decker laughed. "Amen to that, my friend."

They had barely started eating when Swenson's tablet chirped again. He picked it up and checked the status. "Our chimp is approaching. Cautiously." He pointed into the darkness.

When everyone turned to look in his direction, the chimp froze. Guerrero pulled another protein bar out of

61

his vest pocket. He made a show of unwrapping it and then walked slowly over to one of the crew quarters buildings. He gestured toward the chimp. "Welcome back, Mikey." He placed the snack on a ledge on the edge of the building and walked back to the campfire.

Mikey looked back and forth between the protein bar and the assembly of strangers. He finally made his way over to the building and picked up the snack with one hand. Then, eyes locked on Guerrero, he reached up with the other and put something on the ledge. Then he turned and disappeared into the darkness.

They got up to see what Mikey had left behind. Guerrero pulled out a flashlight and shone it on the ledge, where they found a small pile of nuts that looked like almonds still in the shell. He picked one up and sniffed it.

"I know what you're thinking," Decker said. "You'll survive on emergency rations until we can get the kitchen up so we can cook some Earth food. No native food is on the menu for the duration of this mission."

Day 2, 2315 Hours

The man behind the desk read the decrypted message again, not sure what to make of it.

Project code-named Two. Mission is ostensibly to explore another planet. Team includes four military officers, one engineer, five scientists. Skeptical. Possible hoax. Objective unclear. Seem very interested in minerals, petroleum reserves. May lose access to communications. Need backup plan. Team will be sending reports through restricted channel.

Most interesting.

Petroleum reserves. That would fit with Kreitzman's investments in the energy sector. But why the blather about exploring another planet? Obfuscation? Keep the participants confused so they didn't realize where any resources they found were actually located? A scam to gain access to government funds? Or was he really planning to drill for oil on Mars?

Backup plan.

He turned his computer back on.

TEN

Day 3, 2030 Hours

They were busy from dawn to dusk the following day. Guerrero got up before the sun came up and, true to his word, got to work assembling the kitchen. The beef stew they had for lunch was hardly gourmet but after two days of emergency rations, no one was complaining.

Mikey showed up again not long after lunch. At first, he lurked about fifty feet outside the perimeter of the camp. But as the day wore on, the chimp moved in closer to watch what the curious strangers were up to. By evening, he was following Guerrero every step he took, often getting underfoot.

When they sat down for dinner around the campfire, Mikey came over beside Guerrero and pulled one of the protein bars out of the man's vest. He sat down beside him, unwrapped the bar, then turned and held out a fist. Everyone watched in stunned silence. After a moment's hesitation, Guerrero bumped fists with Mikey, who then started eating.

64

Decker, Steadman, and Guerrero were all staring slack-jawed at Mikey.

"You know where he got that, don't you?" Swenson asked.

Everyone looked back with blank stares. "You and Steadman have been doing that all day. Every time you finish a task, you do a fist bump and then move on to the next project. He's been watching how we interact, learning how to socialize in our community."

Decker tipped his head to Mikey. "Welcome to the team."

Guerrero looked at the empty wrapper in his hands. "That's great and all, but I'm running out of protein bars."

Steadman chuckled and pulled a bar from his own vest. "Here, you can have this one back." He tossed it at Guerrero, but Mikey reached out with his long arms and snatched it out of the air. The chimp looked at Steadman and let out a short hoot.

"I think that means 'thanks,'" said Swenson.

Steadman shook his head. "Yeah, I got that." He watched the chimp eat as its gaze shifted around the campfire from one man to the next. Steadman gestured toward Mikey. "We discussed before we left Earth why we don't want to eat anything from this planet, at least until the science team has cleared it. We didn't discuss feeding Earth food to local animals."

Decker nodded. "Yeah. In hindsight, that may not have been a good idea. I'm sure our zoologist will have something to say about it when he gets here."

Steadman waved dismissively. "That's not my point. By my count Mikey has eaten three, soon to be four, servings of Earth food that are made of a whole bunch of different ingredients." He tried to read the fine print on the label in the dim light. "Grains, dairy products, sugars, nuts—artificial ingredients even. He seems to really like them, and forty-eight hours later no sign of any problems."

Swenson looked at Mikey. "It's noteworthy. I'm sure both the zoologist and the medical doctor will want to study that in great detail. I hope Mikey can tolerate spending some time in the lab. The first thing they'll tell us, though, is just because Mikey can eat Earth food doesn't mean we can eat … Two … food."

Guerrero groaned and muttered, "We have to do something about that name."

Decker laughed. "No argument there."

Steadman waved his hand again. "But getting back to my point … the cosmology people were bewildered by how much this place, the first planet we've taken a serious look at, looks like Earth."

"That's true," Swenson said, "albeit slightly overstated."

Steadman scowled at him.

The engineer leaned forward in his chair. "When I originally targeted this planet, I selected it from a database of more than five hundred 'possible' planets that astronomers had studied. Most of those are believed to look nothing like Earth. This was the most similar of the whole group. So in some sense, this is the most Earth-like of the first five hundred planets we've looked at. It's just the first one we've looked at up close. But, to your point, the reality we found when we got here, from a cosmological perspective, was a lot more 'Earth-like' than even the astronomical data suggested."

Steadman nodded. "Exactly. And then we see plants and animals here—trees, grass, flowers—that could have come from Earth. Squirrels, bears, monkeys. So similar to Earth life that animals here can eat Earth food, enjoy it, and see no ill effects. I'm not a scientist, but I don't think anyone expected this."

"Chimps." Swenson pointed to Mikey. "We haven't seen anything yet that looked like a monkey."

Steadman scowled.

Swenson held up his hands in mock surrender. "But your point is well made. Science is, fundamentally, the search for causes. Every effect has a cause. When we wonder how things came to be, we're looking for a cause. The way this normally happens, we first observe a repeatable pattern of events in the world around us. Then we come up with a theory—a guess—that explains how that might happen. Then we test that theory to see if the things it predicts actually happen. It's quite rare that you can actually prove a theory to be correct. Sometimes you can prove it's wrong—if testable things predicted by the theory don't work—but you can't really prove it's right. The best you can hope for is that a preponderance of evidence supports the theory.

"Sometimes a theory will seem to be right for years … decades … even centuries, but eventually be proven to be flawed. Newtonian physics is a case in point. It works. Most of the time. For centuries it was the accepted explanation for how things work. But over time we found more and more cases where it wasn't quite right. These errors are what led Albert Einstein to develop the theories of special and general relativity, which became the new standard for more than a century. But even general relativity has flaws. General relativity doesn't explain what happens in quantum physics. Until Dr. Kreitzman's very recent work, no one had been able to develop a theory that reconciled general relativity with quantum field theory that could muster enough physical corroboration to be accepted.

"I say all that to say that when you get results that diverge from what your theory predicts, it may be time to question whether your theory is correct."

"And what theory is it that you think may be incorrect?" asked Decker.

Swenson shrugged. "With apologies to Douglas Adams, the theory of life, the universe, and everything."

ELEVEN

Dr. Teresa Culpepper stood in the small room with her backpack at her feet as she waited impatiently for the rest of the team to arrive.

Not even allowed a proper suitcase.

As the others began to file into the room, backpacks in tow, she silently rehearsed their names. They had only met the day before, and now they were going to be spending the next three months together. Essentially in isolation.

How many ways can this go wrong?

Still, she was willing to take the risk. The offer they had made was a good one, even if she hadn't been desperate. A three-month commitment in exchange for funding her research for the next two years. They didn't even want a share in anything her future work produced.

As for the next three months, they would own the majority interest in anything she discovered. But she was still skeptical this was on the up-and-up.

Another planet. Sure it is.

This looked more like some kind of group psychology experiment. Dump a bunch of incompatible strangers into an isolated environment and watch the fireworks. Too much of the background data, limited as it was, wasn't credible. Another planet—and they could have her there this morning. Not years, or months, or even days from now. She looked at her watch. Five minutes from now.

How does that work, exactly?

Another planet, almost exactly like Earth, right down to the flora and fauna. None of it was credible for a new planet, but exactly what you'd expect for a psychology experiment that, in fact, had to be executed on Earth.

The chamber door closed and a voice came over the intercom. "Looks like everyone is present and accounted for. Remember to watch the sign on the wall. When it changes, you'll know the transfer is complete. Oh, and I've been advised to warn you that gravity is a bit higher over there. You'll feel a sudden increase in your weight and the weight of your gear. We advise you to stow your pack on the floor to minimize disorientation."

Now, that'll be a trick. How are they going to fake increased gravity?

"If I can get a thumbs-up from everyone, we can start the final sequence."

Might as well get on with it.

She forced a smile and raised her thumb, as did the others.

"That's a go. Ten seconds to transfer ... good luck ... five ... four ... three ... two ... one. Initiating transf—"

Day 4, 0900 Hours

Culpepper's eyes were fixed on the sign on the wall when it suddenly changed from "ONE," hand-scrawled in blue chalk, to "TWO," written in green. Simultaneously she felt an increased downward force in her knees that threw her ever so slightly off balance. She quickly recovered and looked around at the others.

Must be some kind of biosphere mounted in a centrifugal frame. I may have underestimated the budget for this experiment.

She was about to ask the petty officer what they were supposed to do next when she heard a hiss of air exchange and felt the pressure change in her ears.

After a few seconds, the hatch cracked open and bright sunlight streamed in. She reflexively put her arm up to shield her eyes before reaching into a side pocket on her pack for her sunglasses. When the hatch was fully open, Culpepper followed the other five out onto the planet's surface.

The panorama was breathtaking.

The air was crisp like an autumn morning. The sky was deep blue, accented with a few wispy white clouds.

To the west loomed a wall of mountains. They were covered in a forest of tall trees that looked, at least from this distance, like some kind of pine. The dense vegetation was broken in patches by rocky areas, some showing signs of smaller scrub brush.

TWO

A river cut through the terrain on the near side of the mountains, marking an abrupt transition from tall mountains to low hills. The hills were covered in swaths, some of smaller trees (maybe fruit trees?), some of wildflowers, and some of tall grass.

The base camp was set in a grassy clearing nestled between three of these low hills and adjacent to the river.

Her eyes were drawn back to the mountains and a spectacular double waterfall that cut through a cliff face and cascaded several hundred feet down to the river.

As her eyes followed up the waterfall, they were drawn to the moon hanging low over the mountaintops. Her gaze fixated there, something feeling not quite right. It took her a moment to realize the moon was all wrong. It was a little too large. And the contours weren't right.

The man in the moon was missing.

She felt a mild sense of panic as she quickly scanned the rest of the sky and noticed a second, much smaller moon almost directly overhead. It took her a moment to find an explanation.

Projections onto a dome. Get set for three months on The Truman Show.

As she turned her gaze back to the grassy hillsides, her mind was flooded with unbidden memories long buried of her childhood on the family farm; of dreams of a future that were dashed when her father died while she was in college studying agriculture. Tears began to well up as she remembered her father and brothers working in the fields while she helped her mother tend the livestock.

She forced herself to look away as she struggled to regain her composure. She suddenly realized that while she and the rest of the science team were taking in their new environment, the four members of the advance team had seen all this before and were instead looking at the newcomers.

In particular, at her.

So she yelled. "Who's in charge here!"

She immediately identified Decker from the photos she'd seen before she left Earth.

"Do you really think you're fooling anyone with all this smoke-and-mirrors stuff?" She waved her arm expansively. "Just because I don't know how you did it doesn't mean I believe for a minute that we're really on another planet. And before we're done here, I'll prove it."

Day 4, 0900 Hours

Dr. Henry Zindell was a quiet man. In his late thirties, he still had a full head of (mostly) black hair. Dark prescription sunglasses protected his eyes from the alien sun.

Zindell was in heaven. As he stood with the rest of the newly arrived science team taking in their new surroundings, he couldn't wait to get started. He was already making a mental list of the things he wanted to look at and beginning to prioritize and sort the list in his mind.

He looked ahead and saw the mountains where the caves had been reported that were most likely home to a population of bears.

To the right, he saw the trees where the squirrels and the chimpanzee had been spotted.

A flock of birds flew overhead.

So many species. So little time.

Zindell's moment in heaven was shattered by the sound of someone yelling.

"Just because I don't know how you did it doesn't mean I believe for a minute that we're really on another planet. And before we're done here, I'll prove it."

It was that Culpepper woman.

What's she going on about now?

One of the advance team people looked at Culpepper and said, "I'm Commander Decker. I'm the one in charge."

Zindell recognized Decker from the photos they'd been shown before they left Earth. The man standing beside Decker would be Swenson, the engineer, and the other two men in tactical gear must be Steadman and Guerrero.

Decker stepped forward to greet the newcomers. "For what it's worth, I share your skepticism. This seems far-fetched to me too, but I lack the scientific acumen to dismiss the claim. Or to corroborate it, for that matter. That's why you're here." He gestured to include the whole scientific team.

"So please, maintain your skepticism, and when you think you have evidence, one way or the other, by all means, bring it. In the meantime," Decker expanded his address to include the whole group, "let's get you all settled in and then bring you up to date on what we know. Then we can start talking about a strategy to move your respective research efforts forward."

The advance team members turned to lead the way to the center of the compound. As they turned, Zindell caught sight of Mikey, who had been hiding behind Guerrero's legs.

"Pardon me ... please ... is that the chimp?"

Everyone stopped to look. Weaver took a quick step backward so that Zindell was between her and the alien creature.

Zindell could barely contain his enthusiasm.

Guerrero knelt down beside Mikey, who wrapped his arms around Guerrero's shoulders and pressed his head against Guerrero's chest. He seemed to be frightened by the new strangers.

Guerrero stood up, holding Mikey in his arms protectively. "Dr. Zindell, I presume. Meet Mikey. It took him a couple of days to warm up to us. I think the sudden appearance of the six of you may have scared him a little."

Zindell was back in heaven. "This is extraordinary. On Earth, when we first started studying chimps in the wild, it took years for researchers to establish enough trust with them to get close enough to interact with them directly.

Here, you've done it in a couple of days?" Zindell looked at Guerrero. "How?"

Guerrero shifted Mikey around to his hip, reaching into a vest pocket and producing a protein bar. "Snacks." Mikey promptly reached out and grabbed the bar and clenched it tight against his chest.

Petty Officer Weaver smiled as she peeked around Zindell's shoulder. "That explains the extra case of protein bars you requisitioned."

Zindell's face reddened. "You fed him Earth food! What were you thinking! You could have killed him. We have no way of knowing what that could do to him."

The scientist rushed forward, intending to take the snack away from Mikey.

Mikey twisted in Guerrero's arms to face his attacker's onrush. He let out a scream, waving his arms menacingly. That stopped Zindell in his tracks, just out of reach of Mikey's arms.

Mikey jumped out of Guerrero's grasp and ran off toward the nearest grove, still gripping the protein bar.

Zindell felt everyone's eyes boring into him.

"Don't you understand?" Zindell pleaded. "You could have killed him."

TWELVE

Steadman wasn't looking forward to this. He wasn't too worried about Zindell, but Culpepper had already established that she wasn't into teams. That didn't change the fact they had a job to do.

He entered the second crew quarters building where Weaver, Tornquist, and Culpepper were busy stowing their gear and settling in.

Each of the crew quarters had shower and restroom facilities. The other one had four bunkrooms, each with two beds. This one had three bunkrooms, each with one bed. This building also housed the shared kitchen facilities and a small dining area. They'd have to eat in shifts if they were all going to eat in here.

The door to Culpepper's room was open. She sat on her bunk making notes on her tablet.

Steadman introduced himself. "Dr. Culpepper, I'm Commander Chris Steadman. I'll be responsible for your safety while you're here."

Culpepper looked at him with disdain. "I don't think that'll be necessary. I can take care of myself."

Steadman was ready for that. "Glad to hear it, ma'am. It'll make my job easier. I do need to go through a few items of training and procedure with you and Dr. Zindell. Five minutes, at the storage building."

Steadman didn't wait for a response. He turned and walked out.

He found Zindell outside the other crew quarters building, chatting with Drs. Sakhr and Solansky. Dr. Khaled Sakhr was the team geologist. Dr. Jacob Solansky was a cosmologist.

"Gentlemen, I'm Commander Chris Steadman. Chief Petty Officer Guerrero and I will be responsible for your safety while you're here. For the next few days, we'll be operating in three-person teams. Dr. Sakhr, Dr. Solansky, you'll be paired together and Chief Guerrero will provide security and logistical support. Dr. Zindell, you'll be paired with Dr. Culpepper, and I'll be seeing to your security and logistical needs. If you're done stowing your gear, we can head over to the storage building and get started with a few orientation tasks."

Dr. Zindell extended his hand to Steadman. "By all means, Commander. I look forward to working with you. Please lead the way."

Steadman shook his hand and the two men walked across the compound to the storage building.

To Steadman's surprise, Culpepper was there waiting. He'd expected her to be late if she showed at all. Steadman nodded to her. "Thanks for joining us."

Expanding his remarks to both of them, he said, "First rule: No one leaves the compound alone. Always have at least one other person with you, and always let someone else know where you're going and how long you expect to be gone. Understood?"

Steadman looked to both of them for confirmation. Zindell nodded. Culpepper just stared.

Steadman confronted Culpepper and repeated, "Understood?"

Culpepper crossed her arms and scowled at Steadman. "No. Why?"

"To give you a better chance of living long enough to get home. I'm not asking whether you agree to abide by the rule. I don't expect you will. I'm asking whether you understand it. That way when you turn up dead, I'll still be able to sleep at night knowing it wasn't because I didn't do my job."

Steadman repeated, "Understood?"

"Understood," Culpepper hissed through gritted teeth.

Day 4, 0935 hours

Guerrero, Solansky, and Sakhr arrived at what looked like a small, red, extended-cab pickup truck, except that it had no wheels or axles. It had wheel wells, but no wheels, as though someone had taken a production vehicle and hacked away the parts they didn't need.

It was resting about a foot off the ground, standing on four legs extending from the corners of the vehicle.

Guerrero opened the driver's door so they could see inside. "We call this a four-wheeler. Right now this is the only one we have, but we're expecting two more in tomorrow's supply shipments."

Solansky bent down to look underneath. "Do the wheels come in tomorrow's shipment too?"

Guerrero smiled. "It's a functional title, not physical. Don't ask me how it works. Even if I knew I couldn't tell you. This is one of those things—per your nondisclosure agreement—you'll be asked to forget you ever saw when you get back to Earth. Rather than using wheels to roll across the ground, it levitates above the terrain. That enables it to go places even a real four-wheeler can't, like over water, ravines, or up a cliff. We'll be using these whenever we leave camp. The controls are biometrically locked. I'll add both of you to the authorized user list after we go over the basic operation."

Sakhr was visibly impressed. "This is fantastic. I never imagined I'd have access to such tools. How high can it go? Being able to observe the geography from a few hundred to a few thousand feet would be tremendously helpful."

"Right now they're locked to about fifty feet off the ground," Guerrero said. "I think that's an artificial limitation imposed for the safety of the passengers. We'll have to talk to Mr. Swenson about whether we can relax that restriction, and Commander Decker about under what circumstances."

Day 4, 1000 Hours

Dr. Grace Tornquist put her blood pressure cuff away and made a few notes on her tablet. She tucked a lock of hair behind her ear as she looked across the medical lab at Decker. "I appreciate you setting an example for the others in cooperating with the physicals, Captain. It's been my experience that military men don't like doctors."

He finished buttoning his shirt. "It's 'Commander,' and I think you'll find that Steadman and Guerrero will be very cooperative. Neither of them would hesitate to take on that bear with their bare hands, and they'd both be confident they could win the fight. I doubt you can get either of them to admit it, but they're a lot more worried about getting taken out by some unseen microorganism than an alien predator. They're counting on you more than you know. And likely more than they'll admit."

Glad I'm not the only one worried about that, she thought.

"I understood that it's traditional to refer to the commander of a naval vessel as 'Captain,' regardless of actual rank. I realize this isn't a submarine, but surely the circumstances aren't that different."

Decker nodded. "True on both counts, but I think tradition would be better served by sticking to 'Commander,' seeing as we're on dry land and all."

He turned toward the door. "Who do you want to see next?"

81

"Steadman. But it doesn't really matter. I want to be in the way as little as possible, so whoever is available is fine. As long as I get to see everyone today, I'd rather work around their schedules than have them working around mine. But don't you worry about it. I'll ask Weaver to help with the coordination."

Decker smiled as he walked out the door. "Yes ma'am."

Day 4, 1230 Hours

Zindell sat beside Swenson and Sakhr in the science lab as they scanned through video collected by the survey drones during the initial sweep three days earlier.

Swenson pointed to the screen. "I thought you'd find this interesting, Dr. Sakhr. Tracing the main river upstream, back to the south, it starts abruptly here, coming out of the mountain."

Swenson panned the image farther south. "But then here, about a mile away, what would otherwise appear to be the same river abruptly ends with a small lake nestled up against the same mountain. It's almost like soil from the mountain eroded to cover and block the river. But the lake isn't large enough to contain the volume of water coming downstream, and clearly, most or all of that water is coming back out of the mountain here."

Sakhr panned the image. "Yeah. I'm guessing these mountains are mostly limestone. We'll probably find a lot of limestone caves. Like the one your bear disappeared into. The river is disappearing into an aquifer, then reemerging on the other side. This isn't soil erosion to cover the river—that would wash downstream—but the river taking advantage of the natural breakdown of the rock to forge a path through the mountain. It does create a convenient land bridge between the two shores. Still, I think the caves will be more interesting than the aquifer."

Swenson continued scanning through the reconnaissance video, then paused and zoomed in on a lump on the side of a tree. "This is the squirrel, or I should say, squirrel-like creature, that Guerrero mentioned."

Zindell zoomed in tighter on the creature, then started the video forward in slow motion. "I appreciate your effort at precision, Mr. Swenson, but I think we'll quickly grow tired of appending '-like' to everything we say. 'Bear-like,' 'squirrel-like,' 'chimpanzee-like.' If we just call that a squirrel, I think everyone will know what we're talking about." Zindell zoomed in on the image of the creature. "For all I can prove right now, that *is* a squirrel. My father was fond of saying, 'If it looks like a duck, walks like a duck, and quacks like a duck, it's a duck.'"

Zindell rewound the video and watched it again. "With that said, I really can't wait to get a closer look at it. The resolution of these scans is insufficient to be deterministic. I sure would like to get some of its DNA. Assuming it even has DNA. It would be very illuminating to see how it compares to various Earth species."

Swenson jumped up from his seat and pulled a sample case out of a refrigerator. "I can't help you with the

83

squirrel, but our friend Yogi may have left you a sample of *his* DNA."

Swenson held the bag out to Dr. Zindell, whose eyebrows shot up.

"Is that what I think it is? How did you get it?" Zindell took the bag, handling it as if it were a fragile, ancient relic of enormous value.

"We had a severe thunderstorm the day before yesterday. We think Yogi was caught too far from home, so he sought another shelter. He mistook our unfinished supply building for a cave and crashed in the back of it until the storm subsided. After he evacuated, we found that. Evidently, he thought we would find it of sufficient value to cover his tab."

Zindell laughed. "You have no idea, Mr. Swenson."

Swenson turned back to the console. "So I've shown you how to access the sensor logs, including the squirrel and bear footage. I've also tagged all the footage we have of our early encounters with Mikey. Tomorrow morning I'll show you how to operate the survey drones manually. You can do a lot of preliminary exploration remotely from here and then head out into the field when you want to observe firsthand or collect specimens."

Zindell shifted uncomfortably in his seat. "You were supposed to wait for me before you initiated any interactions with local fauna. That's my field. None of you have the training."

Swenson drew back, shifting in his chair away from Zindell. "That's true. But to be fair, we didn't initiate interaction with Mikey. Or with Yogi either, for that matter. Mikey saw us before we saw him. We steered clear, as per the mission protocol. Until he came to us. I can't speak for the commander's thought process, but in my mind, he was faced with two options: try to scare the chimp away, as we did with Yogi, and risk burning a bridge that might prove irreparable, or try to establish ourselves as friends. The mission protocol did call for us to steer clear of local animals until after your arrival. It was Commander Decker's decision to preempt that directive. I'm not defending his decision, but I believe as the mission commander he had the authority to make it. You should take that up with him."

Zindell's nostrils flared as he crossed his arms.

Swenson straightened up in his chair. "I'm curious what you would have done differently."

Zindell's neck muscles corded. "I wouldn't have sent half a team. They should have held you back until we were all ready to come together."

Day 4, 1300 Hours

Dr. Tornquist wasn't there yet when Steadman entered the medical lab for his baseline physical. Not given to wasting time, he started surveying the contents of the medical lab while he waited for her. He was checking through the contents of a refrigerated medicinal storage locker when he heard Tornquist enter the lab behind him.

"Can I help you find something?"

He could hear the disapproval in her voice. He put the bottle he'd been looking at back on the shelf and turned around to face Tornquist. "Sorry, ma'am. Force of habit. Always inventory your surroundings. You may not have time to do it later when the … excrement hits the ventilator."

Tornquist fought to suppress a smile. "Duly noted, Commander, but those are the implements of *my* trade, not *yours*. If they need to be used, *I'll* be the one using them."

Steadman grinned. "Yes ma'am."

"That cabinet was locked. How did you get into it?"

Steadman glanced back at the cabinet. "Yes ma'am. It is. Redundancy is part of the mission protocol. Everyone and everything has a backup. As the second most qualified person on the team for medical emergencies, I'm also coded into the locks."

Tornquist tilted her head as she gave Steadman a mystified look.

Steadman answered the unvoiced question. "A distant second, but second. Special forces training includes significant instruction in battlefield triage. Most special ops mission profiles can't accommodate medical specialists for contingencies, so we train every operator to be able to handle emergencies until we can evac to appropriate facilities."

"So how 'trained' are you?"

Steadman smiled. He glanced back at the cabinet. "I know what about half of that stuff is, what to use it for, and how to use it. And I can use a needle and thread."

Tornquist shook her head. She motioned Steadman to the examination table. "Okay, Rambo. Let's get this over with."

With a smile and a "Yes ma'am," Steadman climbed up onto the table.

Tornquist started her exam with a stethoscope on his chest. "Did the Navy teach you that?"

"Ma'am?"

"Yes. That."

"Oh. That. No ma'am. My dad taught me that. He figured you shouldn't expect other people to respect you if you don't respect them. He said those few extra words may not add any content to the communication, but they wield influence facts can't buy."

Tornquist moved the stethoscope around to his back. "So, how did you get chosen for this mission?"

"No idea, ma'am."

"You're not curious?"

"Sure. But you don't get very far in the Navy if you ask, 'Why me?' every time a commanding officer gives you an order. It's not my job to make that decision. My job is to execute it."

Tornquist flashed a penlight in Steadman's eyes. "I get that. My late husband was career navy. Did they at least let you pick your own team?"

Steadman's mouth twisted. "I'm sorry for your loss. And for your service. Military spouses don't get enough credit for what they give up."

Tornquist nodded.

"To answer your question, sometimes. Usually. But not in this case. Sometimes the information that drives decisions is above my pay grade, as it appears to be in this case. The mission planners picked Guerrero."

"Any concerns about that?"

Steadman scowled.

"Sorry." Tornquist held up her hands. "I'm not trying to stir up trouble. My job is to see to the health of the team. Physical *and* emotional. I'm just looking to get ahead of any personnel problems that might crop up."

She smacked him below the kneecap with a small mallet.

Steadman chuckled. "Alex Guerrero's been part of my team for more than two years. I trust him with my life on a regular basis. He's saved it more than once. I'd have been comfortable with any of the men on my team. If I weren't, they wouldn't still be on my team. Special Forces isn't where you come to prove you have what it takes. You don't get here until you've already proven it. Guerrero has it. And if they'd asked me to pick someone for this mission, he's the one I would've chosen."

Day 4, 1920 Hours

Swenson and Guerrero both kept tabs on Mikey throughout the day. Swenson had tasked one of the drones to track him, worried he might run away and not come back.

The first couple of hours Mikey spent foraging in the trees on the surrounding hills. After he seemed to have his fill, he set up camp in a tree on the edge of a grove facing the compound and watched.

As the activity moved from building to building with different people going about assorted chores, Mikey would from time to time move to other vantage points. Later in the day, he started edging slowly closer to the camp. Anytime he saw Dr. Zindell he would hunker down in the tall grass and try to hide.

That night's campfire was significantly expanded. The bulk of the day had been spent getting laboratory equipment up and running, refining research strategies, and getting baseline medical data on everyone on the team. Now that the sun had set, everyone was looking forward to a real meal and a chance to talk to the others.

Dr. Solansky looked across the circle at Swenson. "Something about this has been bothering me. If this transit portal is so fast and easy, why are we stuck here for three months? Why don't we just go home at night, come back in the morning?"

Dr. Tornquist edged forward in her seat. "It's primarily a medical quarantine issue. One of the big fears is that when we go back, we'll take something with us that might wreak havoc on Earth. So if any of us went home today, we'd have to be quarantined for as long as it took for them to convince themselves that we didn't bring anything risky back."

Solansky nodded. "I guess that makes sense. And we'll probably still have to do that when we finally do return. Though I don't remember that being part of the bargain."

Tornquist smiled. "I can't promise you there won't be a period of quarantine when we get back, but the time here counts for something. If there's anything dangerous here, it should affect us while we're here. If we don't encounter any problems in three months, it's unlikely there's anything problematic for us to bring back. And we're not just waiting for someone to get sick. My main job is to actively look for any infectious agents or toxins that might be problems. If three months doesn't answer that question, it should at least give me a good feel for how large the task is and how big the risks are. When we go back through the transit portal, I expect a day or two —a week tops—in quarantine for standard medical lab work and then we'll be good to go."

As the conversation progressed, Mikey finally worked his way in and joined the group. He sat beside Guerrero, huddling close to his side and giving Zindell, seated on the opposite side of the circle, a warning glare.

Zindell reached under his seat and picked up two bottles of water. He opened one of them and offered it to Mikey. Mikey scrunched up closer to Guerrero, his eyes darting back and forth between the bottle and Zindell. He made no move to reach for it.

Zindell proffered the bottle again. "Mr. Guerrero, she seems to trust you more than me. Would you take this bottle of water and offer it to our friend?"

Guerrero took the bottle and held it out for Mikey, who still ignored it. Meanwhile, Zindell opened the other bottle and drank from it, making a show for Mikey.

The chimp looked up at Guerrero. Guerrero offered the bottle again.

Mikey took the bottle and looked at it. Then he looked back at Zindell.

Zindell took another swallow from his own bottle. "Go ahead. Drink."

The chimp held the bottle out at arm's length. After a moment he turned the bottle upside down, eyes locked with Zindell as the whole bottle poured into the edge of the fire pit.

Weaver giggled, causing everyone to turn to look at her. She covered her mouth and let out a muffled "Sorry."

Guerrero looked at Zindell. "Sorry, Doc. It looks like he still has trust issues."

"I can see that."

Keeping his eyes locked with Mikey, Zindell held his own bottle of water out at arm's length, and after a brief pause turned it over and poured the rest of it out.

Mikey matched Zindell's stare for about ten seconds before he turned to Guerrero and extracted another protein bar from a pocket in Guerrero's tactical vest. The chimp looked back at Zindell as he unwrapped the bar and started eating it.

Everyone tensed up, eyes on Zindell. Guerrero asked, "Do you want me to take it away?"

"What?" Zindell glanced up at Guerrero. "No. If there's any harm, it's probably already been done. It doesn't help matters for both of us to make her mad."

As everyone watched Mikey eat, Zindell said, "I think I'm beginning to understand why she bonded with you so quickly."

Weaver turned to look at Zindell. "Why is that?"

"On Earth, chimps usually live in groups. Clans. But it isn't uncommon for young female chimps to leave their birth clan and join up with a different one."

Weaver's eyebrows squished together. "Why would they do that?"

"Well, no one really knows for sure. It certainly helps maintain the DNA of the species by mingling between populations, but the chimps don't know that. They just do it. In any case, when the young female finds a new clan, she has to earn acceptance. From everything I've seen, and what you've told me, there doesn't appear to be a group of chimps in the immediate area. So she's probably recently left the family of her birth but hasn't yet found another. When she found you, she must have figured, 'Hey. They're weird, but let's hang out and see what happens.'"

Weaver's face lit up. "You keep saying 'she' …"

Everyone stopped eating and looked at Guerrero, who was blinking rapidly.

Weaver laughed. The others joined in.

Guerrero stammered, "Of course I knew that. How was I supposed to know that? Do I look like a zookeeper?"

Guerrero shook his head. He reached over and rubbed Mikey's scalp and said, "So it's Michaela. 'Mikey' still works."

Mikey looked up at Guerrero and stuck out her tongue.

Guerrero lowered his brow. "What? What'd I do now?"

Zindell laughed. "I think that means she's still hungry."

"Oh." Guerrero patted his vest pockets and came up empty. "I'm all out of protein bars. Does anyone else have any?"

Weaver pulled one out of her vest and offered it to him. "Here."

Guerrero reached for it but then said, "No, you give it to her." He nudged Mikey toward Weaver.

Weaver abruptly stiffened in her chair as she pulled her arms against her chest. "No, that's all right. You do it."

Guerrero laughed and smiled at Weaver. "It's okay. He … she … won't hurt you. Go ahead."

Weaver looked furtively back and forth between Guerrero and Mikey before she tentatively reached her hand out toward Mikey, offering the bar.

Mikey looked up at Guerrero and then over at Weaver, then at the snack. The chimp fixed her eyes on Weaver as she slowly reached out and took the power bar. She turned her head toward Zindell and bared her teeth again, warning him to keep his distance.

Everyone—except Zindell and Weaver—laughed. Mikey sat down beside Weaver where she unwrapped her snack and took a bite. Weaver shifted to the edge of her seat, leaning away from the chimp. As Mikey chewed, she turned her head to look up at Weaver but reached with her free hand in a loose fist in the opposite direction toward Guerrero.

Guerrero responded with a fist bump.

"Extraordinary!" Zindell mumbled.

Dr. Culpepper threw her plate into the fire. "I don't believe this!" Looking at Zindell, she said, "You're not actually buying this, are you?" She pointed at Mikey. "It's a trained chimpanzee. Probably from a zoo, or a circus, or something. It's all part of the scam."

Zindell drew his head back. "I beg to differ. Look at her." He pointed at Mikey. "Look at her hands. Her thumbs."

Culpepper looked. "What of it?"

"On Earth, there are two species of chimpanzee. One we call chimpanzee, the other we call bonobo. Within the species of chimpanzee, there are four subspecies. I can assure you, Mikey is none of those. They all have opposable thumbs on both their hands and feet. As does Mikey. But in all of those, the thumbs are relatively short. Look at Mikey's thumbs. On her feet, they're short. Similar to chimpanzee species on Earth. But look at the hands. The thumbs are comparable in length to the fingers."

Everyone was looking at Mikey; Mikey was looking for an escape route.

Zindell continued. "There's more. This is subtle, and I wouldn't expect any of you to notice, but the shape of her head is also distinct from any known population on Earth."

Culpepper sat back in her chair in a huff. "You're all crazy." She looked again at Zindell. "As far as I'm concerned, you're just part of the conspiracy."

Everyone around the campfire was silent, glancing around at each other. Decker was about to speak when Swenson jumped in.

"So, what say we take a scientific approach to all this? We've all made a lot of observations. We've seen things that are out of sorts with our expectations. Let's itemize those observations. Then we can posit theories that might explain them. Then we can test those theories to see if they hold up. Who's in?"

Swenson looked around the circle, making eye contact with each of the scientists one at a time. Each nodded assent, though Culpepper seemed somewhat reluctant.

Swenson looked back at the group. "So, what do we have?"

Guerrero and Zindell both answered in unison, "Mikey."

"Mikey," Swenson echoed. He looked around at each of the other scientists in turn. "Come on, people. You're trained observers. You've been here more than twelve hours. What else have you observed that seems out of the ordinary?"

Commander Steadman looked at Sakhr, the geologist. When Sakhr remained silent, Steadman said, "Gravity seems to be stronger than what we're accustomed to. Mr. Swenson says about ten percent. We should be able to measure that."

Looking at Solansky, the cosmologist, Steadman continued. "There are two moons. The sun is brighter than it should be, and the color seems slightly off. The day is twenty-four hours and sixteen minutes long. That much we've already measured. Mr. Swenson says the year is about six weeks longer than on Earth. Once your instrumentation package arrives, you should be able to verify that. There are no detectable radio frequency transmissions other than our own comm systems. No radio, no TV, no telephone, no GPS, no nothing."

Steadman looked back at Swenson. He nodded. "That sounds like a good start. We can add to it if, or when, new irregularities are found. So, theories?"

Culpepper harrumphed. "Scam."

Swenson nodded. "Fair enough. But to be a useful theory, it needs to be testable. Do you have any testable theories that suggest how each of these observed effects was faked?"

Culpepper started ticking things off with her fingers. "Trained chimp. Something slipped into our food or water to diminish our physical capacity to make us think gravity is stronger. Projections on a dome covering the habitat. Watches and computers modified to misreport time. Equipment modified to report no signals present despite their existence. And let's add this to your list. How is it we managed to travel fifty-seven light-years in the blink of an eye? And how is it that life on this 'alien' planet evolved independently to be indistinguishable from life on Earth?"

Culpepper looked around at her scientific colleagues. "And how is it that supposedly educated and intelligent people can be taken in so easily?"

After a moment of awkward silence, Sakhr said, "The other theory that is obviously in contention is that this is, indeed, another planet, and the life we see around us is, indeed, distinct from Earth life. The discord with that theory seems to be that the life we see around us appears so similar to Earth. And then there's the question of how we got here."

"How we got here is not something I'm at liberty to discuss," Swenson said, "or frankly could explain even if I were. But as to the similarities in life, how do we explain that?"

"Aliens," Guerrero said.

Culpepper rolled her eyes.

Zindell leaned forward, resting his elbows on his knees. "I need more data before I even consider positing a theory regarding the similarities in the fauna." He looked at Culpepper. "I expect that's true of the flora as well."

Culpepper ground her teeth.

Day 4, 2255 Hours

The man standing in the doorway smirked. "The boss didn't seem very happy with your lack of progress on the Kreitzman op."

The man behind the desk waved dismissively. "These things take time. Kreitzman is a smart man with vast resources who runs a tight ship. *Pospeshish' - lyudey nasmeshish*"[1]"

"Russian proverbs aren't going to satisfy the boss. He's more a fan of rushing subordinates."

"That's my problem, not yours. Close the door on your way out."

His unwelcome visitor turned and left, not bothering to close the door behind him.

The man behind the desk turned back to his computer. *I'll tell him what I want him to know when I want him to know it!*

---

1 Translation from Russian: "If you rush things, you'll only make others laugh."

He read the message on the screen.

Arrived at destination. Base camp established by military. Commander David Decker. Commander Chris Steadman. Chief Petty Officer Alex Guerrero. Petty Officer Pam Weaver. Engineer, Rusty Swenson, works for Kreitzman. Looks like Earth, but they went to great lengths to create a few apparent discrepancies. Some team members voicing skepticism. Several schisms to be exploited. Exploration for resources begins tomorrow. Waiting for large astronomical instrumentation package to be delivered.

Excellent. Let's see what we can learn about Commander Decker and his associates.

THIRTEEN

It was another chilly morning, the downtrodden grass of the camp covered with dew. A thin overcast was already beginning to burn off as the sun rose above the hills to the east. Birds could be heard in a nearby grove going about their morning rituals, oblivious to the newcomers whose strange buildings and campfire stood in stark contrast to the natural beauty surrounding them.

As the team huddled around the campfire, some were discussing their plans for the day while stragglers in the group finished their breakfasts.

Decker walked into the middle of the circle by the campfire. "If I can have everyone's attention for a few minutes, we can get the day started."

Conversation stopped and everyone looked at Decker. "I know you're all anxious to get into the field today to start exploring. Unfortunately, we have a couple of key resource limitations, so, for the time being, you'll need to pair up. Dr. Culpepper, Dr. Zindell, you'll be working together today. Commander Steadman will ride along

100

with you to handle the four-wheeler and to provide logistical and tactical support. You'll be in the red vehicle."

Culpepper shook her head. "I have a job to do and I know how to do it. It doesn't help me get it done to have an overgrown Boy Scout and a circus animal trainer tagging along. I can take care of myself."

Zindell bent over, elbows on his knees and forehead in his hands. Decker didn't know whether to think he was insulted by her remark or discouraged at the idea of being paired with her.

"I recognize this is not the most efficient strategy for you to get your job done. It's also not the most efficient strategy for Dr. Zindell to get his job done. I do believe, however, it's the most efficient strategy for the team to get the team's job done, given the resource limitations we're working with."

Culpepper started to jump back in, but Decker cut her off. "I can give you one other option. If you prefer to work alone, Dr. Zindell and Commander Steadman can take the four-wheeler and start exploring, and you can remain here at the compound and focus your efforts inside the secure perimeter."

Decker didn't give her an opportunity to respond. "The second team will be Dr. Sakhr and Dr. Solansky, accompanied by Chief Petty Officer Guerrero. You'll take the blue four-wheeler. There is a third four-wheeler scheduled to come in this morning's supply shipment. For the time being, we'll always try to keep at least one of the three here at the base camp for contingencies. Each field team will have three drones tasked to it. You'll need to coordinate with Mr. Swenson regarding how those are deployed and utilized. He'll be remaining here at the compound to monitor the drones, support the field teams, and help me with the morning supply shipment. Petty Officer Weaver will also be here coordinating data collection and reports. If you have logistical issues, please route those through her. Any other questions or issues?"

Culpepper bounced out of her seat. "Yes, I do. I still —"

Decker ignored her. "Glad to hear it. Let's all get to work." He turned to leave the campfire. Everyone else headed off in eight different directions.

Culpepper stood speechless for a moment and then charged after Decker. She grabbed him by the elbow and spun him around to face her, her face glowing red. "You have no authority to tell me what I can and can't do. I'm not one of your tin soldiers."

Decker looked down at her hand gripping his elbow. He made no move to dislodge it, nor did he respond to her statement until she finally released him. "You're right, Miss Culpepper. I have no authority over anyone on this team—except what they grant me. That truth applies to the military personnel under my command just as much as to the civilians. That's part and parcel of being a human being. We're all created equal. No man has an inherent right to rule over another. But when we join together, whether in a team, a community, a family, or a corporation, we recognize that while we're all equal, we're not all identical. Each of us has strengths; each of us has weaknesses. We join a team believing that we complement each other; that we can accomplish more together than we can as individuals. None of us has inherent authority over another, but we choose some among us to be leaders, believing first that leadership is necessary to the efficient operation of the team, and second that some are more capable leaders than others. When you join a team as a contributing member, you implicitly agree to comply with the directions established by the leadership of that team.

"Now, you've made it abundantly clear that you haven't joined this team. I'm under no illusions about that, and there's nothing I can do to change it. You're the only one who gets to decide whether you will or will not commit yourself to the success of this mission. What I do have authority over is the material resources allocated to us. Those resources are the property of the corporations and government who are underwriting this project. As the owners of that property, they have rights that are absolute, and they've delegated the administration of those rights to me. That includes every building, tool, instrument, article of clothing, and food ration we brought with us."

Her eyes lit up when Decker mentioned clothing and food rations.

He continued. "Now, I don't intend that as a threat. I have no intention of withholding food rations to force

103

compliance. And it wouldn't further the objectives of this mission to deny you access to your analytical instruments. What I will do, and have done, is take measures to limit your ability to go off lone ranger on us. That would put the team and the mission at risk. To say nothing of your own life."

Culpepper crossed her arms across her chest and opened her mouth to speak, but Decker held up a hand to silence her. "Commander Steadman isn't going to wait for you. If you want to get into the field today, you need to have your gear and be on board the four-wheeler when the commander and Dr. Zindell are loaded up and ready to roll."

He glanced over her shoulder to where Steadman and Zindell were already preparing for their expedition. "I'd guess you have about ninety seconds to make ready."

A look of panic washed over Culpepper's face as she jerked her head around to look behind. When she turned back, Decker was gone.

Day 5, 0900 Hours

Weaver came out of the storage building. She and Swenson had set up a workstation there to monitor communications and logistics without being underfoot in the medical or science lab buildings. She circled around behind the building to the staging area for the four-wheelers.

The second team was still finishing preparations as she joined them and handed a tablet to Solansky. "Here you go, Doctor. I pulled your reports to include in today's mission update. I also transferred several files over for you that were sent from Earth."

"Why, thank you, my dear. And please call me Jacob. I very much appreciate this. I expect that Dr. Sakhr will be a lot busier today than will I so this will give me something to read if I get bored."

"I did have a question" Weaver's brow wrinkled. "I noticed an application on your tablet that isn't part of the mission protocol. Do you know what it is or how it got on there?"

Solansky's eyes widened as he pulled the tablet into his chest and glanced sideways at Steadman. "I ... I have no idea."

Weaver tilted the tablet in his hands so they both could see it and pointed to an item on the screen. "This."

Solansky's face paled. "Oh, that." He forced a laugh. "It's just an algorithm I've been working on to translate astronomical coordinates. All of our star charts are based on observations from Earth. Because this planet is in a different place in the galaxy, the same stars won't appear in the same patterns here, so I'll need to translate the data in order to make sense of it."

Weaver tilted her head. "Oh. Okay. Just curious."

Solansky smiled and pulled back his tablet. "It's nothing you need to worry about, my dear."

Sakhr and Guerrero boarded the four-wheeler and took the two forward seats. Solansky used the opportunity to excuse himself. "It looks like my train is getting ready to leave the station."

FOURTEEN

Steadman had parked the four-wheeler near the river. It was a compromise location, a decision he had to make himself and force on his two charges. Culpepper had insisted they explore the wooded areas of the neighboring hills; Zindell said he needed to start his work in the mountain forest.

Zindell's stubbornness seemed out of character to Steadman, but he guessed Zindell had figured out that, paired with Culpepper, if he didn't put his foot down and stand for something, he'd never have a chance to get his own work done.

So Steadman proposed the river. Neither of them liked the idea, but they both grudgingly agreed they could be productive there.

They'd been alongside the water about an hour. Steadman sat on the tailgate of the four-wheeler scanning the horizon. Culpepper had been all over the area within about fifty feet of the vehicle collecting plant specimens and cataloging them.

Zindell had studied the area for about fifteen minutes, mostly looking for signs of animals that might have frequented the area. That was enough for him to decide there wasn't much to see here and ask if they could relocate a little farther upstream where the river broke out from the limestone aquifer.

Culpepper had declined, saying she needed to finish working this area before she moved on. She generously offered to let them go and leave her here. She'd catch up with them later, or they could swing back and pick her up. Steadman couldn't do that, and he suspected Culpepper knew it.

After about fifteen minutes of sitting in the four-wheeler watching Culpepper work, Zindell prevailed upon him for a little handgun target practice and coaching. Steadman showed him how to attach the silencer so they wouldn't need ear protection and so they wouldn't scare any wildlife in the area. Then he tossed various pieces of driftwood they found along the edge of the stream out into the middle, coaching Zindell on posture and grip as he fired at the slow-moving targets.

They hadn't thought to bring extra ammo with them, so it didn't take long for Zindell to exhaust his two clips. Steadman traded a full spare clip for one of Zindell's empties so the doctor would have a live weapon in the unlikely event he actually needed to shoot something before they got back to camp.

Then they went back to sitting on the tailgate of the four-wheeler and watching Culpepper work.

That gave Steadman time to think about things Swenson had said regarding how this planet might have come to be.

"Dr. Zindell, I'm curious what you, as a scientist, think about how life here could look so much like life on Earth."

Zindell harrumphed. Nodding in the direction of Culpepper, he said, "I still don't have enough data to even begin to posit a theory."

"I understand that," Steadman said. "But I'm just trying to work this out logically. Science wasn't my strong suit in school. Most of what I thought I knew about life on other planets I now realize is just fiction. The product of someone's imagination. Until we found this place, no one had ever actually seen life from another planet. But here's the rub: I was taught that life on Earth was a product of millennia of evolutionary processes. Random accidents that occasionally happened to have a beneficial outcome. If that's the case, then it stands to reason that life could happen elsewhere in the universe, but also that life elsewhere would look very different from life on Earth. Because it would be the product of a different series of random events."

Zindell smiled. "That's a reasonable line of thinking and is probably consistent with what the vast majority of people believe. What might surprise you is that modern science contradicts most of that."

Steadman's eyebrows shot up. "What do you mean?"

Zindell shifted on the tailgate. "Well, it's a deep and complex subject. Even if we sat here the rest of the day, and I sincerely hope we won't"—he nodded again toward Culpepper—"we couldn't begin to scratch the surface. So let's keep it simple and start with DNA. DNA is incredibly complex. But it's not just complex. It has specified complexity."

Zindell pointed toward the river. "Look at the gravel in the riverbed. Millions of individual pebbles arrayed in a complex pattern. But the pattern is random. There's nothing specific about it. It doesn't specify anything. But look at this text." Zindell pointed to the screen of his tablet where he'd been reading. "It's composed of a few hundred thousand individual symbols, like the individual pebbles in the riverbed. But these symbols are arranged in a specific pattern, a pattern that specifies something. DNA is like that. Like the book, not the riverbed. DNA has an alphabet. It is composed of exactly four letters. Human DNA has more than three billion of these letters. The letters are grouped together into gene sequences, much like the paragraphs in a book. The gene sequences are grouped together into chromosome pairs, much like individual books. And every cell in the human body contains a complete set, twenty-three, of these 'books.'

"If you printed it out, three billion letters would fill more than a million pages, or more than five thousand typical books. All that information, identical copies, packed into every individual cell. And, as I said, it isn't just a random collection of letters. Every gene sequence has a specific purpose. Many of them are instruction codes that are read by molecular machines within the cell that instruct the machine in precisely how to construct particular proteins. This is where things like the color of your hair, or eyes, or skin come from. Your unique DNA has the precise gene sequence to tell the cells in your eyes to produce the specific protein that results in the particular color of your eyes.

"Other gene sequences perform other tasks. But the point is that DNA is not just a random collection of letters. It is a five-thousand-volume set of instructions for how to build and operate a human being. Evolution theorists would have us believe that these volumes organized themselves by random chance over millions of years. But they've been unable to demonstrate a credible mechanism by which this could happen."

Culpepper, who had been studiously ignoring their conversation, looked up from her work. "Now, you should know that isn't true, Doctor. The Miller-Urey experiment showed that the complex molecules necessary to form the basis for protein synthesis could be generated spontaneously from conditions in the prebiotic atmosphere. And natural selection has been demonstrated to enable the transformation of DNA over time. Neither process needs to make any appeal to a god."

Zindell grinned. "I've made no such appeal. I've merely pointed out that the evidence points strongly to design. In fact, if the Miller-Urey experiment proved anything, it is that intelligent intervention is required.

They had to intervene with the apparatus to prevent interfering cross-reactions and other chemically destructive processes from destroying the assembled molecules faster than they were generated. Further, they had to assume an atmosphere dominated by methane, ammonia, and hydrogen, while evidence strongly suggests that helium and nitrogen dominated the early atmosphere. These neutral gases would have suppressed the requisite chemical reactions. There were likely also significant amounts of oxygen present, which would have further disrupted the production and accelerated the destruction of such molecules. Further still, natural selection has been demonstrated to explain variation within a species, but never transformation from one species to another."

Steadman raised a hand to stop Zindell. "Sorry if I'm asking a dumb question, but what does that mean?"

Zindell smiled again. "Not at all, Commander. About 0.1 percent of the DNA in humans varies from person to person. The 'genome of the species,' as we call it, includes the 99.9 percent that is the same for every human plus all the different variations that exist across the entire human race in that other 0.1 percent. Those variations are things that control eye color, hair color, skin color, gender, and everything else that makes one person physically different from another. Natural selection has been shown to provide a mechanism by which some traits, some genes, become more common in the species as a whole. This is a bad example, but suppose blue eyes made it easier to survive. Over time, more people with blue eyes would survive and reproduce, and blue eyes would become more common in the species. But there would still be people out there with the genes for brown eyes. If the environment changed so that suddenly brown eyes were better for survival, over time brown eyes would displace blue eyes as the more common characteristic.

"That's natural selection. Nature selects—or prefers—one characteristic over another. But the important thing here is that nature didn't create a new gene. It just selected one that already existed that it found more favorable."

Culpepper shook her head. "But gene mutation happens. There are sometimes errors during the gene replication process. While it's admittedly rare, all that is required is for a beneficial mutation to occur. Then natural selection will favor that benefit and it will be propagated."

Zindell chuckled. "Well, first, no one has ever observed a 'beneficial' mutation. When they happen they always represent deficiency—usually catastrophic. Meaning that the cell can no longer function and it dies. But even supposing that once in a million years a truly beneficial mutation did occur, evolution still runs into a problem with irreducible complexity. Charles Darwin himself said that if you ever find an organ or system that is irreducibly complex, his theory would fail."

Steadman rubbed his temples. "Sorry, Doc, but you're over my head again."

113

Zindell turned back to Steadman. "Charles Darwin, who first postulated the theory of evolution, said that 'If it could be demonstrated that any complex organ existed which could not possibly have been formed by numerous, successive, slight modifications, my theory would absolutely break down.' Now, in his defense, in Darwin's day they didn't know about DNA, or even very much about the cell. The crude microscopes available at the time could see a cell, but not the complexity of what's inside. Darwin imagined a cell as a balloon filled with protoplasm. Basically goo. 'Irreducibly complex' means you have to put all the pieces together at the same time or you don't have something that can survive. Evolution requires that a single change happen, Dr. Culpepper's 'mutation,' that the mutation survives into successive generations, and then be augmented by an additional mutation, and so on. Darwin's 'multiple successive mutations.' What Darwin was saying was that if you could find something that required two or more individual, distinct but interacting changes in order to be functional, evolution could not explain that. Today we can point to many such organs and systems. One is the cilia found on the surfaces of many animal and lower plant cells. These are hairlike structures that move fluid over the cell's surface, or sometimes 'row' a single cell through a fluid. Human lung cells have these structures to sweep mucus toward the throat for elimination. There are at least three distinct structures required to make this work. If they don't all come to exist at the same time, in the same cell, the mutation doesn't work. It won't be sustained as part of the genome."

Steadman watched Culpepper dig up another plant. *I would swear she's already collected at least two samples of that plant.*

She looked up at Zindell. "Just because we haven't worked out all the answers doesn't mean some fanciful god had to do it. That isn't science, Doctor. Science is the study of nature. If you start imagining causes outside of nature, it isn't science anymore."

Zindell grinned again. "I beg to differ, Doctor. Science is the search for causes. Every effect has a cause, and we search for what caused the effects we see. If one precludes a whole class of causes before the investigation begins, without any rational basis, *that* isn't science."

Culpepper thrust her shovel into the ground again, this time with more force than necessary. "But what possible rational basis could you have for suggesting deity is the cause?"

Zindell held his hands up. "Again, I'm not suggesting a divine hand. I'm saying that it's reasonable to consider the possibility that living things were designed. The evidence, to me at least, is compelling. If not overwhelming. I'll grant that design requires a designer, and that a designer must necessarily be intelligent. But to preclude that possibility simply because it isn't an idea you're personally comfortable with is not, well, rational."

115

Steadman shook his head. "That's all great, Dr. Zindell, but I'd like to get back to my original question. How is it that life here looks so much like life on Earth?"

Zindell leaned back against the sidewall of the vehicle. "It seems to me there are three possibilities. One, that, as Dr. Culpepper asserts, evolution is true and life evolved independently on both planets. I consider that possibility infinitesimally small for a variety of reasons, most notably how much things look alike on the two worlds, but it must be considered. Two, that evolution is true and life evolved on one planet and then that life was transferred to one—or more—other planets. I've already said what I think of the viability of the theory of evolution, but I grant that the theory must be considered. Three, that life in both places was designed by an intelligence. That intelligence could have designed life once and then transported it to multiple planets, but that would be an unnecessary complication. If you have the knowledge and power to create life once, you would be more likely to just do it again on the new planet. That would further allow you to customize your creations to the unique environment in each location."

Zindell cocked his head to one side. "As I say that, it will definitely be something we want to evaluate. Where we find differences between a chimpanzee on this planet and a chimpanzee on Earth, do the differences make each species better adapted to their respective planets?"

Culpepper dug up another plant. "If so, that would support the evolution theory."

Zindell's face contorted. "Well, not exactly. It wouldn't contradict the evolution theory, the argument being that the environment here favored the particular variations. But it would also be consistent with the design theory, whereby the designer optimized his creations to their environment. What it would undermine is the transport theory. At least as far as design is concerned. Evolution plus transport could still be considered, but the transport would have to have happened long enough ago to allow continued evolution in the new environment. We would also have to consider whether species that evolved on one planet, whichever came first, could have survived on the other long enough to evolve into its optimized form."

Culpepper pulled another empty container from her pack. "There's a fourth theory still to be considered."

"And that is?"

"That this is all a hoax. We're still on Earth and everything we see is from—and originated on—Earth. It looks like Earth life because it is Earth life. That's the simplest explanation and therefore most likely the correct one. Occam's razor."

"It's the simplest theory, but it doesn't explain some very significant observations." Zindell looked up at the pair of moons overhead.

Steadman shook his head. "So you're telling me there's a pretty good chance this place was, in some form, created by aliens. Whether they created it independently or transported life from Earth or another planet,

117

someone else was involved. Someone who might take offense at our uninvited presence on their planet."

Culpepper smirked and shook her head. Zindell shifted to sit upright. "Well, I wouldn't use those words. 'Aliens,' in particular. It's a loaded word that suggests people from another planet. That's a more specific conclusion than I'm willing to draw. In some form or another, what we see here required intelligence. And power. It also required what I would call 'personhood.' A will to change things in a particular direction. Whether that's 'aliens' or 'supernatural deity,' I can't say."

Steadman looked at Culpepper.

She shrugged. "I still say we're on Earth and this is all an elaborate scam."

FIFTEEN

Decker zipped his jacket against the chill of the night air. The sun had set more than an hour ago, and with clear skies overhead the temperature had already fallen more than ten degrees. The smell of burning wood accompanied by the occasional hiss and pop of the campfire reminded him of weekend excursions with his family when he was younger. Much younger.

As he approached the campfire, he noted that most of the team had finished their meals and were engaged in conversation.

"I can't get over how beautiful everything here is," Tornquist said. She looked at Zindell, seated to her left. "I envy you getting to go out and explore today. I've been stuck here in the compound since we arrived, buried under medical evaluations."

Zindell smiled. "It is, indeed. I'm sure before we're done you'll have plenty of opportunities to get out and see it for yourself."

Solansky leaned forward in his chair. "What about Dr. Culpepper's theory—that this is all fake?"

Zindell pursed his lips. "It has to be considered. I certainly can't disprove it yet. At this point, Dr. Culpepper has a lot more data to work with. I wasn't really able to do any meaningful research today."

Decker caught Steadman's eye. Steadman nodded.

Sakhr looked around the circle. "Where *is* Dr. Culpepper?"

Tornquist gestured toward the women's quarters. "She's in her bunk. Said she had work to do and would eat in there."

Zindell quipped, "That's probably better for the rest of us."

Tornquist glared at him.

Zindell held his hands up in mock surrender. "I'm just sayin'."

Weaver looked up at the sky. "Even the stars seem more sparkly than on Earth."

Solansky laughed. "Well, if we *are* in a different part of the galaxy. They *should* look different."

Swenson shook his head. "Actually, in astronomical terms, we're still within spitting distance of Earth. More than ninety-nine percent of the stars you see are more than a thousand times further away from us than Earth's sun. If you pointed a camera in the same direction on both planets, you'd see exactly the same patterns with very few exceptions. We'll see that confirmed when your astronomical instrumentation package arrives."

Solansky shifted uncomfortably on his chair. Weaver's eyebrows squished together. Swenson looked up at the sky. "They seem more sparkly because there's no light pollution here and probably fewer contaminants in the atmosphere to filter the light."

As Weaver turned to say something to Solansky, Decker caught sight of Mikey coming out of the shadows, walking toward the group. He was about to announce her presence when he noticed Guerrero looking directly at the chimp and gesturing. Guerrero grabbed the bill of his baseball cap and tipped it up, then put it back on and made a strong-arm gesture with both arms, baring his teeth. Then he gestured at Weaver, who was seated on the opposite side of the fire.

Weaver was engaged in conversation with Solansky, who was sitting on her right, so her head was turned away where she couldn't see Guerrero's antics. Nor, evidently, did she notice Mikey's approach.

Mikey slipped up behind her, reached over the top of her head, grabbed the brim of Weaver's cap, and in one smooth motion pulled it off, flipped it over, and put it on her own head. Then she mimicked Guerrero's gesture and bared her teeth.

Weaver, startled by someone stealing her cap, turned around to see who had taken it. Mikey's face only inches from Weaver's when Mikey hooted. Weaver screamed and jumped up and away, almost landing in the fire.

Now everyone was watching, most trying hard not to laugh. But Guerrero couldn't contain himself. He nearly fell out of his chair.

Weaver spun around and glared at him. "You!"

She took two quick steps toward Guerrero and grabbed his cap, then proceeded to whack him over the head with it repeatedly. After several blows, Guerrero put his arms up to block her, but he couldn't stop laughing.

Weaver finally let up. She moved her chair to a different spot, as far as she could get from both Mikey and Guerrero and still be around the fire.

Mikey took the cap off and held it out to her.

Weaver looked at it and crossed her arms. "You keep it. I couldn't wear it again anyway."

Mikey put the cap back on, then walked over to a spot beside Guerrero and sat down. Then she and Guerrero exchanged a fist bump.

That started everyone laughing again. Except for Weaver, who gave Guerrero a smoldering glare.

Guerrero decided to change the subject. "I think we should have a contest to pick a better name for this planet. Who's in?"

Swenson raised a hand. "I'm in, but my contribution is to stick with 'Two.' It's simple. Elegant. Descriptive."

Guerrero frowned.

Sakhr raised his eyebrows. "Descriptive? How does 'Two' describe this planet?"

Swenson held out his hands. "It's the second planet with human footprints. You have something better?"

Sakhr straightened up and smiled. "I think we should call it 'Opportunity.'"

Weaver had picked up her tablet and searched for something. Her face lit up. "I like that. But how about '*Benignitas*'?"

Guerrero tilted his head. "Ben is what?"

Weaver smoldered at him again. Looking back at her tablet, she said, "Ben … ig … knee … tas. *Benignitas*. It's a Latin word that can mean benevolence, bounty, or favor." She glared at Guerrero again. "So what's your contribution, meathead?"

Guerrero held up his hands in surrender, trying to defuse the tension. "*Tejas Nuevo.*"

Weaver shook her head.

Guerrero grinned. He looked around the circle. "Dr. Solansky?"

"Well, I really hadn't given it any thought. These things are normally decided by committees of academics after years of discussion and input. I'm not sure it will make any difference what we decide."

Guerrero looked at the ground and shook his head before he continued his lap around the circle. "Dr. Zindell?"

"I hadn't really thought much about it either. I think I'll wait until I've seen more of the planet before suggesting anything."

Guerrero tilted his head and took a deep breath. "Fair enough. But I, personally, am going to go with '*Tejas Nuevo*' until something sticks."

Swenson laughed. "And I'm going to stick with 'Two.'"

For the last few minutes, Steadman had been staring into the fire, elbows on his knees. He looked up at Swenson, who was sitting opposite him on the other side of the fire. "So, Mr. Swenson …"

"Will someone *please* call me Rusty!"

Decker chuckled.

Steadman cast a dark glance in Decker's direction, then turned back to Swenson. "Rusty. I had a long conversation today with Dr. Zindell about why life here and on Earth seems to be so similar. He seems to be on board with you that there's some kind of intelligence behind the connection. But he doesn't have an opinion on whether that points to aliens or God. What do you think?"

"Thanks," Swenson said. "Now, was that so hard?"

Steadman forced a smile.

"From an objective science perspective, I don't think we can rule either out. But from a philosophy perspective, I lean heavily toward deity."

"Why?"

"I'm guessing your conversation with Dr. Zindell was around biology. Biology makes a solid case for design, at least as far as the question of the origin of life is concerned. But I think it's easier to address your question by examining the origin of the universe."

"How so?"

"Are you familiar with the big bang theory?"

Steadman nodded.

"The big bang theory says that the universe had a beginning. That all matter and energy, even space itself … and time itself … had a beginning. Before that, nothing existed. It isn't that space and time *existed* but were empty. Space and time themselves had a *beginning*. That's a big problem for the atheist, the person who says there is no God."

"Why?" Steadman asked.

"One of the fundamental principles of science is that every effect has a cause. Any time something changes, something caused it. Without that principle, science couldn't exist. So every change requires a cause. The universe wasn't. Then it was. What caused it? Well, the universe didn't exist, so the cause for the universe can't be part of the universe. If it doesn't exist, how can it cause itself to exist? So the cause has to be something outside the universe. Something that existed before the universe and exists beyond it. Something that is beyond nature. Something supernatural. That something must also have a will. It must be able to make a decision, to choose."

"Zindell said that too. Why?"

"There are two types of causes; some say three. One type of cause is that, by its very nature, it simply *must* be. The logs in this fire burn because of the chemical composition of the wood, the presence of oxygen, and the presence of sufficient heat to initiate combustion. It simply must burn.

"The second type of cause is that someone made a decision to change things. Before Guerrero lit this fire, it didn't burn. There wasn't enough heat available to initiate combustion. But he decided he wasn't happy with that condition, and he acted outside the system of stacked wood and available oxygen and added an external heat source. A person acted to cause change.

"The third type of cause is random chance. When you flip a coin, it might come up heads, it might come up tails. Random chance. But in reality, nothing is random. The toss of the coin can be reliably predicted if you model enough of the parameters that control its trajectory. Gravity, air resistance, height off the floor, rate of spin, force applied when it's flipped. We use 'random chance' to explain things we haven't studied enough to adequately model the underlying physics. As Albert Einstein once said, 'God does not play dice.'

"So to argue the first type of cause for the universe, that it simply must be … why wasn't it? It had a beginning. Before that, it wasn't. If it simply must be, why wasn't it? The only type of cause left is that some 'person' chose to create it. Thus the designer of the universe is a person. I can argue along similar lines that this person is eternal, which is to say that he exists beyond time. He is also supremely powerful. In the context of the universe as we know it, he created it, and that makes him more powerful than anything in it. And he is supremely intelligent. The complexity of what he has created is beyond our ability to comprehend."

"So you don't think there are any aliens?"

"That's a different question. I think there is a God. I think he created the universe. I think he created life, both on Earth and here. I think he created humans. Did he create aliens—intelligent life, human analogues—on other planets too? He's certainly demonstrated that he's capable of doing it. The question is whether he chose to. So far we haven't seen any evidence of it here, but unless he comes and tells us otherwise, or we find an actual example, we'll never know. We'd have to search the entire universe."

Steadman shifted in his chair. "Okay. But I still don't see how that explains why life here looks so much like life on Earth."

"The same designer created life in both places."

Steadman shook his head. "I'm not following."

Swenson pointed to the gun strapped to Steadman's thigh. "If you ask a gunsmith to design a pistol, you'll get a pistol. If you ask the same gunsmith to design a rifle, you'll get a rifle. It will look different than the pistol. But if you look closely at the details, you'll find the two have a lot in common. Part of that commonality is driven by similarities in the functional requirements. Both devices, at some level, do the same thing. They shoot bullets. Likewise, part of the *difference* is driven by the *unique* functional requirements. The pistol needs to be compact. The rifle needs to be accurate and powerful. But another part of the commonality is driven by the personality of the artisan. Every engineer has his own preferred solutions for particular problems. Every artist has his own style. You can often tell who designed or painted something by looking at what they created, without regard for whether they signed it. Even if this planet were a complete work of fiction—or a hoax, as Dr. Culpepper asserts—the design pattern evidence on Earth alone is a compelling argument that life on Earth was designed. If you look at the animal kingdom, you see the same design patterns used over and over, in slightly different ways. Eyes. Ears. Arms. Legs. Tails. Fingers. Toenails. Tongues. Hair. Stomach. The list goes on, components large and small. This reality is so commonplace we scarcely notice it.

"The evolutionist will say that each of these components evolved once, and every creature that has that feature is descended from a common ancestor. The problem is, when you stack up all the different components that make up all the different known animals, there's no way to construct even a hypothetical evolutionary tree that explains it all. It requires, at many points, parallel evolution of similar features in multiple branches independently. It's possible. But almost infinitely improbable.

"Faith is believing something you can't prove. I would argue that it requires a lot more faith to believe evolution explains life on Earth than to believe all those forms were created by a single designer. That same designer, the one who created the whole universe, created life here. Common designer. Common design patterns. And so it logically proceeds that life on Two would look a lot like life on One."

Day 5, 2305 Hours

The man behind the desk stared at the new message.

New tech. 'Classified.' Vehicle floats. No wheels, no fans, no sound. Low speed, extremely limited altitude. Team is dysfunctional. Lots of personality conflicts. Plan for resource exploration not well thought out or executed. Incompetence? Not a priority? Looking more like a scam. Engineer is trying to explain away similarities as an act of God. Was concerned about being able to sustain the legend, but no one here seems to be doing any real science. Might go months without anyone noticing.

Flying cars. Now we're getting somewhere. It sounds like I need to increase my focus on Mr. Swenson.

SIXTEEN

Day 6, 0615 Hours

Decker zipped his jacket against the chill as he left the kitchen with a steaming cup of coffee. If he'd been back home, he'd have assumed that fall was turning into winter. He had to remind himself that they didn't yet know enough about the seasons on this planet, or this particular location on this planet, to know this wasn't the middle of summer. Or winter, for that matter.

He found Guerrero at the campfire working to rekindle it. Decker set his coffee on a chair and grabbed an armload of wood stacked nearby. He figured that was probably Guerrero's work too. Alex really seemed to get into this campfire thing. Decker was glad of it. It was proving to be a valuable bonding experience for the team.

Well, most of them anyway.

Decker set his armload of firewood down beside the pit. "Morning, Chief. Can I give you a hand there?"

"Thanks, Skipper. It's a bit cool out this morning. I thought breakfast might go a little better with a good fire."

The kindling had a healthy flame by now, so Guerrero started adding Decker's wood. It didn't take long to have a decent blaze. The two men sat by the fire and nursed their cups of coffee.

Decker picked up a stick to poke the coals. "The story between you and Petty Officer Weaver: Is that anything I need to know about?"

Guerrero smiled as he shook his head. "No, sir, but it's not exactly a secret. We grew up in the same town but didn't really run in the same circles. I helped her out with a problem once. Football practice had ended, and everyone was flooding into the parking lot to leave. She was trying to get into her car, but some guy claiming to be her boyfriend—she clearly didn't agree—was harassing her. I intervened so she could leave, and then I explained to him that he would probably live a longer, happier life if he forgot about her and moved on. He seemed to get the message. She joined the navy about the same time I did, but we were on different paths. We've connected a couple of times briefly when one of my missions overlapped with one of her postings. It's never been more than sitting at a table in the mess hall and catching each other up on hometown gossip."

Decker suspected there was more to the story but decided to let it go. "Thanks for letting me know, Chief."

He heard a door open and saw Tornquist and Weaver coming out of the kitchen with their breakfasts and heading toward the campfire.

He put a hand on Guerrero's shoulder as he stood. "Just as a friend, Alex, you may want to think seriously about looking her up after we get home."

Day 6, 0645 Hours

Half an hour later everyone had collected around the campfire. A few stragglers were still eating their breakfasts, but the conversation was lively. The one notable absence was Culpepper.

Decker excused himself from the group. He found her alone in the science lab. "Good morning, Dr. Culpepper."

Culpepper nodded curtly. "Commander. Now, if you'll excuse me, I have a lot of work to do before I head out into the field. I wouldn't want to delay anyone's departure this morning."

"That won't be necessary, Doctor. You'll have all day to get it done."

She glared at him. "What's that supposed to mean?"

"It means you're grounded. You're staying here today so Dr. Zindell will have the same opportunity to do his work today that you afforded yourself yesterday."

"But you can't do that!"

"I can. I did. I read Commander Steadman's report of yesterday's field trip. If you're going to behave like a child, I'm going to treat you like a child. Until you learn to share and play well with others, you're in time-out."

Decker turned to leave, but Culpepper called after him. "That's not fair! I don't know what they told you, but it isn't true. I was very cooperative yesterday."

He turned back to face her. "No, you weren't. Dr. Zindell corroborated every word of Commander Steadman's report, and it's completely consistent with my own observations of your behavior. You had your opportunity to work in the field yesterday. Today you can work here in the lab. Tomorrow? We'll see."

Day 6, 0900 Hours

"Where to?" Steadman asked as Zindell climbed into the passenger seat.

Zindell glanced over his shoulder at the empty back seat and grinned. "The waterfall!"

Steadman pointed the vehicle toward the mountains. Both men scanned the landscape intently as they cruised a few feet above the grass navigating between the hills and orchards.

As they approached the base of the cliff, Steadman glanced at Zindell. "I'm curious what you think of Dr. Culpepper's theory that this is all a hoax?"

Zindell tilted his head and raised an eyebrow. "It's a theory. And it's not without merit. Good science requires objectivity—a willingness to consider alternate explanations. Until and unless we find facts that contradict her theory, it must be considered. Today, we collect facts. And we see where they lead."

"Dr. Culpepper doesn't seem to share your objectivity."

Zindell chuckled. "To be fair, no one is completely unbiased. Even me. I *want* this to be real. The prospect of

133

studying real alien life? It's been a fantasy since I was eleven years old. But to do good science, I have to set that bias aside. And the first step is to recognize that it exists."

They arrived at the base of the waterfall and both men got out of the four-wheeler. Steadman had his rifle at the ready as he surveyed their surroundings. Zindell's attention was captivated by the panorama.

The cliff face ran roughly north and south, facing toward the campsite to the east. Even from the base of the cliff, the view was spectacular. The lower fall was about fifty feet tall. A pool formed at the bottom where the water cascaded down the cliff face. The pool fed a stream that led out to the east a short distance before merging into the river.

Above the lower fall was another that was closer to two hundred and fifty feet tall. A ledge about twenty-five feet across interrupted the cascade of water down the cliff face. Over time, the impact of the water on the shelf had hollowed a deep crevice, collecting water to form another pool that fed the lower falls.

"What's the plan, Doc?"

Zindell seemed not to hear.

"Doc?"

"What?" Zindell turned to look at him. "Oh. My apologies." He turned his gaze back to the waterfall. "You have to admit, whoever put this hoax together spared no expense making it look stunning."

Steadman laughed.

Zindell's eyes followed the stream to where it met with the river. "I don't think we'll see much here we didn't see by the river yesterday. We should move up to the ledge between the two falls. I expect that to be more interesting."

They loaded into the vehicle and headed up the mountain. The area around the upper pool was much rockier than down below. The continuous rush of water from the upper falls served to wash away any soil, and even most smaller rocks. The water in the pool was crystal clear, at least around the edges where the turbulence was less dramatic. Medium and large stones lined the bottom of the pond. The bare rock gave little opportunity for vegetation beyond the green moss that covered most everything.

Steadman looked at the pond. "Now I wish I'd brought a fishing pole."

Zindell chuckled. "There aren't likely to be any fish in there. The vertical drop of the fall would prevent fish in the stream below from getting here. It's possible some might wash down from the stream above, but the reproductive patterns of fish make that unlikely. Assuming fish here are anything like Earth fish. With that said, there's a good chance we might find amphibians—frogs or snakes or the like—in there."

Steadman had worked his way around to the other side of the pool. "Over here."

Zindell looked in his direction. Steadman motioned toward the rocks. "This looks to be where they come for water. The trail leads along the cliff face to the south."

As Zindell turned to make his way to the other side of the pool, his foot slipped and he lost his balance. Everything slowed as he saw the water rushing up toward him.

He shifted his weight and managed to get his right foot planted on a large submerged rock, arresting his fall. He quickly reversed direction, stepping back out onto dry ground, but his boot was soaked and his pant leg dripping wet.

Steadman rushed around to help. "Are you okay?"

"Yeah. I'm fine." Zindell shook his leg. "Just a little wet. For the record, the water is cold."

Zindell made his way carefully around to the other side of the pool where he found a shallow inlet lined with coarse gravel. Unlike the rest of the perimeter, there was very little moss growing here despite the wet surfaces.

"You have a good eye, Commander. It looks like animal traffic has forced out most of the moss. But where do you see a trail? There's nothing but bare rock in every direction."

"Over here. See the scratches on the rock surface along this path? They're much more concentrated along here in this direction."

Zindell's eyebrows shot up. "You're right." Zindell crouched and ran his fingers over the scratches in the rock surface. He shook his head. "Unfortunately, scratches on limestone won't tell me much about what kind of animals were here."

Steadman took a few steps along the path. "You're not going to get a mold of a footprint, but I'm pretty sure some of these scratches were made by hooves, and others were made by claws."

"Is there enough of a trail for us to follow?"

"Sure." Steadman activated his comm. "Mr. Swenson, we're about to go for a hike. How's our perimeter?"

Swenson's reply was immediate. "Looks good. Lots of small critters nearby, but they're all steering clear of you. No sign of anything big."

"Roger that. I trust you'll be able to hang with us as we hike."

"You got it. Just stay out of the caves."

"That's the plan."

Steadman clicked off his comm. "Do we need to set a probe here?"

Zindell shrugged. "We can do it when we get back."

Steadman walked back to the four-wheeler and shouldered his pack, then gestured for Zindell to grab his own.

Zindell's shoulders drooped. "Is that really necessary?"

"Be prepared." Steadman handed Zindell the pack and started walking.

Day 6, 0900 Hours

"Where to, gentlemen?" Guerrero asked as Solansky boarded the four-wheeler.

Sakhr looked to Solansky, who shrugged. Sakhr motioned toward the mountains. "Up."

Solansky nodded. "Works for me."

Guerrero urged the four-wheeler in that general direction and pulled up a topographical map to look for an efficient path up the nearest mountain.

As they approached the cliff face, Guerrero veered to the north where he thought he'd found a good path the vehicle should be able to navigate. Unfortunately, the forest thickened quickly, making it impractical to thread between the trees.

He elevated the four-wheeler to its maximum height—which put them just above the tops of the trees—and started forward again.

It became apparent the trees were getting taller when branches started scraping the bottom of the vehicle as they ascended the mountain. Guerrero maneuvered among the treetops trying to get higher, but progress was slow, and he frequently had to backtrack.

Swenson's voice came over the comm. "I don't think you can get there from here, Alex. I had one of the drones survey between you and the top of the mountain. The trees are too tall and too dense. It doesn't look like there's a way to the top using the four-wheeler with its current operating limitations. I recommend you turn around and work your way back down. We'll have to explore options and try again tomorrow."

Guerrero looked to Sakhr, who ducked his head and slumped his shoulders.

"Roger that," Guerrero said.

"I've had the computer plot an optimal path off the mountain and back to camp based on the survey data. It's already been uploaded. If you engage the autopilot, it should have you back at camp in about thirty minutes."

"Autopilot? What's that?" Guerrero clicked off the radio and turned the vehicle around to begin a winding descent of the mountain.

After he got far enough down the mountain to get a little maneuvering room between the trees, he gradually turned their trajectory to one side, running parallel to the slope of the hillside.

Sakhr had been staring out the window, seemingly mesmerized by the birds-eye view of the terrain, when his head jerked back. "This doesn't seem like a very optimal path down."

Guerrero grinned. "That depends on what you're optimizing for. Are you here to explore your bunk, or that?" Guerrero pointed past Sakhr at the view of the valley below. Though small, their camp was clearly visible below: five geodesic domes and the spherical portal arranged in a neat circle. But the rest of the scene was breathtaking. Rolling hills with their patchwork of grasslands, orchards, and small forests, framed on one side by the river meandering through the countryside as it made its way to a distant ocean. Even at this altitude, the ocean was beyond the horizon, but that added to the illusion that the river went on forever.

"It *is* beautiful. I'll give you that."

Guerrero tapped a button on the console and the window in Sakhr's door whipped open.

Sakhr flinched, jerking away from the open panel. He looked at Guerrero with wide eyes.

Guerrero tilted his head back and inhaled deeply through his nose. "Smell that?" he yelled to be heard above the roar of wind blowing past the open windows.

Sakhr turned back to the window and sat up straight, sniffing tentatively. He closed his eyes and inhaled deeply. "Cedar," Sakhr shouted.

Solansky leaned forward from the back seat and yelled, "Now that that's settled, do you suppose we could put the window back up? It's quite windy back here where I'm sitting!"

Guerrero turned to stare at Solansky. He glanced over at Sakhr, not entirely sure he'd heard what he thought he heard.

Sakhr reached over and toggled the control to raise the window.

"Thanks." Dr. Solansky sat back in his seat as Guerrero turned back to piloting the vehicle. "So, what do you think of Dr. Culpepper's latest theory, Mister Guerrero?"

Guerrero raised an eyebrow.

Sakhr looked over into the back seat. "What theory is that?"

Solansky crossed his arms over his chest and nodded toward Guerrero. "She doesn't think they're here to protect us. She thinks they're here to keep an eye on us to make sure we don't get near anything that might expose this … hypothetical … hoax."

Guerrero banked the four-wheeler hard and accelerated down the mountain slope. The sudden maneuver threw Sakhr and Solansky against the side of the vehicle and pinned them against their seats. He banked again in the opposite direction and leveled out.

Sakhr righted himself in his seat and stared wide-eyed at Guerrero. "What was that all about?"

Guerrero grinned. "That." He nodded toward Sakhr's window.

Sakhr edged his eyes sideways, his head following slowly around before he suddenly jerked his whole upper body around to stare out the window, his mouth agape.

Guerrero's hands caressed the four-wheeler's controls as he maintained formation with a large bird less than twenty feet away. It looked like an eagle, floating effortlessly alongside them on wings that must have spanned at least seven feet. "Now that's something you don't see every day."

Sakhr reached for the window control, but Guerrero blocked him. "I'd rather you didn't do that. He'll hear the noise it makes too, and it might scare him off. Or worse, the airflow disruption might draw him in. I don't want to be trying to keep this thing in the air with ten pounds of muscle, beak, and talon flailing about."

Sakhr swallowed hard as he withdrew his hand from the control panel. He turned back to the window.

TWO

Guerrero shadowed the eagle as it began a slow bank down and away. He focused so tightly on the raptor that he forgot about the trees below him until three of them in rapid succession whipped against the bottom of the vehicle.

Sakhr shot up in his seat, avoiding a concussion only because the seat belt held him in place.

Guerrero pulled up and leveled off.

Sakhr stared blankly out the front windshield. "Let's don't do that again."

Guerrero shook his head grinning. "You can't soar with eagles if you're not willing to whack a few trees."

SEVENTEEN

Dr. Tornquist let the door swing closed behind her as she walked into the medical lab with two cups of coffee.

Weaver looked up from her workstation and smiled. "Please tell me one of those is for me."

Tornquist shook her head. "After three hours studying lab results and writing medical reports, I thought I needed two," she said as she set one down beside Weaver.

"You and me both." Weaver took the mug and held it under her nose as she inhaled the aroma before taking a sip.

Tornquist leaned back against the edge of a console nursing her own. "So, how did you manage to get this assignment?"

"What?" Weaver's head jerked around. "Oh. General Fleming assigned me."

Tornquist raised an eyebrow. "I thought you were the one who managed the research of prospective candidates."

143

Weaver turned back to her computer. "Yes, I did. But General Fleming made the final determinations."

"Did he override any of your recommendations?"

Weaver looked up at Tornquist, then looked past her at the ceiling. "No, I don't guess he did. Well, except for me."

Tornquist raised an eyebrow. "What do you mean, 'except for you'?"

She tilted her head. "Well, my name was on the list, but I put it at the bottom. When he asked why my name was so far down, I explained that I had a conflict of interest. As the person responsible for researching the list and making recommendations, it didn't seem right to put my name at the top. I had considered removing it entirely, but that didn't seem right either. I did feel I was qualified, after all."

Tornquist took a sip from her mug. "Did you want the job?"

Weaver beamed. "General Fleming asked me that too. I didn't answer, but I think he could see it in my eyes. I've never wanted anything more in my life. The next day when the list came out, I was on it. And here I am."

Weaver turned back to her computer.

Tornquist blew on her coffee. "So, what's the story between you and Guerrero?"

"Guerrero?" she asked, just a little too quickly. "I ... I don't know what you're talking about."

Tornquist laughed. "Yes, Guerrero. He flirts with you. You flirt with him. And it didn't just start on this mission —you two obviously have a history."

Weaver's face reddened. "I don't know what you're talking about." Her eyes were fixed on the computer and her hands hovered nervously over the keyboard, but she wasn't typing anything.

Tornquist laughed again. "Come on. I'm an old romantic. I notice these things. And as the team physician, I have access to all your files. I know you both grew up in the same town and are the same age. You had to have at least been aware of each other."

"Well, yes." Weaver rested her hands in her lap. "We attended the same church and the same education co-op, but we ran with different friends and participated in different activities."

She pushed back from the console and turned to face Tornquist. "The only significant interaction we had was in the parking lot one day after a football practice. One of the players had told all his friends he was going to take me to the prom. *Then* he told *me* he was taking me to the prom. I tried to be polite … the guy was a real jerk … but I told him I had no interest in going anywhere with him. But he wouldn't take no for an answer." She turned her head and looked down to her right. "I kept trying to get into my car so I could leave, but every time I opened the door he slammed it shut. I was getting worried and wondered if anyone would step in to help me; most of the kids were afraid of him. And then Alex came over."

145

She looked back up at Tornquist. "He looked Chuck in the eye and asked me if there was a problem here. Chuck balled up his fists and said 'This is none of your business, Gordo.' Alex laughed at him. He was standing there all straight and calm like he was afraid of nothing. Chuck didn't like being laughed at. He took a swing at Alex."

Weaver's eyes drifted off into the distance as she shook her head. "Everything else was just a blur, but I'd swear it was over in less than two seconds. Chuck was on the ground screaming in pain, holding his shoulder, with blood flowing from his nose and a cut over one eye. Alex told him, and I quote, 'The day you set foot within ten feet of Pam again will be the day they measure you for a casket.'" She looked at Tornquist again. "I found out later Alex had dislocated Chuck's shoulder and broken his nose. He got into a lot of trouble over the incident. Chuck's dad was the mayor. They were going to have Alex charged with battery. He would have been kicked off the football team, and it would probably have kept him out of the navy. Somehow Alex's dad managed to sort things out. His dad is a Texas Ranger. Not the baseball team."

Tornquist blew on her coffee and took another sip. "And after that?"

Weaver smiled. "Chuck never came near me again."

Tornquist shook her head. "No, not Chuck. Alex."

Weaver's face twisted up. Then she frowned. "Oh. Well, nothing really. When we saw each other around town, I'd smile at him. He'd smile back. Nothing ever came of it. He was just letting me know he was still looking out for me. I think he just assumed I was grateful for what he'd done ... which I was."

Tornquist sighed. "Men can be so dull sometimes."

Weaver sighed. "Tell me about it."

EIGHTEEN

Decker met Guerrero's team as they rolled back into camp. Sakhr was the first out of the vehicle, stumbling out almost before it stopped and grabbing on to the side to keep himself upright.

"How'd it go, gentlemen?"

Sakhr smiled meekly. "A venture I'll not soon forget."

Decker glanced at Guerrero, who shrugged. "Did you learn anything?"

"About geology?" Sakhr straightened up. "No. Mostly we just saw trees, not geology. As to what we should try next? Maybe. I'll need to spend some time with Mr. Swenson discussing options."

Decker turned to Solansky. "And you?"

Solansky shook his head. "No. I'll work with what I can get, but I need a location with a good view of the horizon in every direction, and ideally as high as practical." He gestured toward the high mountain to the west of camp, beyond the waterfall. "It really needs to go on top of that peak."

"Understood. By the way, your astronomical instrumentation package was delayed again. Something about 'calibrating the optics.' They say maybe tomorrow."

A brief hint of a smirk crossed Solansky's face before he closed his eyes and exhaled. "No problem. It'll get here when it gets here. I don't have a location identified for it yet anyway."

"Does either of you want to go back out this afternoon?"

Solansky deferred to Sakhr.

Sakhr stole a furtive glance at Guerrero before he shook his head. "No. I need to work with Mr. Swenson to find a better way to survey the geography. Is there any way we can relax the altitude governor on the four-wheeler? If I could take that straight up to five or ten thousand feet, I could learn a lot."

Decker nodded. "Let me talk to Mr. Swenson. I need to understand why that limitation was put in place before we talk about relaxing it. We may need to consult with Earth before making changes."

Sakhr and Solansky headed for Swenson's workstation in the storage building. Decker and Guerrero walked toward the transit portal, where Weaver was still working to unload the morning's shipment of supplies.

"How did things go with Dr. Culpepper this morning?" Guerrero asked. "I suppose under the circumstances I should offer to take her out to explore on the four-wheeler this afternoon."

Decker smiled. "Bravery above and beyond the call of duty?"

"Just trying to do what's best for the team, Skipper."

"Appreciate that, Chief. But it won't be necessary, at least not yet. She isn't here."

"Isn't here? On the planet?"

"No ... she's still on the planet. The last update Mr. Swenson gave me was that she was in that first grove to the north."

"By herself? Is that safe?"

"Yes and no. We're keeping an eye on her, but there are limits to how well we can protect her when she insists on doing things her own way." They arrived at the portal and started unloading cargo. "She started out this morning trying to steal the third four-wheeler. As soon as she figured out she was locked out of the controls, she loaded her pack and headed off on foot into the hills, doing her best to get there without being seen. Of course, she triggered the perimeter array and a survey drone locked onto her immediately. Swenson has been tracking her discreetly ever since and has a couple of extra drones monitoring her perimeter."

Decker looked over his shoulder at Guerrero. "You'll be interested to know that your friend Mikey has also taken up the cause. One of the drones spotted him ... her ... in the trees keeping an eye on her. As far as we can tell, Culpepper hasn't noticed yet."

Decker turned back to his work. "Realistically it will take us at least two minutes to get to her if anything happens. We'll just have to hope no threats arise faster than that."

Day 6, 1105 Hours

"Commander, we may have a problem."

Steadman crouched and readied his rifle. Zindell nearly crashed into him before he realized Steadman had stopped.

Steadman keyed his radio. "What's up, Rusty?"

"Yogi just popped up. About fifty yards behind you, to your north."

Steadman spun around and lowered his voice. "That puts him on the path we just came down, between us and our four-wheeler."

"That's affirmative."

Zindell felt his gut tighten. "What's he doing?"

Steadman gestured emphatically for Zindell to keep his voice down. He took cover behind a large tree and motioned Zindell to hide behind another.

"If I didn't know better, I'd say he was waking up. He looks kind of groggy. Moving slowly … now he's rubbing his back against a tree."

Zindell pulled out his tablet. "Rusty, can you route the video to me?" He shifted around and sat with his back against the tree as he surveilled the bear. "He probably just woke up from a nap. Must have a cave nearby. That may explain why he didn't show up sooner on your cameras. He'll probably look for water next. Then food."

Steadman surveyed the surrounding terrain. "Which means he's about to head straight for the waterfall where we parked our four-wheeler."

Zindell's heart raced. "Unless he catches wind of us first."

Steadman shook his head. "No, we're downwind of him here. But that only buys a little time. Once he has his fill of water, the trails indicate this is the most likely direction he'll go looking for food. It also means if we try to circle around him to get back to the four-wheeler, we'll be upwind of him before we can get to safety." Steadman pulled out his own tablet. "Rusty, please retask one of the drones to me."

Steadman tinkered with the tablet.

"What are you looking for?" Zindell whispered urgently.

"Options. Keep an eye on Yogi and let me know if he starts moving."

Steadman looked uphill to their left. He motioned for Zindell to join him. "Follow me. Stay close, and stay quiet."

They climbed the hillside between the trees, moving cautiously. After traversing about fifty yards up the slope, they turned north across the face of the mountain to flank Yogi's last location. A short distance forward they found a rocky area devoid of foliage. There were small bushes and patches of grass, but no trees; the terrain wouldn't support them. Instead, several large boulders provided some measure of cover, and more importantly, a clear view of the trail, almost all the way back to the waterfall.

Yogi finished his back-scratching session and started down the trail. As expected, he headed for the waterfall.

Zindell pulled out his binoculars. The zoologist in him wished he could get a lot closer; the human in him wished he was a lot farther away. He took some comfort in his belief Steadman could protect him, though he would have been a lot more confident if they were sitting in the four-wheeler.

They lost sight of Yogi just before he reached the waterfall. Zindell got up to move but Steadman grabbed his arm and pulled him back down.

"Shouldn't we move while he's distracted at the pond?"

"And go where? We're two and a half miles from camp. On foot. He might not follow us. But if he does, we'd be stuck out in the open without good defensive options." Steadman shook his head and looked over the rocks at the trail below. "This is our best tactical option. Be patient and wait him out. If he picks up our trail, it should take him well past where we are now before he turns back. That will put us much closer to the four-wheeler than him and give us a better chance."

Zindell wasn't sure he agreed, but he sat back down and switched over to the video feed from the drone that tracked the bear.

When Yogi arrived at the pool he lumbered over to their vehicle and sniffed all the way around.

153

After a couple of minutes, he lost interest and headed for the water. He stepped into the shallow end up to his ankles on all four paws and drank. Then he sat down in the shallow water.

A few minutes later, Zindell began to worry the bear had settled in for another nap when Yogi got up and headed back toward the trailhead. As he passed the four-wheeler, he sniffed around the edges again before he continued down the path.

Once the bear came far enough that he could be seen from their vantage point, both Zindell and Steadman went back to binoculars. Every few feet the bear would stop and sniff at the air or the ground as he made his way along.

"That's not good," said Steadman. "He's tracking us. He picked up our scent from the four-wheeler, and he's following it."

Zindell fought the urge to run. "But he shouldn't have any reason to associate our scent with food."

"Maybe. Maybe not. We smell like animals; different, but the same. It may well be curiosity driving him more than a hunt for food. I imagine that depends on how hungry he is. The good news is, there appears to be plenty of food around here, so he isn't likely to be starving."

They continued watching Yogi as he followed their trail down the path until he got to the point where they had stopped earlier at Swenson's warning. Yogi sniffed around the area for a couple of minutes, then started up the hill along the path they had taken about an hour ago.

Steadman repacked his binoculars and shouldered his pack. "We need to get moving."

Zindell drew his handgun.

Steadman whispered urgently, "Put that away. In a fight with a bear, it's worse than a last resort."

Zindell heard only the sound of his heartbeat pounding in his ears. He looked at Steadman. He looked at the gun in his hand. He looked in the direction of the bear. He looked at Steadman again.

Steadman slowly reached out and got a firm grip on Zindell's gun, pointing it to the ground. "Listen, Doc. You're the expert on bears. I'm the expert on hunting. You're not going to stop that bear with this handgun. You could empty the entire clip into him and not kill him —at least not fast enough to prevent him from killing you before he dies. If your only option is to use a handgun against a bear, you're dead already. We need to not let this get to that point. Put the gun away. We need to get moving toward the four-wheeler."

They were now upwind of Yogi, which would make it easier for the bear to find them. But they had also managed to swap positions, so they were closer to the four-wheeler than he was.

Steadman's firm grip and confident tone eased Zindell's momentary panic. He holstered his sidearm and nodded for Steadman to take the lead.

Balancing stealth and speed, they worked their way down the side of the mountain toward the waterfall and the four-wheeler. With the steep slope, rocks, loose topsoil, decaying leaves, and fallen branches, it was difficult to move quickly or quietly.

They had covered about half the distance to the four-wheeler when Zindell hit a patch of loose soil and slid about twenty feet down the mountainside. He stifled a yelp but made enough noise to attract Yogi's attention.

Steadman followed Zindell down, surfing the hillside on the loose dirt while somehow managing to keep his feet underneath him. Zindell was already picking himself up when Steadman got there, but as soon as he stood he nearly went down again.

"Can you walk?"

Zindell tried to put weight on his left foot again. Searing pain shot up from his ankle. "I don't think so. I think it's broken."

Steadman pulled Zindell's left arm over his own shoulder to help support Zindell's weight. "Let's go. We need to keep moving."

They had just started a three-legged walk when Swenson's voice came over the comm. "You guys had better get a move on. Yogi heard the commotion, and he's hustling in your direction. If you don't pick up the pace, he'll get to you before you get to the four-wheeler."

Steadman stooped down, still holding tight on to Zindell's arm. The maneuver toppled him across Steadman's shoulders. He wrapped his free arm around Zindell's legs and lifted up into a fireman's carry.

Now with the weight of two packs plus Zindell on his back, Steadman made the best speed he could down the hillside and toward the four-wheeler. Once he made it down to the trail, the firmer, flatter terrain made progress easier.

Swenson's voice came over the comm again. "You're not going to make it. We're engaging plan B."

Steadman and Zindell broke through onto the open ledge of the cliff face, but they were still seventy-five yards from the four-wheeler.

Zindell felt panic encroaching again. He knew he had to fight it off, that it would impair his ability to think when he needed it most. The video of Yogi attacking the drone flashed into his mind. *Not what I need.* He mentally rewound to the staring match that had preceded the destruction of the drone. He slapped Steadman's arm. "Stop! Put me down."

Steadman kept running.

Zindell persisted. "This isn't going to work! Before he breaks into the clearing, we have to stop. You have to put me down. We have to face him."

"Are you crazy?"

"You have to trust me. This is what I do."

Steadman stopped abruptly and stood Zindell back on his feet, supporting him under his left shoulder. They faced the direction from which Yogi would approach and stood still.

Yogi came through the opening in the trees at a full gallop. He slowed to a stop, looking at the two strangers. He tilted his head left, then right, poised as though ready to resume the chase.

Zindell followed Yogi's lead, tilting his head one way and then the other. He whispered under his breath, "No sudden motions. Nothing that might be interpreted as aggression. We need to look big, but not threatening."

Steadman whispered back, "Roger that." Then he activated his comm. "Rusty, can you navigate the four-wheeler remotely?"

"Yeah. But there's no way I can get it to you before Yogi does if he decides to come after you again."

"Understood. I need you to move it very slowly, and primarily side to side with just a little forward angle."

"You mean like tacking a sailboat?"

"Exactly. It should slowly move closer to us, but always appear to be moving side to side. Never toward the bear. Understood?"

"Understood. Starting the first tack."

Swenson started the four-wheeler toward the cliff edge. The motion caught Yogi's eye. His attention shifted in that direction, but he remained poised.

"That's good. Keep it moving like that. I can't see it, so keep me apprised of its position in case we need to make a dash for it. Ideally, you'll be able to position it directly in front of us, between the bear and us, so we can load up and ride out."

"Roger that. I'm at the cliff edge, starting to tack back toward the cliff face. It's about ten feet closer to you than where it started. Still a long way to go."

"Roger that. So what's 'plan B'?"

"Decker's idea. Bring in a swarm of drones to harass Yogi to distract him while you make your escape."

Zindell's stomach churned. "Problem with that strategy is that bears tend to have one-track minds. If he's locked on to us, he'll likely ignore the distraction and keep coming." He noticed that he could get a pretty good read on where the four-wheeler was by watching Yogi's eyes as it tracked the vehicle back and forth.

"Turning back to the cliff edge again. Yeah. We thought about that. That's why it's 'plan B,' not 'plan A.' For what it's worth, we have a 'plan C' too. That entails turning the drones into projectiles. We probably can't stop him outright, but we should be able to slow him down enough to buy you time to get away."

Steadman shook his head. "If the bear charges at us, you won't have time to try plan B and evaluate the results before trying plan C. You'll need to hit him once, hard, to make the drones the bigger threat. Then start harassing."

Decker came on the line. "Roger that."

"I don't know how much control you'll have over targeting," Zindell said, "especially if he's on the move, but if you can aim for the face or head, you'll be more likely to get his attention."

Steadman shook his head again, this time attracting Yogi's attention. "Countermand! Aim for center of mass, and hit as hard as you can. The chance of missing the headshot with him at full gallop is too big."

"Affirmative," Swenson said. "I programmed the drones earlier to target center of mass per Commander

159

Decker's recommendation. The four-wheeler is currently directly behind you, sweeping toward the cliff face, about twenty yards distant. At this pace, it should take about three more minutes to get it into position."

The bear had been alternating his attention between the two interlopers and the slow-moving vehicle. He seemed to have decided the four-wheeler was the more significant threat because as the four-wheeler moved to his left he would slowly take a few steps to his right. As the vehicle tacked back the other way, Yogi moved in the opposite direction.

The bad news was that just as this maneuver was slowly moving the four-wheeler closer to Steadman and Zindell, it was gradually drawing the bear closer to them as well.

Zindell felt his gut tighten again. "I don't think we're going to have another three minutes. His patience has to be wearing thin, and the closer the four-wheeler gets to us, the more likely he'll think he needs to make his move now. I think he feels more threatened by the vehicle than by us."

"That's it!" Steadman said. "New plan. Rusty, next time the four-wheeler passes behind us, bring it around quickly on a path right past us and directly at the bear. Fast enough to scare him, but slow enough to give him time to respond and run back into the forest."

"Roger that. It will be passing you on your left side in five ... four ... three ... two ... one ..."

Steadman and Zindell both heard the whoosh and felt the draft as the four-wheeler accelerated past them. The bear reared up on its hind legs and started a growl, but quickly reconsidered the merits of confrontation. He turned and galloped toward the woods as fast as he could go.

Swenson saw that the four-wheeler was closing too quickly and tried to slow it down, but he wasn't quite fast enough. When the front of the vehicle bumped into the bear's backside, it knocked him forward and caused him to lose his stride. He hit the ground chest-first and rolled in a jumble of fur and paws.

He picked himself up quickly and resumed his race toward the outskirts of the clearing and the safety of the woods. Swenson chased him to the edge and then held position as Yogi disappeared into the woods.

"Status?" asked Steadman.

"Still tracking. And he's still running. I think you should be able to safely evacuate now. Sorry about the bump, Dr. Zindell. I didn't intend to hit him, but it's difficult to control the four-wheeler remotely with precision."

Zindell laughed as relief became euphoria. "No apology necessary, Mr. Swenson. I should thank you for saving my life. In hindsight, it will probably work out for the best. It doesn't look like he was injured in the collision, and it should cement in his mind that he wants to avoid conflict with the four-wheelers."

TWO

"Can you bring it over to us, Mr. Swenson?" Steadman asked. "Dr. Zindell's ankle is injured, and I'd rather not carry him again if I can avoid it." He smiled at Zindell.

Zindell shifted, putting more weight on his good foot. "I'll second that."

NINETEEN

"What's the verdict?" Decker asked.

Tornquist tied off the bandage wrapped around Zindell's ankle. "Bad sprain. Fortunately, it isn't broken. He'll need to stay off it for a day or two, and probably use a cane or crutches—which we don't have—for a week. I'll have Pam put in a requisition for a pair of crutches."

"I can't thank you enough, Doctor," Zindell said. "It feels a lot better already."

Tornquist offered a sad smile. "That's just the painkillers talking, Dr. Zindell. Trust me. You don't want to put any weight on this for at least the next twenty-four hours."

Zindell's shoulders slumped. "I'd really like to get back out and explore. That's why I'm here." He perked up again. "What if I stay on the four-wheeler?"

Decker suppressed a smile and looked at Tornquist. "Doctor?"

She grimaced. "Not my first choice, but if you can keep him strapped into his chair—and find a way to keep that ankle elevated—it should be okay."

Decker turned to Steadman, who hadn't left Zindell's side since they got back. "Commander?"

He nodded. "As long as we stay on the four-wheeler, and stay in open terrain where we have good visibility and can avoid getting hemmed in, I don't see a problem."

"Okay. Both of you grab lunch before you head out."

Zindell's eyes brightened. "Thank you, Commander Decker. And again, I can't say enough about Commander Steadman. He risked his life to save mine. I wouldn't be here if it weren't for him. Can you put him in for some kind of medal or something?"

Decker laughed. "I've already put him in for an award. We call it a paycheck. It's what you get in the navy when you do your job."

Steadman grinned and shook his head.

Decker turned to leave and Steadman followed. Zindell started to get up off the examination table, but Tornquist put a hand on his chest to restrain him. "Not so fast, cowboy. Chris will bring your food."

Steadman looked back over his shoulder. "Hang tight, partner. I've got you covered."

"Just make sure it's none of that hospital food."

Tornquist laughed.

Zindell's cheeks flushed as he turned to face Tornquist. "Unless it's Jell-O."

Day 6, 1310 Hours

"That was a resourceful performance out there," Decker said. "You turned what could have been a disaster on multiple fronts into a victory on multiple fronts."

"Thanks, Skipper. Just earning my paycheck." Steadman grinned as he followed Decker to the kitchen. "Zindell deserves some of the credit. He did have a moment of panic, but he pulled it together and stayed in the game. It was his idea to stand and face the bear. That took guts. I wouldn't have believed he had it in him. It bought us valuable time. He was also the one who first recognized the bear might be afraid of the four-wheeler. That was the key to our escape."

Decker stepped into the kitchen. "The two of you made a good team."

Steadman followed into the cramped space. "Speaking of which, where's Dr. Culpepper?"

Decker shook his head as he activated his comm. "Mr. Swenson, any updates on Dr. Culpepper?"

Steadman opened the refrigerator and pulled out the makings of a couple of sandwiches.

Swenson's void came over the radio. "Still in the grove to the north. She's been looking at trees, collecting leaves, fruits, nuts, sticks. She caught sight of Mikey watching over her a little while ago. She … well … made a rude hand gesture in Mikey's direction. Mikey mimicked the gesture back at her, then stuck out his … her … tongue

165

at Dr. Culpepper. Dr. Culpepper responded in kind, then stormed off in the other direction."

Decker rubbed his brow.

Steadman shook his head. "Any sign of predators around her?"

"No," Swenson said. "Well, I think Dr. Zindell would insist that Mikey is technically a predator, but nothing else is showing any interest in her, at least nothing looking aggressive. I'm not sure but what Mikey is doing the same thing we are—watching for potential threats in an effort to keep her safe."

Decker shook his head. "Thanks, Mr. Swenson. Keep us apprised."

Steadman went back to building sandwiches. "I'm amazed that she didn't come racing back to camp when she heard all the commotion about our encounter with the bear."

"She didn't hear it. She turned her comm off before she sneaked out of camp."

Steadman hung his head.

Swenson's voice came back over the comm. "The afternoon supply shipment just arrived."

Steadman dropped what he was doing and turned for the door, but Decker stopped him. "You and Zindell need to finish your lunch and get back out there. Guerrero and I will handle this."

TWENTY

Decker and Guerrero spent the early part of the afternoon moving the fresh supplies to the storage building. Then they installed a new data storage module that would provide more comprehensive information on Earth plants and animals for comparison to local counterparts. They had just finished when Tornquist joined them in the science lab.

"Has either of you seen Weaver?"

"No," Decker said, "but she should be collecting reports and requisitions for the evening upload. We just finished unloading the afternoon shipment."

"That's why I need to find her. I have several things I need to add to my supply requisition. I've checked all the buildings and she doesn't seem to be here."

Decker activated his comm. "Petty Officer Weaver?"

Their stares became uncomfortable as the silence stretched.

"Has anyone seen Petty Officer Weaver?"

Swenson's voice came over the radio. "The last time I saw her she was sorting through the incoming data packets so she could distribute them. That was a couple of hours ago, not long after the supply shipment arrived."

"Can you locate her comm signal?"

"Checking."

Decker's gut twisted. He barely knew her, but she didn't seem the type to flout the rules, especially on-mission. Why would she be away from camp, alone, without telling anyone where she was going, and without her radio?

"No. I'm only getting seven. I have no signal for Weaver, Culpepper, or Sakhr."

He closed his eyes. He knew where Culpepper was. But Weaver and Sakhr? At least they were together. But no radios and no reporting?

"Explanation?" Decker asked.

"Could be turned off, broken, jammed, or blocked. We know Culpepper turned hers off."

"Jammed?"

"Unlikely," Swenson said, "but possible. Our comms use a spread-spectrum technology that is very difficult to jam. And on a planet with no other radio-frequency signals, the jammer would stand out like a sore thumb. More likely blocked than jammed."

"What would it take to block the signal?"

"Thick metal walls. Or deep underground. How deep depends on the composition of the rock and soil."

Decker set his jaw. "All hands. We have two missing people. Please meet outside the storage building to form search parties. Commander Steadman?"

Steadman replied over the radio. "Here, sir. We've been listening. We're already on the way back. ETA fifteen minutes. We'll keep our eyes peeled on the way in."

Decker looked at Guerrero. "Take one of the four-wheelers and go get Dr. Culpepper. Take a TASER with you, and don't hesitate to use it. I don't care whether she's conscious or not as long as I know she's present and accounted for. I need you back here ASAP to assist in the search."

"Aye, sir." Guerrero headed for the storage building double-time.

Decker followed him there, where he found Swenson staring at live video on his console. "Status?"

"Three of our remaining seven drones are following Steadman and Zindell back from the field. I have the other four starting a search pattern spiraling out from the camp. The dicey thing is that they really don't know what they're looking for. If Weaver and Sakhr are up and walking around, they'll be recognized as noteworthy fauna and flagged immediately. If they're unconscious or otherwise incapacitated, they may not be noticed. If they've taken cover under rocks or trees, the drones would likely miss them entirely. When the other drones get back, I plan to reconfigure them to do a more detailed search of any rocky or forested areas the other four won't

169

do a good job searching. They'll fly lower and weave around to make sure they're seeing everything. Even then they might not see or recognize them. I've been monitoring the video feeds in hopes that I might catch something they miss, but with four fast-moving sources to watch simultaneously, I may miss them too."

"What can we do to help?"

Swenson's eyes were still glued to the monitors. "Even with all this technology, there's still no better image processing capability in the known universe than the human brain. The more eyes we can get on these monitors, the more likely we are to see something the drones missed."

Decker stepped outside the storage building and found Tornquist and Solansky waiting anxiously, watching his interchange with Swenson through the door. "Did you get all that?"

Tornquist pushed past Decker through the door. "Enough." She crouched beside Swenson at his console. Solansky followed right behind her, with Decker bringing up the rear.

Swenson pointed each of them to one of the four monitors. The images were a blur as the drones covered ground as quickly as possible. Decker was tempted to ask Swenson to slow things down, but he had learned long ago that he had to trust his people.

After fifteen minutes of staring at his assigned video feed, Decker wondered if his eyes were even still working. It all seemed to turn into one continuous blur. He was afraid to blink for fear of missing the critical instant, but he knew if he didn't it wouldn't take long before he couldn't see anything.

His concentration was shattered by a commotion outside. He heard Culpepper's unmistakable voice yelling, "Get your filthy hands off me."

About that time Culpepper stumbled into the room, bumping into Decker. "I demand an explanation for this! And I demand this man be punished. He threatened to shoot me!"

Decker turned around and reached into Guerrero's tactical vest and pulled out his TASER. Just as he turned to point it at Culpepper, Solansky yelled out, "There!"

Everyone turned to watch the feed Solansky had been monitoring as Swenson switched to it and rewound a few seconds.

Hearts sank as they saw a crumpled body at the foot of the cliff near the waterfall.

TWENTY-ONE

Decker activated his comm. "Steadman, reroute to the base of the lower waterfall. Swenson will send you coordinates. Best possible speed."

"Roger that."

"Dr. Tornquist, get your Go Bag and meet Guerrero and me at the four-wheeler. Mr. Swenson, Dr. Solansky, keep looking for Dr. Sakhr. Focus your efforts on the cliff area."

Tornquist and Guerrero shot out of the building. Decker turned to follow them out, but Culpepper stepped in front of him.

"Someone needs to tell me what's going on here."

Decker realized he was still holding Guerrero's TASER. He pointed it at her. "Miss Culpepper, you are confined to your quarters until further notice."

He set the TASER on the console in front of Swenson. "Mr. Swenson, if Miss Culpepper interferes in any way with your search effort, you are authorized to shoot her."

Swenson kept his eyes focused on the video as he rested a hand on the grip of the TASER.

Day 6, 1706 Hours

Culpepper walked toward her quarters, trying to sort things out in her head. She was angry. She was baffled. She was hurt.

Why was everyone treating her this way? Why wouldn't they talk to her? Why wouldn't they tell her what was going on?

She saw Tornquist and Guerrero coming out of the medical lab loaded down with equipment. They were coming in her direction but headed for the four-wheeler staging area on the other side of the compound.

She grabbed Tornquist by the arm as she raced past, yanking her to a stop and causing her to drop part of her load.

Tornquist wrenched her arm loose from Culpepper's grip and started picking up her gear.

"Why won't anyone talk to me?" Culpepper asked. "I don't understand why he's treating me this way."

Tornquist looked up at Culpepper from where she had crouched. She stood up and glared at her. "Seriously? For real?"

Culpepper just stared back at her.

"The only thing I don't understand is why he hasn't tied you to a chair and taped your mouth shut." She bent back down to pick up the rest of her gear.

Culpepper was dumbfounded.

Tornquist stood back up, both arms loaded with jumbled equipment. "My advice is that you lock your fanny in your bunk and keep your mouth shut until Commander Decker comes to get you."

Tornquist raced off toward the four-wheeler. As Culpepper watched her go, she saw Decker standing beside the vehicle staring at her. He set his jaw tight and pointed emphatically at the bunkhouse.

Day 6, 1711 Hours

It took them less than two minutes to cover the two miles to the cliff. Decker overrode the governor on the four-wheeler, and Guerrero pushed the speed well above what was considered safe over the rugged terrain. No one complained. They were too worried about what they would find when they arrived.

Decker spotted the body as they approached. One drone had taken up a stationary position about ten feet overhead. Guerrero set the vehicle down a few feet away. Tornquist grabbed her medical bag and raced over to find a crumpled body face down on the ground.

No one needed to turn it over to know it was Weaver, and no one needed a doctor to tell them she was dead.

Steadman and Zindell arrived right behind them. Zindell sat sideways in the back seat so he could keep his foot elevated. Steadman left him there and came to help Guerrero provide defensive cover for the others.

He activated his comm. "Mr. Swenson, how's our perimeter?"

"Nothing in your immediate area."

"Are you still tracking Yogi?"

"Negative. I pulled that drone to assist in the search. He was holed up in a cave about a mile upslope of your position. No way of knowing if he's still there, but he's not within a quarter mile of you."

"Roger that."

Decker stood behind Tornquist, who crouched beside the body. "What can you tell me, Doctor?"

She didn't reply. Her shoulders were quaking, and tears were streaming down her face. He knelt beside her and put an arm around her.

Speaking softly, he said, "I know this isn't easy, but I need you to stay in the game. We need to know what happened. More lives could be at stake."

Tornquist nodded. In a pained voice she said, "We should get pictures before we move anything."

Decker pointed up at the drone. "Mr. Swenson has already done that. I'm sure he's continuing to record everything that's happening."

Tornquist nodded. "Help me turn her over."

Decker moved to the head and took Weaver by the shoulders. Tornquist had to straighten the arms and legs before they could roll her.

"From what I can see here, it looks like she fell from the cliff and the impact killed her. I'll need to get her back to the medical lab to say anything more."

Decker motioned to Steadman. "Help me load her onto the four-wheeler."

"Aye, sir."

As they carried her, Steadman said quietly, "With your permission, I suggest we load her on my vehicle and let you, Dr. Tornquist, and Dr. Zindell return to camp in that. I'd like to take a look around before I head back."

Decker activated his comm. "Mr. Swenson, any updates on the search for Sakhr?"

"Yes, sir. I was just about to call you. Dr. Sakhr has been found safe here in the compound."

Decker didn't know whether to be shocked or relieved. "Explain."

"I'd prefer to do that in person when you return."

"Roger that."

Decker disengaged his comm and turned to Guerrero. "You stay here and watch his six," Decker said, nodding toward Steadman.

Decker looked at the setting sun. "We're already starting to lose daylight. I want you back at camp before it gets dark."

"Aye, sir."

Decker and Tornquist climbed into the four-wheeler with Zindell and Petty Officer Weaver's body. Decker took the controls and turned them back toward camp.

Day 6, 1805 Hours

The ride back to camp was substantially slower than the trip out. The urgency was gone, and it seemed somehow disrespectful to hurry the pace with Weaver's body on board.

As they rolled into camp, the rest of the team was waiting for them. Culpepper was missing, presumably in her quarters, but Sakhr was there.

Decker parked by the entrance to the medical lab. Tornquist went inside to get the stretcher. He saw the somber faces of the rest of the team looking at the body on the back of the four-wheeler. This wasn't the first time he had wished they'd brought something with them to cover her.

He closed his eyes and said a prayer, then looked at the assembled crew. "I know this is difficult. We're still trying to piece together what happened. For now, I need you all to eat something and rest."

Tornquist came out with the stretcher. Decker helped her transfer the body into the medical lab.

When he came back out, the crowd had dispersed, but Swenson was waiting for him. Decker headed straight for the storage building, Swenson falling in behind.

Inside Swenson's workroom, Decker closed the door. "What's the story on Sakhr?"

Swenson took a deep breath and let it out slowly. "Solansky and I were in here monitoring the surveillance feeds as the drones continued the search for Sakhr when we heard his voice behind us asking, 'What's going on around here? Where is everyone? It's time for dinner.' I nearly fell out of my chair. Part of me was glad he was here and safe. After we spotted Weaver's body, I feared the worst. Another part of me wanted to throttle him. I told him you were all out looking for him. I asked him where he'd been. He looked genuinely puzzled ... said he'd been in his quarters all afternoon reviewing recorded survey data. I asked him if he was aware his comm was turned off. His hand jerked reflexively to his wrist, and he said—and I quote—'Oh! I'm so sorry. I forgot to turn it back on.' I suggested he go get something to eat while I recalled the search parties. He had just left the building when you called."

Decker rubbed his chin. "Thanks, Mr. Swenson. You handled that well."

He looked at his watch. "We were scheduled to make a data shipment to Earth an hour ago. Where are we with that?"

Swenson looked down at his shoes. Decker knew it was a question for Weaver, but the mission had to continue, and Swenson was the logical person to pick up those tasks.

Swenson looked up at Decker. "I've only had a few minutes to work on it. From what I can tell, she hadn't even finished processing the data we received from Earth in the afternoon shipment, much less begun finalizing the evening return packet. With that said, she's very organized. A lot of what needs to go into it is already collected. I'll need maybe an hour to check with everyone to make sure I have their latest stuff."

"Okay. I'll have a report for you within the hour that needs to go in the packet. Don't ship without it. Also, make sure you check with Dr. Tornquist. She said she needed to add a few things to the requisition she had given Petty Officer Weaver."

"Yes, sir." Swenson sank in his chair.

Decker put a hand on his shoulder. "I need you to keep it together until that packet goes out. Can you do that for me?"

Swenson nodded. "I'll get it done."

"Good." Decker turned to leave. "I'll send someone over with food."

"And coffee!" Swenson called after him.

Day 6, 1830 Hours

Decker knocked on the door to Culpepper's bunk-room. He heard her quickly get off the bed and step to the door.

When the door opened and she saw Decker, she folded her arms across her chest. She turned her back to him and sat on the bed.

Decker remained outside. "Where were you today?"

She stared at the wall. "That's nothing you need to worry about."

"Where was your security detail?"

"I don't need a security detail. I can take care of myself."

"Why was your comm turned off?"

She looked up at him. "Because you made it quite clear you weren't going to offer any help with my work, so I really didn't see any need to communicate further."

"So you probably weren't aware that while you were out picking fruits and nuts, Dr. Zindell was almost killed by a bear."

Her eyes bulged as she stared at him unblinking. "Is he okay?"

"He has a bad ankle sprain. He'll be limping for a few days, but he'll be fine. Fortunately, Mr. Steadman was there with him, and Mr. Swenson was on the comm with them, and together they were able to effect their escape. If only narrowly."

Culpepper crossed her arms and looked away again. "I'm glad he's okay, but me being with them wouldn't have made any difference."

"On that point, I'm inclined to agree."

Culpepper jerked her head around to glare at Decker for the perceived insult. Then she turned back to face the wall.

"So you probably weren't aware Petty Officer Weaver and Dr. Sakhr also both went missing this afternoon."

Culpepper harrumphed. "You can hardly blame them."

She turned back to look at Decker. "Can you not see we're all adults here? We don't need a petty dictator with a dad complex looking over our shoulder every minute."

Decker's chest felt heavy as he voiced a silent prayer. He wished there was another way to bring this news, a way to soften the blow.

"Petty Officer Weaver did not go missing of her own volition."

Culpepper just stared at the wall, waiting for him to continue.

"I regret to inform you we found her body just before sunset. Petty Officer Pamela Weaver is dead."

Culpepper's head swung around again. Decker's heart ached as he saw the color drain from Culpepper's face. She slipped off the bed onto her knees on the floor.

He felt a pang of guilt for putting it to her this way, but she had to understand what was at stake here. It could as easily have been Dr. Culpepper found dead. It could yet be.

"Your confinement is ended. You're free to go. I suggest you get something to eat. I'll have Dr. Tornquist check in on you later."

Decker turned and left the building.

Day 6, 1845 Hours

Decker's next target was Dr. Sakhr. Steadman caught up with him on the way.

"It's a little past dark, Commander."

"'Dark' is a relative term, Skipper." Steadman held the back of his hand up to the twilight skyline to show that, at least according to his standard for dark, they weren't there yet.

Decker wanted to laugh but it didn't feel appropriate right now. "I'll give you that one. Did you learn anything?"

"Not sure. Something doesn't feel right but I can't put my finger on it. I'd like to go back out tomorrow at first light and have another look around."

"No objection. Keep me posted, and make sure Swenson knows what you're doing and where, and has drones watching your six."

"Will do."

Day 6, 1847 Hours

Decker found Sakhr sitting in the common area of the men's quarters sweating profusely and rubbing his hands together. Sakhr abruptly rose to his feet. He stood rigid, looking straight ahead, apparently doing his best civilian imitation of standing at attention.

"Commander Decker! I am so sorry for all the trouble I caused."

Decker walked around to stand in front of Sakhr. "Exactly what trouble is it you think you've caused?"

Sakhr's posture slackened as he drew his head back. "Swenson said … he said you thought I was missing and sent out a search party. When they came back … Petty Officer Weaver … I feel responsible. If I hadn't turned my radio off, she wouldn't have been out there looking for me."

"What makes you think she was looking for you?"

Sakhr's eyes narrowed as he stared at the floor. "Well … the search party … I just assumed …"

Decker took a seat at the table and motioned Sakhr to a chair opposite him. "I need you to account for your whereabouts from the time you and Dr. Solansky returned to camp this morning until you checked in with Mr. Swenson this evening."

Sakhr pulled the chair back slowly, his eyes darting around the room. He settled lightly into the chair. "I've been here." He twisted around to point to the room he shared with Swenson. "In there, actually."

"The whole time?"

"Yes. Well, I went over to the kitchen for lunch. I grabbed a ration pack and came back here to eat. I've spent the day reviewing satellite and drone data. Trying to get a feel for the geography and develop a plan to explore and study."

"Can anyone corroborate that? Anybody stop by to check in on you? Did Swenson come by during the day?"

Sakhr shook his head. "No. Commander, why all these questions? If you don't believe I was here, where do you think I was?"

"Why did you turn off your radio?"

"I didn't want to be interrupted during my mid-day prayers. They are a long-standing habit—a discipline, of sorts—that helps me maintain focus. I've been doing them since childhood. I saw no harm in turning the radio off for a few minutes while I was safe in my quarters." Sakhr looked down at the floor and shook his head. "The radio is new to me. I'm not accustomed to carrying one. I guess it escaped my mind when my prayers were ended."

Decker rose to his feet and walked toward the door.

Sakhr called after him. "Commander. I'm truly sorry for whatever role my actions had in the circumstance of Petty Officer Weaver's death. One thing I don't understand: why send out a search team without checking my quarters first?"

Decker walked out into the night.

Day 6, 2358 Hours

The man behind the desk stared at his computer.

Where is his report?

They'd been coming in like clockwork. Did he not send one? Did something happen to it? Had something happened to delay it? Maybe it was just a logistical problem. Or something big happened that caused them to abandon their normal protocols.

Don't panic. It's too soon to start worrying. Besides, even if he's been exposed and they pick up the trail, it won't lead to me.

He didn't find great comfort in that thought.

Maybe I need to do a little more work to make sure of that.

An alert popped up on his computer.

Finally! See. Nothing to worry about.

Trouble. Encryption software discovered on this end. Don't think it has been reported to the other side, but had to take aggressive action to cover tracks. Staged to look like an accident. So far they seem to have bought it. Will keep you advised. Where do bears and chimpanzees live in proximity?

He pounded the desk.

Imbecile! You take "aggressive action" and expect to not blow your cover?

And why the riddle? Chimpanzees are exclusive to Africa. African bears have been extinct for more than a century.

Zoos?

What do bears and chimps have to do with anything?

He set his jaw and turned back to his computer.

It sounds like the risks of this operation are beginning to exceed the likelihood of further rewards. Time to tie off a few loose ends.

TWENTY-TWO

Day 7, 0008 Hours

Decker hit the sack a few minutes before midnight. One of the things submarine warfare had taught him was the importance of sleep to readiness, even, especially, in times of crisis. Guerrero had the watch and would wake him if needed. His confidence in his team gave him the peace to fall asleep quickly.

He'd only been out for a few minutes when a knock at his door awakened him. He rolled out of bed and opened the door to find Dr. Tornquist wearing a coat.

"I'm sorry if I woke you, Commander, but we need to talk. *Now*."

Decker motioned for her to continue.

"Not here. In the medical lab. I'll wait for you out here. You might want to bring a jacket." She walked out to the common area to wait for him.

Decker grabbed a jacket and followed. "Has it gotten cold that quickly? It was still warm when I was outside a few minutes ago."

Tornquist was already out of the building, hustling toward the medical lab.

He trotted across the compound to catch up. As soon as he entered the building he understood why she recommended the jacket. He put it on and zipped it. "Is something wrong with the environmental controls?"

"No. We don't have a proper morgue, so until we can send the body back to Earth I'll need to keep it cold in here to slow decomposition."

"I assume I'm here because you found something."

She rubbed the back of her neck. "Nothing concrete. Just things that don't add up." She nodded toward Dr. Zindell, who was sitting in a chair behind Decker.

Zindell picked up a stick and used it to push himself up and limp over to the examination table.

"How's the ankle?" Decker asked.

"About the same." Zindell grimaced. "The good doctor will tell you that I'm not following orders and staying off it to let it heal. She's right, of course, but there are priorities." He nodded toward Weaver's body on the table.

"So what do you have?"

"First, I need to say that I'm not trained as a medical examiner," Tornquist said. "This is not my field. I might be misinterpreting things. I might be missing things that are important. I might be destroying, or have already destroyed, important evidence."

"Evidence of what?"

187

Tornquist took a deep breath and let it out slowly. She looked up at Decker. "I think Pam was already dead before she hit the ground."

Decker closed his eyes. "What makes you say that?"

"Mostly little things that don't add up. Again, I'm not trained in this. The first thing that didn't make sense to me was how little blood there was where we found her. This head injury alone should have resulted in massive bleeding if her heart was still pumping, and it should have been. The injuries to the chest cavity were not that severe, and the regulation of heartbeat is managed by the sinus node that is part of the heart itself, not by the brain."

Decker looked at Tornquist—mostly because that was easier than looking at Weaver. "You said 'things.' What else?"

"I x-rayed the whole body and started documenting all the fractures. I tried to stay focused just on identifying and documenting, but as I worked through all the breaks, my mind kept trying to piece together exactly how she impacted the ground. Did she hit feet-first? Head-first? On her back? Did she make any effort to break her fall, increase her chances of survival no matter how remote? Again, I'm not an expert in this field of study, but I think she hit the ground completely limp, like a rag doll. Even with a suicide, it's instinctive to try to orient your body in a particular way. Which particular way depends on your frame of mind, but regardless you'll assume that position and then tense up waiting for the impact. That should produce torn muscles and ligaments. But except for the trauma caused by the fractured bones, and bruising from direct impact, there's no sign of muscle strain. Further, the pattern of broken bones is not consistent with any *intentional* orientation of the body I can imagine."

Decker nodded. "Okay. You've made a strong case. Let's send her body back to Earth in tomorrow morning's return shipment along with your report. We'll see what the experts there think."

"There's one more thing," Tornquist said as she moved over to a diagnostic console and displayed an X-ray on the monitor. "This is her neck."

Decker studied the X-ray. "Okay. It looks broken."

"Obviously. But it's broken the wrong way."

Decker's eyebrows shot up as he looked at Tornquist. "Meaning?"

Tornquist pointed at the fracture on the X-ray. "This should have been a shear fracture, where the two vertebrae dislocate laterally. Worst case, a compression fracture. If she hit head first, the force of her body down the spine might compress the vertebrae to the point that they're crushed. These vertebrae aren't crushed, and while there is significant head trauma, it doesn't indicate that she landed head-down. This is a torsion fracture. Her neck was twisted until the spinal cord was severed, releasing the vertebrae."

"And this couldn't have happened in the fall?"

Tornquist shuffled on her feet. "Again, I'm not—"

Decker held up his hand to cut her off.

189

Tornquist closed her eyes and hung her head, taking a deep breath. She looked back up at Decker. "I can't say it isn't possible, but it seems highly unlikely. Taken with the other evidence, including the blood, I think someone, or something, broke her neck and then threw her off the cliff."

"Attacked by a wild animal maybe?"

Tornquist nodded toward Zindell. "That's why I asked Dr. Zindell to take a look."

Decker turned to the zoologist. "Doctor?"

Zindell shook his head. "No. We've certainly encountered any number of creatures here that are capable of killing, but this is not the way a wild animal kills. They slash. Tear. Bite. Rip. Crush. I hesitate to call it a 'crime of passion' because when an animal kills, it's never a moral decision. But it is an act of extreme violence. Usually quite messy. Animals don't care how big a mess they make. Messes don't bother them. If they're killing to eat, they'll make a much bigger mess before they're done anyway, and there will be other creatures along to clean things up later. If they're killing to eat, they'll kill, and then eat; not kill and throw their hard-earned dinner off a cliff."

Zindell looked back down at the body, resting his free hand on the rail of the bed. "There were no signs that anything tried to eat her. Not bite or claw marks either, which would be expected if she were attacked by a wild animal. Even if their motivation was to defend themselves or their territory, throwing her dead body off the cliff wouldn't make sense. This was a calculated killing, decisive and efficient. Breaking a neck is an act of willful choice, the trademark of intelligence. Executed with precision, it's decisive and efficient. But efficient only in the sense that it's quick and quiet and doesn't create a big mess. Inefficient in that it's difficult to execute with precision. It also requires specific knowledge of human physiology."

"So it had to be someone on our team?"

Zindell tilted his head. "Probably. But not necessarily."

"I'm not following. You said it wasn't a wild animal, and it was someone with specific knowledge of human physiology."

"Yes. But that doesn't rule out the possibility of a human analogue here on this planet. We haven't seen one yet, but we've only scratched the surface of what's here. Everything we've seen so far is a near copy of something on Earth. I see no reason to rule out the possibility that there is something very similar to us here as well."

Decker didn't like where this was going. Was there an intelligent predator on the planet they hadn't found yet? Or had someone on his team done this? And why was she out there alone?

Decker locked eyes with Tornquist. "Get some sleep. We'll talk again in the morning. Don't mention any of this to the others until I've had time to process it. And lock that door. No one besides you gets in here until further notice."

Decker slipped quietly into the bunk-room Swenson shared with Sakhr. Swenson was asleep on the upper bunk. Decker laid his tablet on the bed beside Swenson, positioning it so the light from the tablet would illuminate Decker's face.

He placed one hand softly over Swenson's mouth and gently shook his shoulder with the other. Swenson sat up with a start and a stifled yelp. Decker held a finger to his mouth to gesture for Swenson to keep quiet and then motioned for him to follow as he padded out of the room.

He waited in the common area with Steadman and Guerrero until Swenson stumbled out wearing an unbuttoned shirt and carrying his shoes. Swenson opened his mouth to say something, but Decker gestured for silence again and pointed to the door. They waited while Swenson put on his shoes.

Decker led the way as the quartet walked across the compound to the storage building. Once they were inside, Decker closed the door.

"I need a drone in the air overhead. I need to know if anyone moves in the compound, and in particular, I need to know if anyone is trying to listen in on this conversation."

Swenson sat down at his console. A few keystrokes later, he said, "Done. All clear for the moment. What's this all about? If you don't mind me asking."

Decker turned to Steadman. "You said earlier that something about the scene at the cliff didn't feel right. Can you elaborate?"

Steadman ran his fingers through his hair. "I want to believe Weaver's death was accidental. That would mean either she slipped and fell off the cliff, or she got too close to the edge and the ground collapsed beneath her. In either case, there should have been loose dirt and rock around and on top of the body. There wasn't."

Swenson said, "Maybe she tripped over something and went over the edge without knocking anything loose."

Steadman shrugged. "Maybe. I can't rule it out. It just seems very unlikely."

"Anything else?" Decker asked.

"Something just didn't feel right about the scene when we found the body. I still can't put my finger on what."

Decker nodded. "Tornquist and Zindell felt the same way. They spent several hours studying the body and have a long list of things that 'just don't add up.'"

Steadman's eyebrows shot up. "Like what?"

"I'll let Dr. Tornquist go through all the details with you in the morning. The bottom line is this: her best theory to explain the evidence is that Weaver was dead at least several minutes before she fell from the cliff, and the most probable cause of her death was a broken neck. A break she doesn't believe was caused by the fall."

Guerrero stood bolt upright. "She was murdered."

Swenson stared at the wall, blinking. "So we're all gathered here to figure out who might have done it?"

193

"Or *what* might have done it," Steadman said, looking directly at Guerrero. "We don't know it wasn't done by something native to this planet."

Decker nodded. "Dr. Zindell made a strong case that it was a rational act, not a wild animal. But he can't rule out the possibility there might be a humanlike species on this planet we haven't seen yet. But let's start by making sure we have our own house in order. Eliminate everyone with solid alibis. We know Weaver was here when the afternoon supply shipment arrived. Guerrero and I were together unloading cargo until Tornquist reported her missing. Then Guerrero headed in the other direction to the north grove to pick up Culpepper while I came in here with Swenson. Guerrero returned with Culpepper quickly enough that he wouldn't have had time to detour to the cliff area, and she was probably already dead by the time Tornquist reported her missing. That puts Guerrero in the clear, and it puts me in the clear."

"What about Culpepper?" Guerrero asked. "She was out of the camp for several hours."

Swenson shook his head. "Yes, but we had her under surveillance from mid-morning until you picked her up. She has the best alibi of any of us: seven hours of continuous high-resolution video showing her working in the grove."

"Zindell was with me all afternoon," Steadman said. "I'll vouch for him. And I trust he'll vouch for me."

"I'll vouch for the both of you," Swenson said. "While I didn't have a drone trained directly on you like I did

194

with Culpepper, I had three drones tracking you to monitor your perimeter. If either of you had left the four-wheeler, I'd have been alerted and there would've been a record."

Steadman rubbed his chin. "What about Tornquist?"

Decker felt a surge of anger at the suggestion, but he quickly suppressed it. "I can't absolutely rule her out. She was working in the lab by herself most of the day. Guerrero and I both saw her many times through the course of the afternoon, but I can't absolutely say there wasn't a gap somewhere where she would have had time to get to the cliffs and back unnoticed. In her defense, she's the one who first reported Weaver missing, and she's the one now making the strongest case that Weaver was murdered. If she'd kept her mouth shut, we likely would never have had more than a paranoid suspicion this was anything other than an accident. On the other hand, having Dr. Zindell watching over her shoulder may be forcing her hand."

"I'm in a similar bind," Swenson said. "I was in here all day, but I can't prove it. I had contact, direct and indirect, with almost everyone through the course of the day, but it would be hard for me to produce solid documentation. Especially without a more specific time of death."

Guerrero clinched his fists. "That leaves Sakhr and Solansky."

"Both of whom were largely unaccounted for through the course of the afternoon," Swenson said. "Both supposedly spent the afternoon in their respective quarters, but with no one to corroborate."

Guerrero raised a fist. "Yeah, but when we started looking for Weaver, Solansky was here and assisted in the search. He was the one who first saw her in the video as the drones searched. Meanwhile, Sakhr's comm was offline and he was nowhere to be found."

Decker ran a hand over his head and rubbed his neck. "So we have two good suspects and two weak suspects. But a circumstantial case at best. How do we tie this conclusively to the real murderer?"

Steadman froze. He turned to Decker. "You said Dr. Tornquist believed Weaver was killed several minutes before she fell. Taken with the conditions at the scene, it would seem she was probably thrown off the cliff."

Decker nodded. "Your point being?"

"That we've been studying the location where we found her body, but it seems that isn't the scene of the crime. Either she was murdered at the top of the cliff, or she was murdered elsewhere and carried to the top of the cliff. If we can find where it happened, there might be more evidence that could tie this to an individual."

Decker nodded. "Okay. So you head back to the cliff at first light to have another look around. What happens if you don't find anything?"

Swenson looked up at Steadman. "I have an idea."

TWENTY-THREE

Day 7, 0635 Hours

Dr. Culpepper had barely slept at all. Nothing was going the way it was supposed to. She had been promised three months to be the first botanist to get an up-close look at life on an alien planet. She would've been famous. And not just in her field. This wasn't just her name in a footnote in a botany textbook. Dr. Teresa Culpepper would have been recorded prominently in history texts for generations to come.

But it was all a pack of lies. She was still on Earth, not an alien planet. Part of some kind of demented psychology experiment, not the exploration of a new world. The team that was supposed to be here to support her work was clearly in on the conspiracy. Or just too stupid to see through the charade.

And now this business with Weaver. Culpepper was already beginning to question the morals of whoever was behind this experiment, but it was still inconceivable to her they would have actually killed one of the participants. But an accident like that should have immediately suspended the program.

So what really happened? Was Weaver's death an accident, now being incorporated into the experiment? What kind of research justifies such a low regard for loss of life?

Or was Weaver murdered by one of the other participants? The people running the program would have been monitoring everything that happened. Even if they couldn't stop it, they would have seen it and immediately shut things down.

But they didn't.

Was she really even dead? No one had been allowed to see the body. Except for Decker and his two henchmen. And Tornquist. It was a foregone conclusion the four military thugs were part of the conspiracy, but now she had to consider the possibility Tornquist was in on it too. Especially after the way the woman had treated her last night.

Who else?

Swenson? Definitely.

Zindell? Maybe. Probably not. Just too stupid to see anything other than what he wanted to see.

Sakhr? Solansky? Hard to say. But if Weaver was murdered, Sakhr looked like a good candidate. His alibi for the time of death—"I was praying."

Another religious extremist.

And how did so many religious nuts wind up in this experiment? Sakhr. Swenson. Zindell. It must be a component of the study. But why? What question were they trying to answer? And why was she the only rational actor in the program?

It looked more and more like she was the only one not in on the conspiracy.

But for what purpose? What end could possibly justify this much effort ... this much *money*?

She looked at her watch. The others would be starting to collect around the campfire for breakfast—at least if yesterday's events didn't disrupt everyone's schedule. She wasn't looking forward to going back out there, but she wasn't going to get any answers sitting in her quarters alone.

She got up and headed outside where she saw everyone except Steadman had already gathered. Then she noticed some of them were still finishing breakfast. She hadn't even thought about eating since ... she couldn't remember when. But now she was hungry.

She was about to head back to the kitchen to grab something to eat when Decker started talking.

Day 7, 0645 Hours

The sky was overcast and the air bordered on cold, accentuated by a faint mist that was almost a drizzle when Decker stepped out of the storage building. He ignored the weather as he surveyed the team huddled around the campfire. He'd had less than four hours of sleep last night, waking before dawn to get a head start on what had to be done today.

Swenson and Guerrero followed him out of the building and joined the others around the campfire. Decker noted the only one missing was Culpepper. He was about to ask Tornquist to go find her when she came out of the women's quarters.

Decker joined the circle. "I doubt any of us had a good night's sleep last night, and I know you all have a lot to work through in dealing with yesterday's events. Unfortunately, I have to make this worse for all of you." Decker felt the weight in his chest grow as all eyes focused on him. Times like this were what he loved least about command. "We have reason to believe that Petty Officer Weaver's death was not accidental."

Culpepper's face perked up and she stepped forward. "What do you mean 'not accidental'? You think someone killed her?"

Sakhr's head jerked around, looking first at Culpepper, then Solansky, Swenson, and Decker in rapid succession.

Solansky bit his lip. "You mean like an alien or something?"

Decker nodded to Solansky. "That's a possibility we're still investigating. It could also be one of us. The evidence at this point is inconclusive."

"What evidence?" Solansky asked.

"I'm not prepared to discuss those details just yet. We're still investigating. The next step will be to interview each of you."

Culpepper's nostrils flared. "Let me get this straight. GI Jane breaks your rules by wandering off on her own and gets herself killed. That sure wouldn't look very good on your record, Mr. Officer-in-Charge. So you're going to find a scapegoat to hang this on and fabricate a case against them so this doesn't go against you. Have I got that about right?"

Decker pursed his lips. "We're not in a position to provide you the legal counsel you would normally be afforded. However, I think you all know that you civilians have the right to say nothing and to decline to cooperate with the investigation. I will fully respect that decision if anyone feels they need to make it."

"And what of the non-civilian members of the team?" Solansky asked.

"The investigation will go where the evidence leads. The distinction is that according to the Uniform Code of Military Justice, the military members of the team don't have the legal right to decline to answer questions or to cooperate with the investigation."

"Speaking of which, where is GI Joe?" asked Culpepper.

"Commander Steadman is back at the cliff where we found the body. Investigating."

Culpepper's face reddened. "Investigating? Alone? How do you know he's not the murderer?"

"Commander Steadman was with Dr. Zindell the entire afternoon. Dr. Zindell, was Commander Steadman ever out of your sight from the time you left here after Dr. Tornquist patched you up until we recalled you from the field?"

Zindell was quick to respond. "No. He was with me the entire time. Neither one of us ever left the four-wheeler. In fact, I don't think we ever even set it down from the time we left until we arrived at the cliff."

"That's a convenient alibi," Culpepper said. "They each vouch for the other. They could be in on it together."

Decker held up his hands. "I remain open to that possibility, but for the time being, we have to work with the available resources and prioritize. It won't surprise me at all if Earth sends an independent team to perform their own investigation. In the meantime, we need to collect as much information as we can while it's still fresh. And if this was indeed a murder, we need to figure out who did it and isolate them to prevent further loss of life or interference with the mission."

"I personally think that sounds very reasonable," Solansky said. "If we have a murderer in our midst, I certainly want him to be caught and brought to justice before anyone else gets hurt. I'm just glad that Dr. Sakhr was found safe and sound."

All eyes turned to look at Sakhr as he shrank in his chair. "You *can't* think I had anything to do with this. I'm innocent! You have no proof."

Decker stepped into the middle of the circle. "He's right. Everyone here is innocent until and unless we can prove otherwise. Unless one of you knows something I don't, right now we can't prove anything. To that end, you should all see interviews scheduled on your calendars throughout the day. Please be sure you're here when you're scheduled."

As Decker stepped away from the campfire, Culpepper blurted out, "I want to see the body."

Decker turned back to look at the botanist, as did everyone else.

"Why?" Decker asked.

"I'm on record as believing this whole thing is a scam —some kind of rogue psychology research experiment. I'm on record as believing some … most … all … of you are in on the conspiracy. If you want me to continue to play along, I want to see the body. I want to know whether anyone really died or not. I want to see for myself whether there's evidence it wasn't an accident."

Decker nodded. "Fair enough. We'll do your interview first."

Decker turned to Tornquist. "Dr. Tornquist, if you could join us in the medical lab."

When they reached the building, Decker stepped aside to let Tornquist unlock the door. He and Culpepper followed her inside. Decker zipped his jacket against the cold. Tornquist stood on the other side of the table where Weaver's body lay covered in a sheet. Culpepper stopped just inside the door and stared at the table.

"Are you sure you want to do this?" Tornquist asked.

Culpepper's eyes were glazed as she stared at the sheet draped over the body laying on the exam table.

Tornquist grasped the edge of the sheet, her gaze still fixed on Culpepper. "This is something you can't unsee. It will haunt you for the rest of your life."

Culpepper looked up at Tornquist, her face already pale. She nodded.

Tornquist slowly drew the sheet back from Weaver's head as far as the shoulders. A tear crept down her cheek.

Culpepper abruptly turned away, looking frantically around the room. She lunged for a nearby wastebasket where she fell to her knees, heaving the bleak contents of her empty stomach.

Decker moved to the table to cover Weaver's body as Tornquist knelt at Culpepper's side. She offered her a damp towel. "Are you going to be okay?"

Culpepper buried her face in the towel until her breathing returned to normal. She looked up at Decker. "I promise you, I had nothing to do with this. I'm sorry I went off on my own yesterday against your orders. I'm sorry I turned off my comm. But I didn't do this."

Decker motioned to the other side of the room. Tornquist helped Culpepper up and followed as Decker pulled three lab chairs into a circle.

He leaned in toward Culpepper. "I know. You have a better alibi than anyone on the team—even me. From the time you left camp yesterday morning until Chief Guerrero came to get you yesterday evening, you were under continuous surveillance. Not because we didn't trust you. Because we're in an unknown environment with unknown threats, and it's my sworn duty to protect you. We have more than eight hours of high-resolution video that proves you couldn't have done it. You were, in fact, diligently doing your job the entire time. But as you can see, Petty Officer Weaver is dead. And it doesn't look like an accident. Have you seen or heard *anything* that might suggest someone else might have had motive, means, or opportunity to do this?"

Her gaze shifted into the distance. "Nothing comes to mind. How did she die? What makes you think it wasn't an accident?"

Decker straightened up in his chair. "Those are fair questions; questions I hope to answer in due time. But right now the investigation is still in process, and I need to keep that information confidential."

Culpepper frowned and shook her head. "Right. And how exactly do the rest of us know you're not guilty? Or you're not covering up something by one of your men?"

Decker held up his hands. "All fair questions. Normal procedure in a situation like this is for an independent investigating team to be sent out as soon as possible. I filed a report of Weaver's death under suspicious circumstances in last night's data upload. It's possible that an investigatory team will arrive with the scheduled transfer of supplies this morning. Given the unique nature of our mission, it may take them longer to put a team together. In the meantime, you're also free to make your own reports. I'll see to it that you can personally make sure they're included unedited in the next data upload."

205

"Fair enough. Are we done here?"

"I think so."

Culpepper started for the door.

Decker said, "Dr. Culpepper …"

She stopped with her back to him.

"I'm sorry you had to see that. I understand you have reservations about whether this is real or not. I'm doing what I can to help you resolve those questions. But we still have a mission to complete, and we can't get it done without your help. You have critical skills that are not duplicated anywhere on the team. Anywhere in this part of the galaxy, for that matter."

"I'll do my job. You needn't worry about that."

TWENTY-FOUR

He kept himself low in the tall grass as he approached the foot of the cliff. He was close enough to be confident he would have been able to see anyone who might be lurking around the base. He didn't.

He looked up to the ledge fifty feet above. He couldn't see anyone there either, but he knew he didn't have a good angle. He needed to get higher.

Doing his best to keep his profile low and his visibility minimized, he started working his way parallel to the cliff face toward an area where erosion had collapsed the cliff into a slope that he could scale without ropes.

He was almost up to the ledge when he caught a glimpse of motion off to his left. He quickly crouched and pulled out his binoculars.

A figure in jungle camouflage appeared to be following a trail that ran mostly level along the side of the hill. The figure was moving away from his position—slowly, sporadically, as though looking for something.

He crept up the hill and then began arching his path forward to get directly above his target.

The man's slow progress made it easier for him to catch up, but the need for stealth slowed him down almost as much. If he dislodged any loose rocks or soil, it would signal his presence. He could quickly become the hunted rather than the hunter if his target discovered him before he was ready.

He finally worked himself into a position behind a big rock a little behind and about fifty feet above the figure who was still facing away. Crouched behind the rock, he drew his sidearm and attached the silencer.

He cautiously stood from behind the rock and extended the weapon, resting his forearms on the boulder for stability. His target would be wearing body armor so this would have to be a head shot. He wished he had a rifle instead of the pistol as he gently squeezed the trigger. He felt the weapon recoil and heard the muffled spit as it discharged. A fraction of a second later, he watched Steadman fall to the ground.

Day 7, 1058 Hours

As quickly as the rough terrain would allow, he worked his way down the hillside to where Steadman had fallen. It would be difficult to make this look like an accident, but he had to buy time. The longer it took them to discover the body, the better his chances.

Maybe if he could find a way to get that bear over here. It just might do enough damage that they wouldn't be able to tell Steadman had been killed by a bullet. Maybe the bear would even carry the body off, never to be found.

As he pondered how he might make that happen, he came around a bend in the trail to the spot where he'd dropped Steadman. He still had his gun drawn and pointing forward, just in case.

Unfortunately, Steadman's body wasn't there.

Day 7, 1058 Hours

"He's up the hill about fifty feet—on your four," Guerrero said over the radio. "Crouching behind the rocks."

Steadman stood his ground, keeping his eyes focused on the brush around him along the trail. He pictured the rock formation in his mind and whispered into the comm, "Roger that."

"Drawing his handgun ... attaching the silencer ... standing up ... bracing against the rock."

Steadman turned his head just a bit in his pursuer's direction so he could see the rock out of the corner of his eye.

"He's taking aim. He just fired! Say your status!"

Steadman raced down the narrow trail. "I'm sweet. Status on Tango?"

Guerrero couldn't keep a hint of relief out of his voice. "Scrambling toward your last position. In a hurry."

So far, everything was going according to plan. Decker had put everyone on notice that Steadman was out here alone looking for evidence and then staged a distraction to give the perpetrator an easy opportunity to sneak out of the compound. Steadman had scouted the area and positioned himself on a trail protected by a low ridge where he could scramble away unseen.

Thirty feet down the trail, he broke downhill and then cut back through the dense foliage to circle around, relying on the contour of the hillside and vegetation for cover as he doubled back.

It would have been a lot easier to just kill the man. Steadman could have found a perch uphill and patiently waited with his rifle. But Decker wanted him alive. That meant avoiding a shootout, and that required getting within arms reach of him while he was distracted ... and he wouldn't be distracted for long.

Steadman had a lot of ground to cover quickly.

He made the cut back uphill. Stealth was important now, but so was speed. If his target was where he was supposed to be, Steadman would be coming up behind him.

Steadman was about to break out onto the trail when Guerrero's voice came over the radio. "Hold!"

Decker stopped short and took cover behind a tree.

"He's not quite there yet. He'll be about fifty feet down the trail to your left."

Steadman didn't reply. He quietly drew his handgun.

"Now!"

Steadman lunged onto the path and charged. He felt every ounce of the increased gravity as his legs pounded the trail. It felt like running in a dream as he put everything he had into moving forward but seemed to be barely managing to crawl. He could see the shooter up ahead, gun held in both hands and pointing down the trail in the opposite direction.

He has to hear me coming. There's no way I can get there in time.

Even as he continued to run, he raised his own gun to sight in on his adversary, prepared to take the defensive shot if he had to.

The man began to spin around, but too late. In reality it had taken Steadman barely two seconds to cover the distance. Solansky's eyes went wide with shock an instant before Steadman's left fist crashed squarely into his cheekbone.

Day 7, 1230 Hours

Decker, Steadman, Swenson, and Tornquist huddled in the medical lab with Solansky's unconscious body on the diagnostic table. Steadman had improvised restraints to make sure he stayed there as Tornquist attended to a gash on the back of Solansky's head.

Swenson pulled Decker aside and whispered. "We may have another problem, sir. The morning supply shipment was scheduled to arrive two hours ago. It hasn't come yet."

Decker closed his eyes and took a deep breath before letting it out slowly. "Theories?"

Swenson started ticking things off with his fingers. "Delay in getting some of the supplies we requested for today's shipment. But I've reviewed what was scheduled and requested for this morning and can't imagine that anything on the list would have created problems."

He raised a second finger. "They're assembling an investigation team. That decision would put them in a bind. Mission protocol was to minimize our footprint here. Putting together a compatible group of investigators on short notice would be difficult and contrary to the protocol, but such an investigation would have to be addressed quickly. If they're going to be serious about it, they really need to get them here this morning. Keep in mind they don't know what has transpired here last night and today."

He raised a third finger. "Something has gone wrong with the equipment, preventing a connection."

Swenson raised a fourth finger. "Something has gone wrong on Earth that prevents them from sticking to the schedule."

Decker closed his eyes and rocked his head back. "By 'something,' you mean something non-technical?"

"Yes."

"What do you think most likely?"

"I would prefer it to be one of the first two, but that isn't what you asked. If either of the first two were the case, protocol would have required them to make a shipment anyway, even if it was only a note to let us know what's happening. More likely it's either the third or fourth. Something—maybe technical, maybe not—has gone wrong."

"Recommendations?"

"Protocol is that we sit and wait another twenty-four hours. If nothing comes by then, I take the system down and run a full set of diagnostics."

"Anything more you can do before then?"

"Everything I can run without taking the equipment offline comes up green. Unless the problem is on their end and they fix it between now and then, it will be this time tomorrow before we know anything more."

Day 7, 1235 Hours

Tornquist finished stitching up the gash on Solansky's head. She pulled out a small light and used it to test his pupil dilation for any signs of a concussion.

Solansky woke with a start. He tried to sit up but found himself restrained. He pulled against them but quickly realized he wasn't going to break loose, particularly with Steadman's imposing figure standing over him.

"Headache?" Steadman asked.

Solansky stared at the ceiling.

Tornquist retrieved a vial and a syringe from the medicine cabinet. She loaded the syringe and injected Solansky's arm. "That should help with the pain."

Decker stepped up beside the bed. "So, Doctor, care to explain why you're taking potshots at my man?"

Solansky clenched his jaw and kept his eyes on the ceiling.

"I've got you on video for the attempted murder of Commander Steadman. That's an open-and-shut case. And I've got a pretty strong case against you for the murder of Petty Officer Weaver. If you don't want to go down for that one too, you should probably start talking."

Solansky's breathing began to slow.

"I'm curious as to why. Steadman, I think I understand. You were concerned he might discover something that would tie you to Weaver's murder. But why Weaver? You don't 'accidentally' break someone's neck. It's actually not an easy thing to do, even with professional training. Why?"

Swenson's head jerked up. He moved quickly to one of the computer consoles and started punching buttons.

Decker stood his ground at the foot of Solansky's bed. He needed answers. It didn't make sense that this was just something between Weaver and Solansky. There was something bigger here. And was the missing supply shipment related?

Decker motioned for Steadman and Tornquist to join him in the corner of the lab. He whispered, "Dr. Tornquist, I need answers, and I need them quickly. Can you give him something that will induce him to talk?"

Tornquist gave Decker a hard squint. "Commander Decker, I'm a physician. Even if I had any kind of truth serum in the limited supplies available, I couldn't do that."

She looked at Steadman. "I gave him an anesthetic to alleviate the pain from his injuries."

She looked back at Decker. "Now if you'll excuse me, I'll check back in on him later." Tornquist turned and walked out the door.

Decker started to follow, but Steadman grabbed him by the elbow and turned him back. He led Decker over to the medicine cabinet and pulled out the vial from which Tornquist had drawn the anesthetic.

Steadman whispered, "She injected him with ten ccs of this about five minutes ago. As she said, it is a common anesthetic. What she didn't tell you is that most truth serums are anesthetics used off-label. That's why she looked at me when she made mention of having given it to him. I've used this one in the field before, for exactly this purpose."

Steadman looked at his watch. "In a couple of minutes, his tongue should get a lot looser."

Day 7, 1240 Hours

Decker was about to try again with Solansky when Swenson called for his attention. Decker leaned in beside Swenson. "Can this wait, Rusty?"

"I think you'll want to know about this before you question him. You asked, 'Why Weaver?' That got me thinking there might be clues in Weaver's logs regarding her interactions with Solansky. I think I found something. It will take time to understand the details, but it looks like Weaver found software on Solansky's tablet that didn't belong. She spent some time—and made some notes—trying to figure out what it did. From the timestamp in the log, I think this was what she was working on just before she disappeared."

"Good work, Mr. Swenson. Keep digging. Let me know what you find."

TWENTY-FIVE

Decker opened the door of the medical lab. He saw the rest of the team milling around the burned-out campfire, kept away from the lab by Guerrero, who had been posted at the door. He asked Guerrero to step inside and join them but left the door open.

"Mr. Guerrero, please see to it that Mr. Solansky stays put. Use any necessary force. I'm going outside to address the rest of the team. Mr. Swenson will link the discussion into your comm so you can hear it."

"Aye, sir." Guerrero pulled a chair over where he could keep an eye on the unconscious and restrained Solansky.

The rest of the group in the lab left with Decker and joined the team around the campfire.

"I know you're all wondering what's going on. A lot has happened this morning, and I apologize for not having kept you in the loop. Events were unfolding quickly, and I felt it was necessary to stay on top of things. Mr. Solansky has a head injury and a minor

217

concussion. Dr. Tornquist has treated him and believes he'll be okay. Chief Guerrero is in the medical lab now keeping an eye on him, and Mr. Swenson has arranged the comms so that Guerrero can hear this discussion. Earlier this morning Mr. Solansky attempted to kill Commander Steadman."

Culpepper gasped. Sakhr and Zindell stared wide-eyed.

"Mr. Solansky has subsequently admitted to killing Petty Officer Weaver, although his admission will likely not be admissible in court. Even without that admission, we still have a compelling case against him and believe we may yet be able to collect more evidence."

"Why did he do it?" Zindell asked.

"We believe he tried to kill Commander Steadman because he was afraid the commander was about to find evidence that would tie him to the murder of Petty Officer Weaver. As to why he killed Miss Weaver, we're less clear on that. We believe he was acting for a foreign government. Likely part of a sleeper cell that had penetrated the program. We believe he was sending and receiving coded messages from his compatriots on Earth, and that he may have feared Weaver had discovered this … or she soon would. There's another matter we need to discuss, but before I move on, are there any questions?"

"What was his mission?" Sakhr asked. "Why is he here?"

"I really wish I could answer that. We believe Solansky was only here to observe and report, not to interfere. But we don't know the objectives of those who sent him. And unfortunately, that may be connected to the second issue we need to discuss. You may have noticed no one is working to unload the morning supply shipment. That isn't because we're too distracted. It's because it hasn't come." He looked at his watch. "It's now three hours overdue."

Everyone started talking at once. Decker held his hands up for silence but to no avail. A loud whistle from Steadman finally got everyone's attention.

Decker gestured with his palms to tamp things down. "Before you get too concerned, this may be nothing. They may be having a hard time finding some of the resources we requested for the morning shipment—like crutches for Dr. Zindell. The last data we sent included my report detailing our suspicions about the circumstances surrounding Miss Weaver's death. Protocol for such an event would be to assemble an independent team to take over the investigation. They may be having difficulty putting that together, and may be delaying the scheduled shipment accordingly."

"Or," Sakhr said, "Solansky's people on Earth may have taken action that has shut things down on Earth. The timing can hardly be coincidental."

Culpepper and Zindell started grumbling.

"That's certainly a possibility that must be considered," Decker said. "For now, we need to keep our heads clear. We need to do more than just wait. Mr. Swenson is running diagnostics on the equipment to see if he can identify any issues. The rest of us need to inventory what food, water, medical supplies, and other critical resources we have. If this doesn't resolve itself quickly, we'll need to develop a plan to stretch those resources."

"Do we need to start rationing?" Tornquist asked.

Decker shook his head. "I don't think we're there yet. The shipment is only three hours late. Let's not panic. But at the same time, use your heads. Waste nothing."

Decker noted a lot of very concerned faces in the crowd. Culpepper, on the other hand, seemed completely unfazed. Probably the result of not believing any of this was real to begin with. She asked, "What will we do with Solansky?"

"We wait for the portal to come back online. Then we ship him back to Earth and let them deal with him. In the meantime, we keep him restrained, and we keep a guard on him twenty-four/seven."

"If this turns into a long-term problem," Sakhr said, "that would tie up critical resources. Manpower. Food. Water."

"The portal will come back online. Until then, we came here to do a job. We still need to get it done."

Day 7, 1600 Hours

Dr. Culpepper sat at a computer console in the science lab, her eyes fixed on the monitor, but her mind in a completely different place.

I have a good mind to just walk out on this "project." A scam cover for a psychology experiment is one thing, but this has gone completely off the rails. There's no excuse for them to have not stepped in and shut this down after Weaver's death.

And that's to say nothing of the unprofessional way they're treating me. Keeping me in the dark on the real goals of the experiment is understandable. Threatening to tie me down and tape my mouth shut is something else entirely. And threatening me with a TASER?

Granted it probably isn't real. Or if it is, they wouldn't have actually shot me with it. But what objective justifies this?

Culpepper's reverie was interrupted when the door opened. She looked up to see Dr. Tornquist walk in wearing a jacket and rubbing her hands together.

"Do you mind if I work in here for a while? The medical lab is frigid, and I can't think straight when I'm shivering."

Culpepper pointed to a console on the other side of the lab. "Knock yourself out. Just stay on your side of the room."

Tornquist's head perked up at the comment. Culpepper turned back to her console.

Okay. That sounded meaner than I intended. But she hasn't exactly been on my side in any of this.

Tornquist looked at the floor. "Dr. Culpepper, I need to apologize for my behavior toward you last night. It was unprofessional and inappropriate."

Culpepper ignored her, pretending to be engrossed in the data displayed on her monitor.

"I wish I could say I've never done that before, but I can't." Tornquist looked up. "It's a pattern of behavior

221

that I recognize and am trying to change, but it still sometimes comes out."

Culpepper continued to stare at her screen, wishing the woman would just shut up.

"I've never had children of my own. I already had a busy medical career when I married, and we knew my husband's career would have him away from home for long stretches. We didn't feel that would be fair to children, so we didn't have any."

She sat down at one of the workstations. "Without realizing it, I tend to become attached to younger professionals who come into my circle—medical students, interns, younger doctors. My husband called it 'mama bear syndrome.' I start thinking of them as the daughters I never had and feel the need to nurture and protect them. When I first saw Pam's crumpled body on the search video, I was crushed. I knew she was dead. All I could think was that I'd lost my little girl. Then when my other ... Well, I should have recognized you were operating from a lack of information. I had no right to judge you or to speak to you the way I did, and I'm sorry."

A silent war waged inside Culpepper's mind. Part of her hurt for what Tornquist was going through—what she herself had done to compound that pain. Not staying in the loop so she would know what was happening. Not being there to help with the search for Pam. Actually being a burden to the people looking for her when they needed her help.

But another part of her was still angry about the entire situation. And she was convinced that Tornquist was in on the conspiracy. Was this whole sob story just another attempt to manipulate her?

How twisted are these people?

TWENTY-SIX

It was dark when Decker left the kitchen. There was no sign anyone had fixed dinner. He found everyone sitting around the campfire. The mood was somber, but at least there was conversation. That much was good.

As he sat down, Culpepper had the floor. "I think we need to execute him, and sooner rather than later." She cut her eyes at Decker. "You all heard the numbers. Two weeks of food left. That assumes we keep feeding him. If we cut our losses, that adds what, ten percent, to our time?"

Decker wondered whether she really felt that way, or whether she was just trying to test the boundaries of the observers of her hypothetical psychological simulation.

"Twelve and a half percent," Swenson said. "Less than two additional days."

"We can't kill another human being," Zindell said. "That would make us no better than him. Besides which, with rationing, we can extend our food to last as much as six weeks, even continuing to feed Dr. Solansky."

"*Mister* Solansky," Swenson said. "It turns out he's probably not really a cosmologist. That was part of his cover. He knows less about cosmology than I do."

Zindell waved a hand in the air. "Mister. Doctor. It makes no difference. He's a human being."

Swenson looked at Sakhr. "What do you think, Doctor?"

Sakhr had been looking at his shoes. He looked up at Swenson and the others. "I seem to recall that for a few hours there, some of you were ready to execute me. I think I'd prefer to stay out of this discussion."

Culpepper shook her head. "I think there's a difference between executing a murderer and murder itself."

Decker thought Culpepper's attention seemed focused more on her colleagues than on the subject at hand. *She's baiting them, studying their reactions.*

"How is that different, Doctor?" Zindell asked. "In both cases, a human life is lost. One of our founding principles is that we're all equal. If we're all equal, how is it okay if we kill this person, but wrong if we kill that one?"

"The difference," Swenson said, "is that Solansky acted in his own interest and against the interest of the rest of the community. Us. While you might stretch reality to argue he was protecting himself, he was protecting himself in the midst of an endeavor to betray both our nation and us. By law, that's not a legitimate exercise of self-defense. We, on the other hand, are doing

225

precisely that. Protecting ourselves. I'll admit I'm not comfortable using the argument of limited supplies to contend for a speedy execution. But I'm very comfortable with the argument that he still poses a threat to the rest of us. The nature of that threat, combined with his demonstrated capacity for the lethal use of force, justifies a lethal response."

Swenson looked over at Decker, who was still standing just outside the circle. "For the sake of debate I'm ignoring the chain of command, but each of us has a moral obligation to help protect the others. That's intrinsic in the definition of a community. I can't say I've done what I can to protect my community if I leave alive someone committed to its destruction."

"Again I ask," Zindell said, "how is he different than any of us? We're all equal in the eyes of the law."

"*Created* equal I think is the precise term," Swenson said. "But we're also created with free will, the freedom to choose what path we follow. Each of us individually. Solansky has chosen to set himself against the survival of this community. We haven't. We have a right to protect ourselves."

Zindell opened his mouth to respond, but Tornquist interrupted. "Captain Decker, it seems to me this is an academic discussion. You alone have the authority here to decide what happens to Mr. Solansky."

"It's Commander, and—"

Tornquist shook her head. "I chose that title deliberately. We're more like a ship at sea than we've ever been. We're nine people stranded fifty-seven light-years from home with no supply lines, no channels of communication, and where our very survival depends on discipline and the execution of our assigned duties."

Decker felt everyone's eyes focus on him. He shook his head. "I don't disagree with your assessment of our current situation. But the 'ship at sea' metaphor doesn't work. There are two possibilities here. The first is that the portal will come back online soon. In that case, we turn Solansky over to the authorities on Earth. They'll want to do their own investigation, and they'll want him alive to help uncover the rest of his cell. Part of our job is to keep him breathing so that can happen."

He scanned the faces around the circle, trying to assess their state of mind. "The second possibility is that whatever is interfering with the portal will not be resolved quickly. And while I do believe I have the authority to decide how we deal with Solansky, I also believe it's important for the team that we have this discussion and decide collectively—as a community, to use Mr. Swenson's term—how to deal with this. Some of you signed up to live within a military chain of command. Some of you didn't. If I start deciding to execute people appealing solely to my authority, pretty soon the rest of you will start worrying if you'll be next. How inconvenient do you need to be to get shot?"

He looked at Culpepper. She stared back defiantly.

He looked around at the rest of the team. "That's why civil governments have concepts like 'innocent until

227

proven guilty' and 'trial by a jury of peers.' It takes the power of life and death out of the hands of the king. Or captain."

Decker scanned the faces again. "For the time being, Solansky stays alive so we can send him back to Earth to face justice. He'll be chained up and under guard twenty-four/seven. Meanwhile, our job is still to research this planet. We need to stay focused on that job, now more than ever."

Culpepper sat back in her chair and crossed her arms.

"If I may change the subject," Sakhr said, "you've made the case that we need to work as a team to accomplish our mission. If the portal doesn't come back, I would argue that we need to work as a team if we're to survive. Getting the portal working again would seem to be very important."

Decker nodded. "Your point being?"

"I'd like to know more about how it works. Perhaps with more of us thinking about it … brainstorming … we might find something that Mr. Swenson overlooked."

Sakhr glanced at Swenson. "Meaning no disrespect, of course."

Swenson looked at Decker, who nodded. He leaned forward, resting his forearms on his knees and clasping his hands. "I wish I could tell you more. I wish I knew more. Theoretical physics isn't my thing. I'm just an engineer. I learned some very generic things from Dr. Kreitzman about how he arrived at his theory, but nothing about the theory itself. He would give me components, specifications for how to interface with those components, but nothing about what was inside or how it worked. They were just black boxes to me."

"Well, tell us what you do know," Sakhr said. "How did he arrive at the theory?"

Swenson looked at the ground. "When Albert Einstein developed the theories of special and general relativity, he started with two postulates. First, that the laws of physics are invariant, and second, that the speed of light is fixed, regardless of the motion of the observer or light source. This second postulate was based on experimental observations, and it contradicted the Newtonian model that had been the established standard for centuries. Kreitzman started in a similar state. General relativity was good, but there were things it didn't explain. In particular, general relativity, which was good at explaining big things like cosmology, and quantum field theory, which was good at explaining small things like atoms, contradicted each other. They couldn't both be right. So he set out to develop a new theory, and he started with two postulates. But his starting point was somewhat controversial. First, he assumed the universe was designed. That some exceptional intelligence engineered what we think of as the laws of physics with the specific intent of creating a universe suitable for life and creating life in that universe. And second, that this designer had the further intent of allowing us to inhabit the entirety of that universe. In real time. Not by spending generations and millennia traveling between the stars in tin cans."

229

Culpepper shook her head and leaned forward. "That's not how you do science. That's how you entertain children."

Swenson smiled and held out his hands. "And yet, here we are. I did say it was controversial. And I can't begin to tell you how he got from that starting point to a coherent theoretical model, or what that theoretical model is. But I disagree with your contention that it isn't how science is done. It's precisely how science is done. Every theory is nothing more than a guess. You observe nature. You guess at what causes things to be that way. Then you look for ways to test your theory—test to see whether it really explains things or not. Dr. Kreitzman's theory predicted a lot of things that had never been seen or tried. So he started trying some of those things. And they worked. Power for the buildings, vehicles, and tools we're using. Propulsion for the drones and four-wheelers. And the portal itself."

Sakhr became suddenly still. "So Dr. Kreitzman has proven the existence of God."

Culpepper rolled her eyes.

Swenson laughed. "Well, no. Just because his theory works doesn't necessarily mean the postulates that led him to that theory are correct. It really doesn't even mean the theory is correct. Just that it works. Newtonian physics is wrong, but it works for most things."

Culpepper harrumphed. "Well, you can't prove by me that his theory works. I say we're still on Earth. Batteries, or fuel cells, could provide the power. I don't know how you move the drones around, but I can come up with all kinds of theories that are easier to believe than to think we're actually on another planet. Or that God exists."

Zindell leaned forward in his chair. "You know, this wouldn't be the first time that a scientific breakthrough came from someone starting with the assumption that life was designed. In the early days of the study of DNA, it was believed that only a minute fraction of DNA actually served any purpose. Ninety-eight percent of it seemed to be meaningless nonsense. Evolutionists dismissed it as random junk that didn't help but didn't hurt, so it was sustained in the genome. But a group of researchers who believed DNA was designed, not evolved, believed that if it was there, it must serve a purpose. So they kept looking at all the DNA that was being ignored by the rest of the community. That research led to major breakthroughs in immunology and disease prevention as we've learned that DNA does other things besides code for protein synthesis."

"Which brings us back to our study of local plants and animals," Decker said. "And food. How is your research shaping up?"

Tornquist and Culpepper looked at each other with wide eyes. Tornquist looked at Decker. "Wait a minute … you're not thinking of eating things from this planet, are you?"

Decker shrugged. "Why not?"

Culpepper glanced at Tornquist, then she leaned forward in her chair. "Nutrition is more than just

231

chemicals. We don't eat dirt because our bodies can't derive any meaningful resources from it. We need a variety of very specific, and very complex, molecules: proteins, carbohydrates, fats. The plants and animals we eat from Earth are from the same evolutionary tree and share these same constituents. The probability that life here evolved with those same molecules is, well, almost infinitely improbable."

Swenson looked pointedly at Culpepper. "Now you're presuming that we're not actually *on Earth*. You also presume that independent evolution is the right theory to explain life on this planet."

He turned to Zindell. "Tell them about the bear."

Zindell's attention was focused on his shoelaces. Tornquist reached over and touched his shoulder. "Doctor?"

Zindell looked up. "What? Oh. Yes. The bear. We recovered some of Yogi's hair from the bumper of the four-wheeler that collided with him. I ran his DNA profile this afternoon. It confirms the physical observations. He shares ninety-nine percent of his DNA with other bear species on Earth but is an exact match for none of them. Actually, the most profound observation is that he *has* DNA. Precisely the same chemical composition and molecular structure as life on Earth."

Swenson said, "And DNA codes for protein synthesis. So if ninety-nine percent of his DNA is a match for Earth life, his body probably has most or all of the same proteins that typify life on Earth. And by extension, the plants and other animals on this planet are likely similar, since *he* has to get *his* nutrition from local sources."

Decker looked at Culpepper, who had a dazed look. "I'm just looking at this as a contingency plan for now. But until the portal comes back online, I think it behooves us to figure out if there's a viable plan B. What does it take to do that?"

Culpepper sat back in her chair. She looked over at Tornquist as if hoping someone would offer a counterargument she couldn't find.

"I'll queue up everything Mikey gave us—a variety of nuts and seeds—plus a few fruits I collected in the orchard yesterday for toxicology tests. Those will run overnight. In the morning, I'll put anything that didn't show toxicity in for nutritional analysis. Then head out and start collecting more samples."

Steadman shifted on his feet. "What about the samples you collected by the river the other day?"

Culpepper shook her head. "I'll get to those eventually, but right now I think they're a low priority. They have potential as spices, medicinals, sources of vitamins. But what we need most are carbohydrates and proteins. Fruits, nuts, grains, and roots are the most likely plant-based sources."

Decker looked at Zindell. "What about meat?"

"There's a limit to what I can tell you without actually killing a few animals. So far that's been off the table—if you'll pardon the pun. Today, with Mr. Swenson's help, I sent out three of our drones to start a comprehensive

233

survey of wildlife in the area. At some point … soon … we'll need to collect physical samples for analyses similar to what Dr. Culpepper is doing on her plants."

Decker looked at Tornquist to see if she had anything to add.

"My chief concern is time," she said. "We should be spending months to evaluate whether any particular food source is safe, much less efficacious, for human consumption. We have days. We have hundreds, perhaps thousands, of potential sources, but we're flying blind. We have no way to decide which are most likely to work so we can put those first."

Swenson sat up and looked at the assembled scientists. "I know this isn't scientific, but I recommend you start with what the locals eat. Mikey, in particular."

"Why?" Tornquist asked.

"Two reasons. First, we've all observed how similar the plants and animals here are to those on Earth. Dr. Zindell just told us about Yogi's DNA, confirming the parallel. On Earth, for the most part, we eat the same foods other animals eat. The same things are nutritious, the same things are toxic."

Culpepper opened her mouth to speak, but Swenson held up a hand to cut her off. "I do know there are exceptions. Some animals can eat things that are toxic to humans. Humans can eat things that are toxic to some animals. But it gives us a starting point that should dramatically narrow the candidates."

"And the second reason?" Decker asked.

"We've already demonstrated that Mikey can eat cereal bars composed of a variety of nuts, seeds, grains, and sugars from Earth. That's why I suggest focusing on Mikey's diet. That, and because on Earth apes are more like humans than any other animal species."

Decker looked at Tornquist, who was looking at Culpepper and Zindell.

Culpepper felt all eyes on her. "I can't say I like it. As Wonder Boy admitted, it's not objective science. But I don't have a better idea. It's certainly no worse than just picking things at random."

Zindell seemed lost in thought. Decker said, "Dr. Zindell?"

Zindell looked up. "Sorry, sir. With your permission, I'd like to go out with Mr. Guerrero and Mikey tomorrow and see if we can get our host to show us around her orchard."

"I think that's a great idea," Decker said. "How's your ankle?"

Zindell opened his mouth to answer, but Tornquist cut him off. "He's okay to ride along, but I want him to stay in the four-wheeler."

Zindell's face fell.

Decker looked at Sakhr. "Dr. Sakhr, would you mind joining them in case they need help foraging? I'm sure Dr. Culpepper can walk you through what you need to do to collect and document."

Sakhr perked up. "I would consider it an honor."

TWENTY-SEVEN

It was close to midnight when Zindell decided to call it enough and go to bed. He'd been working with Swenson to modify the search parameters for the drones based on the earlier discussion around the campfire.

He hobbled into the men's quarters on a makeshift crutch Guerrero had fashioned from a tree branch. The common area had been reconfigured so there was now a bunk against one wall. Solansky was lying on the cot, a chain attached to his ankle with the other end bolted to the wall.

Decker sat in a chair on the other side of the room making notes on a tablet—probably keeping up his status reports—positioned so he could still see Solansky in his peripheral vision. Solansky was awake, staring at the ceiling.

Decker looked up and greeted Zindell as he entered the room.

"How long have you been standing watch?" Zindell asked.

Decker looked at his watch. "About two hours now. Mr. Steadman will relieve me at 0200."

"Mr. Swenson asked me to see if you could check in with him. Something about the portal status, I think."

Decker looked at his watch again, looked at Solansky, and frowned.

"I'd be happy to stand watch for a few minutes if it helps," Zindell said. "It doesn't look like he's going anywhere."

Decker set his tablet down. "I'd appreciate that."

He stood and stepped toward the door. "One thing. Consider him dangerous. This line of tape on the floor shows how far he can travel before that chain stops him. Stay on this side of the line and you'll be fine."

Zindell nodded and Decker stepped outside.

Ever since the campfire discussion about capital punishment, Zindell had been hoping to get a chance to talk to Solansky. Preferably alone. He thought he had a better chance of getting to the truth that way.

Zindell stood squarely in the middle of his side of the room, well away from the tape and Solansky. He stared at the man for a moment. As though sensing his gaze, Solansky tilted his head up and looked at him. "Come by to see the barbarian exhibit at the zoo?"

Zindell ignored the taunt. Solansky sat up on his bunk, his ankle chain clinking as it shifted and part of it fell to the floor.

"Why?" Zindell asked.

Solansky looked at him. He bent over, elbows on his knees and forehead resting on his hands. "It isn't what they're telling you. When I heard what had happened to Petty Officer Weaver, it broke my heart. That a life so young and full of promise should be snuffed out in such a violent way."

Solansky rubbed his hands together and looked at the wall to his left, hiding his face from Zindell. "I needed some time to think, to process. I went for a walk. Before I realized it, I was back near the waterfall. Then I caught sight of something stalking me. I couldn't see it clearly, couldn't be sure what it was. My mind was a fog. Since I was near where Weaver had died, I assumed it was the same creature that had killed her."

He looked back at Zindell, a hint of tears in his eyes. "I managed to get the drop on it and fired one shot. I thought I'd hit it and ran down to see what it was. That's the last thing I remember."

Zindell needed a minute to think. The story sounded plausible, but something didn't ring true. He turned around to sit on the couch opposite Solansky's bed where Decker had sat but forgot about his bad ankle. As he shifted weight onto the ankle while turning, his left leg folded underneath him and he fell across the boundary of Solansky's virtual cell.

Solansky pounced from his bed, grabbing Zindell by the shirt and dragging him further into his lair. He grabbed for the gun strapped to Zindell's thigh.

Zindell was reeling from the pain shooting up from his ankle and realized too late what was happening. He managed to get a grip on Solansky's arm, but not until after his opponent had already gotten a grip on the gun and pulled it from the holster. Zindell screamed for help and fought to keep his grip on the arm in hopes of preventing Solansky from using it until help arrived. He bit at the man's forearm in hopes of forcing him to release his grip.

Unfortunately, that had the opposite effect and the gun discharged.

Zindell heard the powerful echo of the discharge simultaneous with feeling fire rip through his leg. The shock caused him to lose his grip on Solansky's arm.

Solansky pointed the gun at the lock securing the chain to his ankle and fired again. He raced out into the darkness, Zindell's screams of agony ringing out behind.

Day 7, 2415 Hours

Steadman was awakened by the noise of someone yelling something he couldn't understand. As he listened, he heard the unmistakable sound of a gunshot. Already rolling out of bed, he heard someone screaming in pain, then another discharge. He bounded to the door, grabbing his sidearm on the way.

As he raced out into the common area, he heard Guerrero falling in behind him. Steadman turned right to scan the area where Solansky should have been. Guerrero followed immediately behind, turning left to cover the other side of the room.

They both shouted, "Clear!" in unison.

Guerrero holstered his gun and dropped down beside Zindell, who was writhing in pain.

Steadman continued on to the outer door, which was still open. He heard another discharge outside, followed by a screech. He looked out in the direction from which he thought the gunshot came and saw a silhouetted figure disappear into the darkness.

Looking back the other way, he saw what he believed was Mikey bounding off in the opposite direction.

"Get Tornquist over here stat!" Guerrero said. "The bullet hit an artery."

Day 8, 0003 Hours

Grace Tornquist sat beside her husband holding hands under the starry night skies. The fireworks were beautiful this year, and it was a perfect night for it. Clear skies, the moon low on the horizon. Not too hot with just a slight breeze.

This had been a tradition for the two of them since they first started dating. They missed a few times—when her husband was deployed—but whenever he was home on Independence Day, they celebrated together.

Pow!

Wow. That sounded close. I guess someone brought their own fireworks again.

Screeeeeeee!

Roman candles too?

She looked over at her husband, squeezed his hand. He smiled back at her.

Pow!

Who's setting off fireworks so close?

She tried to turn her head to look, but it wouldn't budge. She looked at her husband again, but now Commander Decker was in his chair, holding her hand.

She tried to pull her hand back, but it wouldn't move.

Bam! Bam! Bam!

Dr. Tornquist woke with a start.

"Medical emergency! Men's quarters!" She recognized Decker's voice on the other side of the door.

She rolled out of bed and grabbed her clothes. "On my way!"

"It's Dr. Zindell. Gunshot wound to the leg. Guerrero thinks it hit an artery. Bring your Go Bag."

Tornquist opened the door and pushed past Decker. "I'll meet you there," she said as she raced out into the darkness.

Decker came through the door to the men's quarters with Swenson not far behind. Zindell was on the floor, bleeding profusely. Steadman was fashioning a tourniquet from a shoelace that appeared to have been taken from the doctor's boot.

Zindell winced as he looked up at Decker. "I'm sorry, Commander. This was my fault. I started talking to him. I forgot about my ankle. I turned to move to the couch and went down. We struggled over my gun and it went off. He has it."

Tornquist came through the door pushing her way past Decker and went straight to Zindell's side.

Sakhr came out of his bunkroom. "What's all the commotion out here?" Then he saw Zindell and all the blood. He clamped his hand over his mouth and raced to the back of the building where he could be heard regurgitating into the toilet.

A moment later, Swenson could be heard having the same reaction on the ground outside the front door.

Decker said, "Steadman, Guerrero. Gear up. I want you on his trail."

Steadman looked up at Decker from where he knelt beside Tornquist, who was working to stop the bleeding of Zindell's leg.

Tornquist shook her head. "If you want me to save the leg, I'll need Chris's help."

Decker looked back at Steadman. "Do what you can to help the doctor."

He turned to Guerrero, who was standing watch at the door. "Guerrero, you and Swenson get over to the control room and get the drones up. See if you can find him and track him before he gets too far away."

Sakhr came back into the room, wiping his face with a towel and studiously looking away from Zindell. "What can I do to help?"

Without looking up from her work, Tornquist said, "Get over to the medical lab and raise the room temperature to sixty-five degrees. Then head over to the science lab and drop the room temperature there to thirty-five degrees. Then move Weaver's body from the medical lab to the science lab."

Decker nodded to Sakhr. "Stop by and roust Dr. Culpepper on your way. Fill her in and get her to help. I'll be along in a minute to help with the body."

Tornquist said, "Medical lab first, Doctor."

Sakhr raced out the door.

"Captain, I need you to go get the stretcher," Tornquist said. "We'll need it to transport Zindell as soon as I get this artery tied off."

Decker was out the door not far behind Sakhr.

TWENTY-EIGHT

Solansky crouched behind a rock to catch his breath. He'd been running full-out for more than two miles. Playing the professor the last two years had taken its toll on his physical training regimen. He was tempted to believe they really were on another planet with higher gravity and that it wasn't his fault. He laughed. The Culpepper woman was right. They'd slipped something into his food or water to weaken him so he'd believe the lie. That would also explain how Steadman had overtaken him so quickly.

He inventoried his situation. They'd taken his comm, which was just as well. He wouldn't be able to monitor their communications, but they'd have switched frequencies and encrypted anyway. And he'd have had to ditch it to make sure they couldn't use it to track him.

He had a gun. He checked the clip: twelve rounds left. He wished he'd had time to grab Zindell's other clip and maybe the silencer. But with Steadman and Guerrero asleep in the next room, and Decker somewhere nearby, he couldn't take the chance.

Without the silencer, shooting would be a last resort. The sound would carry for miles. If he had to shoot, he'd have to run again.

He put more ammunition and a silencer on his shopping list.

No food, beyond the two snack bars he had with him.

No water.

Well, that actually might be less of a problem for him than for them. He'd have no choice but to go native for food and water. They were already talking about extreme rationing to try to avoid it. They'd be focused on survival, not on him.

He'd be focused on survival too, but for him, that meant something entirely different. They were the threat to his survival. And he would eliminate that threat. Patiently. Systematically. Efficiently.

But first, he had to complete his escape. If Steadman and Guerrero weren't already on his trail, they soon would be. They wouldn't be able to track him as quickly as he could run—at least at night—but the drones would be a problem. He was pretty sure they had night-vision capability.

That meant he needed to find a way to mask his body heat. He thought about the river but dismissed it immediately. Hypothermia wasn't part of a winning strategy, and the cold water wouldn't hide him as much as highlight how hot he was by comparison.

245

Caves seemed to be his best bet. Far enough inside, they wouldn't pick up his body heat without coming into the cave. Of course, there was always the risk that he'd be crashing someone else's pad.

The thought of finding a bear in a cave sent a shiver down his spine. But it also made him think that until daylight, when they could get visible imaging, they wouldn't be able to tell whether the heat they were seeing was him or a native animal. And they'd likely assume he was smart enough to stay out of caves.

The line between genius and stupidity is sometimes murky.

It was time to get moving again. Setting a slower pace —one he hoped he could sustain for several miles—he cut methodically between the trees and over the rugged terrain in the faint light of the two moons. He would have to stay far enough out to be confident that the perimeter sensors wouldn't pick him up. Unfortunately, that meant he had about ten miles to cover before daybreak.

If those are artificial lights, why don't they turn them off? Darkness would be to their advantage.

Day 8, 0102 Hours

Decker entered the storage building to find Swenson seated at a computer console with Guerrero looking over his shoulder.

"Status?"

Swenson glanced at Decker. "I have one drone up in a defensive position watching the compound. The other six are executing a search pattern using night-vision cameras.

Right now we're focused in the direction Guerrero gave me for Solansky's departure, but if we don't get a hit pretty soon, I'm going to recommend we restart the search using a spiral pattern out from the perimeter."

Decker looked at Guerrero. "Any chance of picking up a trail?"

"Not at night using remote drones and night-vision cameras. I'd need to be on the ground with a flashlight to spot a trail. That's dangerous work with a hostile out there and without a wingman."

"And counterproductive," said Decker.

They both turned back to watch the camera feeds on Swenson's monitors. Decker heard the door open behind him and turned to see Culpepper carrying a tray with three mugs of coffee. Her eyes were bloodshot and her cheeks rosy. He took two cups. "Thanks, Doctor. This is much appreciated."

She nodded as Guerrero took the third, then she left.

Decker placed one on the console beside Swenson.

"One other thing, Skipper," said Guerrero. "The more time that passes without finding him, the less comfortable I am with only one drone playing defense. It leaves us with a narrow perimeter and several blind spots."

"Options?"

"If our current sweep fails to find him, I recommend deploying three drones for a larger defensive perimeter with cross-coverage. The remaining four can be used for active search beyond that perimeter."

"Do you think we've missed him on this pass?"

Guerrero looked at Swenson's monitor again. "I do. He must have doubled back or circled around and gone in a different direction."

Decker patted Swenson on the shoulder. "Do it."

TWENTY-NINE

Day 8, 0200 Hours

Teri Culpepper hadn't slept well the night before, and tonight wasn't going any better. Tornquist had stabilized Zindell and patched up his leg, but Solansky was on the loose again. With a gun. They weren't safe.

Why didn't the people running this experiment shut it down? It didn't make sense.

As she fell into a fitful sleep, she began to dream of her childhood. She was a teenager, driving the ATV into the field with lunch in an ice chest. She could see her dad driving the harvester over a crop of alfalfa, bales of hay spitting out the back and dropping onto the ground.

Following some distance behind was the old blue pickup truck. Mom would be driving, and her brothers would be in the back, picking the hay bales off the ground and stacking them in the bed.

The tractor stopped in the middle of a row. Her father must have seen her coming.

She pulled up alongside and bounded out of the ATV as her dad climbed down to meet her. He hugged her

249

tightly as though he hadn't seen her in forever. He looked down into her eyes. "What are you doing here, honey? You're all grown up now. You're with a new family. You need to take care of them."

He nodded toward the approaching truck.

Confused, she turned and watched the truck as it pulled alongside them. The windows were rolled up, and she saw a face reflecting in the glass.

Pam? What's she doing here?

Teri shook her head in confusion. When Pam's image reflected the motion, Teri's consternation grew.

The window began to roll down, and where Teri was expecting to see her mom, it was Dr. Tornquist who greeted her.

Beginning to feel panic sweep over her, she looked at the back of the truck where her brothers were jumping out—except it wasn't her brothers. It was Steadman and Guerrero.

She heard a voice behind her—Decker's voice—saying, "These people aren't going to survive without your help."

Enveloped by panic, she spun around to face the voice, expecting to see Decker. But Decker wasn't there. The tractor wasn't there. The field wasn't there.

She was in a hospital room. Her dad's hospital room. Where she had last seen him just before he died. Her dad lay on the bed, his body shriveled by a losing battle with cancer.

No! I can't do this again.

He reached out to her and she took his hand. With great effort, he rolled his head to look at her. With a labored smile and a weak voice, he said, "My dear Teri, this is not who I raised you to be."

The hospital dissolved around them, leaving only the two of them and the hospital bed, now in the middle of the clearing on Two. The persistent beep of a heart monitor stayed with them, but the antiseptic smell of the hospital was replaced by a faint hint of the cedar forest in the distance.

Her father squeezed her hand. "There's a reason why God put you here, Teri. Find it."

Teri turned to look at the surrounding hills. The sound of the heart monitor stopped, and she felt her father's fingers slip from her hand.

She turned back to where he had been, but he and the bed were gone, replaced by the campfire and a ring of empty chairs.

A lone hat lay on one of the chairs.

Motion in the distance caught her eye, and she looked up to see someone hiking up the side of one of the hills, nearing the summit. When the figure reached the top, it turned to face her.

It waved at her and smiled.

Pam?

THIRTY

"How's the leg?" Decker asked.

Zindell looked up with a blank stare. He was still on the exam table in the medical lab, but Dr. Tornquist had propped him up so he was half sitting. Zindell's face suddenly animated.

"Just fine, Mr. President. And yours?"

Tornquist smiled. "He's still a bit loopy from the anesthetic. It'll be a few hours yet before he's completely coherent, and then he won't remember you were here."

Decker gave Zindell a pat on the shoulder. "So, what's his prognosis?"

"He'll live. And he should regain full use of the leg. I wish we had better facilities. I'd argue for sending him home if it was an option. But under the circumstances, I think we can manage. I have him loaded up with antibiotics to minimize the risk of infection. He'll need to stay completely off the leg for at least a week. Crutches for several weeks after that. Physical therapy. He's not feeling it now, but he's going to be in a fair amount of pain for the next few days. I have enough meds to manage it, but it'll significantly deplete our limited supplies. When he's more coherent I'll have to talk to him about how much pain he's willing to tolerate in the interest of conserving irreplaceable resources."

Zindell tugged at Decker's sleeve. "Pardon me, sir, but I've been here for over an hour, and no one has taken my order yet. I'd like the prime rib, cooked medium rare. And a baked potato. Loaded. And could you have someone bring me another glass of tea? I seem to have misplaced my glass."

Decker fought hard not to laugh, but Tornquist wasn't helping. She was standing behind Zindell with her hand covering her mouth, her shoulders shaking.

"I'll see what I can do, Doctor," Decker said, with as straight a face as he could muster.

After Tornquist regained her composure, she said, "I'm getting hungry myself. Is anyone working on breakfast?"

"I ran into Dr. Sakhr in the compound on the way over. He said Dr. Culpepper has already started working on it. Should be ready in a few minutes. Sakhr said he would deliver. Unfortunately for Dr. Zindell, I don't think steak and potatoes are on the menu."

Tornquist nodded. "What's everyone else up to this morning?"

"Steadman and Guerrero got a couple of hours of sleep last night and then headed out at first light to see if they could pick up Solansky's trail. Swenson is still

253

monitoring the drone search. After breakfast, I'm going to have him train Dr. Sakhr on the equipment, at least enough so they can trade off. Swenson is way overdue for some sleep."

Tornquist's posture slumped ever so slightly. "He's not the only one." She straightened back up. "What can I do to help?"

He nodded toward Zindell. "Beyond looking after our dinner guest, food and water are our highest priorities. Anything you can do to help Dr. Culpepper find food we can eat helps. Also, Mr. Swenson thinks he can cobble together a still to purify water for drinking and cooking, but it would be helpful to know how good the river water is. If we can use that for cleaning and bathing, it would significantly reduce the capacity requirements for Swenson's still."

Decker nodded again toward Zindell. "Losing him, even for a few days, is a problem. As soon as he's able, I need him sitting in front of a computer monitoring drone recon. If he can at least identify something to target, I can send Steadman and Guerrero on a hunting trip. You won't be able to tell whether we can eat it until we bag it. If we can get the good doctor out on a four-wheeler with Steadman riding shotgun, so much the better."

Day 8, 1600 Hours

"What do you think it means?" Culpepper asked.

Tornquist cocked an eyebrow. "It doesn't necessarily mean anything. Most dreams are just your subconscious mind sorting through leftovers. I'm guessing the grassland here reminds you of the farm you grew up on. You and I talked about my 'mama bear syndrome' yesterday, and that may have prompted your subconscious to associate me with your mom. And, by extension, Commander Decker with your dad, Chris and Alex with your brothers. Maybe you've also been thinking about Pam and the possibility that could've been you."

An involuntary shudder gripped Culpepper. "Okay, but what about the things my dad said to me? And what Decker said to me?"

Tornquist shrugged. "Decker's been saying that to you all along. Your expertise is critical to this mission, and now more than ever it will take all of us to get through this. As for what your dad said … I don't know. If your dad was actually here with us today, do you think he would've said the same thing?"

Culpepper's stomach roiled and she felt a sudden tightness in her chest.

That was the most real part of the whole dream.

Day 8, 1930 Hours

There was no campfire that evening. Guerrero had always been the one to get the fire started, but he was sacked out. Decker had put Guerrero and Steadman on a rotating watch. Steadman was on now, and Guerrero would relieve him at midnight.

Everyone else was either too tired or too busy to mess with it. "Dinner" had been reduced to a light snack per the rationing plan, so it didn't provide the team much of an excuse to gather.

Swenson had spent the day running diagnostics on the transit portal. He was increasingly convinced there was nothing wrong on their end. He could establish a link between his portal and the one in orbit around the planet. He'd even sent a test package up and brought it back.

Unfortunately, they had available only a small fraction of the power that would be necessary to connect to Earth. Because of the distance involved and the volume of the transfer chamber, transfers in either direction had to be initiated from Earth.

Sakhr spent the day monitoring the drones that were searching for Solansky. He'd also taken over the construction of Swenson's distilled water apparatus. He'd taken enough chemistry in college to understand the operating principles. Armed with Swenson's design concept, he volunteered to put it together.

Steadman and Guerrero had searched for Solansky's trail until about noon. They quickly found one and followed it far enough to determine that he had, in fact, doubled back. That explained why the initial drone search the night before hadn't picked him up. But they lost the trail in a rocky area and hadn't been able to pick it up again.

Decker ordered them back to camp to provide security for Culpepper. She and Guerrero headed out into the foothills to collect more samples of possible food sources. Guerrero volunteered for the assignment, hoping they might run into Mikey while they were out. Decker suspected he also hoped he might get lucky and get a shot at Solansky.

Sakhr had found blood on the ground in the middle of the compound earlier that morning. Zindell was the only one injured as far as they knew. Tornquist ran a DNA profile on a sample, hoping it might have been Solansky's. When it came back as nonhuman, she had Zindell, now mostly coherent, run it through the Earth fauna database. It came back as a close analogue to chimpanzee.

Good news in one way. Bad news in another. No one was happy to hear it; least of all Guerrero, who saw it as one more nail in Solansky's coffin.

Decker and Steadman spent a good part of the day shuffling equipment and supplies. They needed both the medical facility and the science lab up and running, so they had to move Weaver's body somewhere.

Decker still wanted to keep it on ice in hopes of returning it to Earth as part of the case against Solansky, so they needed another location where they could keep it cold. When something like this happened at sea, they would usually empty a refrigerator or freezer to store the body until it could be transported off-ship. The small unit they had wasn't large enough, and they couldn't afford to sacrifice the perishable foodstuffs.

So the supply building became the morgue. Most of the supplies stored there wouldn't be hurt by the cold. In fact, it would probably help them if they had to store up large amounts of fresh meat for the winter they expected would soon be setting in.

Swenson, on the other hand, wouldn't function well working inside a refrigerator. So they decided to move his workstation into the common area of the men's quarters.

This task gave Decker and Steadman time to think about their situation.

"So, what do you think his endgame is?" Decker asked.

"I've been thinking about that. Everything we thought we knew about him turns out to be wrong. I read the file they gave you when they shipped him over. In hindsight, it's clearly a fake legend. But it's not even a very good one. Too many inconsistencies. Too many details that would be easy to fake. Too few details that would be easy to verify."

"If the cover was that weak, how do you think he managed to get past the security checks?"

"That's what worries me. A lot," Steadman said. "Sure, they were in a hurry. But there should have been enough red flags to make someone decide to slow things down. There had to be someone pretty high up in the program greasing the skids for him to get through. Which leads to the question, why was this mission such a rush? Is someone expecting this planet to disappear in the next few days?"

Decker thought for a moment about whether he should answer that question. Then it occurred to him that he might not know.

"I'm not really sure. Secretary Rutledge suggested it was concern about political unrest back home. They were worried if word got out that the Republic had developed this technology and had potentially found a habitable planet, other nations might take drastic steps to avoid being further overshadowed. According to him, the plan was to learn enough about the planet before the information leaked that we could respond quickly with a reasoned plan for the joint development of the new world."

"Do you believe him?" Steadman asked

"I believe he believed it. But he also said part of why they were so worried was they believed they already had a leak. Not so much about this project, but some of the other technology developments that came out of Kreitzman's research."

"Did he say anything about a connection to the Russians?"

Decker shook his head. "No. The first I heard of Russian involvement was what Solansky told us when we interrogated him. And Earth doesn't know about that. But Dr. Sakhr was right—the timing of the portal failure is too much to be a coincidence. I'm convinced someone on the Earth side shut it down precisely to prevent Solansky from blowing their own cover. But for now, that's Earth's problem. Ours is Solansky. It's pretty clear he's not the mild-mannered academic we were led to expect. What do we actually know about him?"

"He's had military-grade hand-to-hand combat training," Steadman said. "The technique he used to break Weaver's neck isn't something you learn at a strip mall karate shop. He knows how to move quickly in the field without leaving much of a trail. It follows he's probably been trained in survival and evasion."

"That tells us something about his strengths, but what's he after? What's his endgame? What will he do next?"

"He doesn't strike me as a religious zealot."

Decker raised an eyebrow. "Meaning?"

"He's not likely to be willing to die for the cause. He expected to survive this when he came here. He didn't plan for this turn of events and likely recognizes his odds are not as good now, but he's still playing to survive."

"But his best chance at survival was as a prisoner," Decker said. "Waiting with us for the portal to be restored."

"Maybe. He may not have seen it that way. Worst case from our side is we would have treated him as a foreign combatant. But he might have feared worse treatment from his own. This was technically an act of war. Getting caught will create a huge international incident that would be very bad politically for Russia."

"So what are his options now?"

"I can think of only three possibilities. First, he's just trying to survive. That means not getting caught by us, and not getting sent back to Earth in captivity. If that's his strategy, he'll run as far and as fast as he can. Find a spot a hundred miles from here where he can carve out his own existence and live until he dies.

"Second, he believes the Russians are coming. In that case, he'll still be trying to survive. But he'll want to stay nearby. Or at least near where he thinks they're likely to come. He'll want to know when they get here."

"Yeah. I've been worried about that one," Decker said. "When we interrogated him, it was clear he was not aware of the Russians having acquired the technology to get here, but it was also clear they had at least one other operative inside the program. So he could be trying to hold out in the hopes Russia will successfully steal the technology and then be able to build their own portal and get here before our people do. But it seems far-fetched to think they could build a first article, even with stolen designs, faster than we could rebuild what we've already done."

"I guess that depends on how much damage they did in this hypothetical scenario where they took out our Earth-side portal," Steadman said. "We still don't know as a matter of fact what happened. If they managed to get to Kreitzman, and could either force or entice cooperation, they would be well ahead of us."

Decker grimaced. "What's your third scenario?"

"The one I think is most likely," Steadman said. "His best chance at survival is to kill all of us and take control of our compound and our portal. Whether or not the Russians are coming, we're a threat he needs to eliminate. And our equipment and supplies greatly increase his

261

chances of survival, regardless of what happens with the portal."

"If he's out to kill us all, why didn't he kill Zindell when he had the chance?" Decker asked. "One more shot to the head before he fled the building."

"He was outnumbered. He knew Guerrero and I were in adjacent rooms and would have been awakened by the shots. He knew you were across the compound at the medical lab and also would have heard the shots. If he got lucky, he might have taken all three of us out, and then likely run the table in short order. But the odds were against him. That's why I say he's not a religious zealot. He's playing to survive. He figured Zindell was more valuable to him alive than dead because we'd have to delay pursuit to help the doctor."

"But you think he's ultimately going to come back after us?" Decker asked.

"He has to assume we'll be coming after him. He killed Petty Officer Weaver. He knows we're taking that personally. If he doesn't take us out first, he has to believe we'll eventually get him."

"So you think we should go after him?"

"Yes and no. We have to make neutralizing him a priority. But going after him plays to his strengths and exposes our weaknesses. He's outnumbered eight to one. He'll be looking to divide and conquer. If Guerrero and I go on a hunt, it leaves the rest of you exposed. It leaves Guerrero and me exposed. It's a lot easier for him to sit tight and wait for us to come to him. We would necessarily be out in the open as we search. Easier for him to see us coming than for us to see him waiting."

"So what's our strength?" Decker asked.

"Tech. And patience. We have drones and perimeter sensor arrays. As long as we're here in the compound, he can't get close to us without us knowing he's coming. And without giving us a clean shot at him. He can't light a fire to keep warm or cook food. He has to be very careful about moving around for fear of being picked up by a drone. Right now he has a perch up there on the mountain somewhere, watching for us to come after him. He'll wait for a day or two, maybe a week, before he realizes we're not playing his game. At that point, he'll have to decide whether he wants to play our game or settle for a standoff."

"And if he chooses a standoff?"

Steadman shook his head. "He won't. He knows it isn't really a standoff. As long as our drones are flying, he's at a profound disadvantage. He'll have to forage for food. Find shelter. Eventually, he'll slip up and we'll find him."

THIRTY-ONE

Guerrero was trying to keep himself busy. Every time he stopped working, he started thinking. And here lately that never ended well.

He would start thinking about Pam. A hometown girl and friend from high school. He knew her parents. He knew he should be the one to deliver the notification, and part of him wanted to. He owed that to Pam. But another part of him cringed at the thought. And he also knew that someone else would have to do it. He was here, not there.

Or he would start thinking about Solansky. He never fully appreciated how many ways he knew to kill a man until he started thinking about Solansky. And he would see Solansky dead. There was no doubt in his mind.

But after the third time he caught himself walking through camp with his KA-BAR knife firmly in his grip, he realized he needed to change the subject.

So Guerrero decided to try to be helpful. He stopped by the kitchen and picked up a hot breakfast tray for

Tornquist and headed over to the medical lab to check in on Zindell.

As he entered the lab, Tornquist was staring at a computer monitor. She turned to look when he came through the door.

"Good morning, Doctor," he said. He set the tray on the counter in front of her. "The skipper said you could use some breakfast."

She grabbed the coffee and lifted it to her face, inhaling deeply before taking a sip. "You're an angel sent from heaven, Alex."

He nodded toward Zindell, who appeared to be sleeping. "How's he doing this morning?"

He thought he caught a hint of worry on her face before she smiled. "He's sleeping, which is good. Between his injuries and the pain medication, he'll be doing a lot of that the next few days."

Guerrero glanced at the medical monitor beside the bed. "A hundred and three. Isn't that a little high?"

Tornquist glanced at her watch. "Yeah, it is. But not unusual in the aftermath of a very messy gunshot wound. An infection has set in. I've started him on an antibiotic that should knock it out. He should be fine in a day or two."

The sight of Zindell's bandaged leg triggered the memory of the bloody scene the night before last. Solansky would pay for this. If Zindell died too, Guerrero would find a way to make him pay twice.

"Alex?"

265

Guerrero turned to face Tornquist. "Yes?"

"I said, she told me about the time you beat the snot out of Chuck."

"Oh! Uh …" Guerrero shuffled his feet. "What about it?"

"I really think that's why she joined the navy. She felt really vulnerable right then. Chuck getting increasingly agitated, increasingly physical. People walking past and pretending not to notice because they were afraid of him too. She seriously doubted anyone would stop to help her. She was terrified. And then Alex Guerrero stepped in and faced him down. Her knight in shining armor … without the armor."

The memory brought a brief smirk to his face. But the idea that she might be here because of him, and was now dead because she was here, only compounded his despondency. "So you think she joined the Navy to follow me?"

"Not you, exactly. Well, maybe a little. But mostly the idea. The ideal. Who's going to stand up for the defenseless? Who's going to do what needs to be done, no matter the cost? Who's going to take the risks, engage the enemy, conquer the unknown, make the world safe for the rest of us? She knew she could never do what you did—what you do. But in the navy, she found a place she could play a role—a role with significance—on a team whose charter was just that. She didn't follow you. She followed what she saw in you."

Guerrero turned to look at Zindell again, more to look away from Tornquist than anything else. He was glad they'd moved Pam's body to the other building. He didn't think he could handle seeing that right now.

That's right, Gordo. Now she's dead. Because she followed you here, and you weren't there to protect her when she needed you.

Tornquist put a warm hand on Guerrero's cheek and turned his head to face her. "Alex, this is important. Pam isn't dead because of you. She came here, she volunteered for this mission, with full knowledge of the risks, because she wanted to be one of those people who took those risks so others wouldn't have to. She died with honor, for a cause she believed in. Don't take that away from her by making this all about you."

Guerrero clenched his jaw. "Solansky."

"No."

She moved her hand to his arm. "Alex, we'll deal with Solansky. He'll get what's coming to him. But there's something bigger going on here. And on Earth. Solansky may be the key to unlocking it—even to getting us home. We need you focused on saving the mission. Decker thinks that means capturing Solansky alive."

Day 9, 0830 Hours

Decker counted heads as the last of his team filed into the cramped medical lab. They looked like a parade of prisoners being marched to their new cells.

Decker closed the door as the last inmate entered. "I apologize for the close quarters. Dr. Tornquist needed to stay close to her patient, but I'd like to have us all together so we only have to go through this once. Doctor, could you start us off?"

Tornquist's eyes grew wide as she bit her lip. Her face relaxed. "We're making good progress on the search for food. We've identified a few things that have chemicals or compounds in them that are known to be toxic. We have a couple of things where every constituent chemical or compound is known to be safe. Unfortunately, those also have little to no nutritional value." She adjusted her lab coat. "Most of the things that we've analyzed so far fit into a third category. Nothing in them we know is toxic, but lots of things we've never seen before. Any one of them might be toxic, or might be nutritious. We don't have the equipment here to assess that."

"So the planet is half-full." Decker smiled. "How are we doing on the rationing plan?"

Tornquist offered an uneasy laugh. "So far we're consuming eighteen percent below the plan. I'm not sure we can sustain that on an individual basis without compromising performance, but I'll continue to monitor."

Swenson, who had been leaning against the wall in the crowded room, edged forward. "I'd like to volunteer to start eating some of the local foods. We're eventually going to have to just try them, and the sooner we start, the sooner we'll know."

Decker motioned him back. "Not yet, Mr. Swenson."

Decker turned back to Tornquist. "What is—"

Swenson interrupted. "I really think the time to start is now. There's a trade-off—"

Decker raised his brow at Swenson. "Not yet, Mr. Swenson. I do want to have this conversation, but I want to know where we are before we talk about where we're going."

Swenson frowned but slid back against the wall.

Decker turned back to face Tornquist. "What's Dr. Zindell's status?"

Tornquist closed her eyes. "It could be better." She took a deep breath and let it out. "The infection is getting worse. It's in his blood now, spreading throughout his body. We've tried every antibiotic we have with us, and none of them seem to be effective. Right now I'm just trying to keep him alive, hoping his own body will figure out how to fight it." She looked up at Culpepper and smiled. "Dr. Culpepper and I are trying to isolate the infection in hopes of learning something that will help."

Decker looked at the botanist. "Your research on Earth was focused on finding plants that could cure diseases. If this infection is unique to this planet, is it possible that there's a cure here somewhere too?"

Culpepper's eyebrows shot up. "Accurate, if oversimplified. The problem is scope. And time. Until the last century, the vast majority of medicines were derived from plants. Or, in some cases, animals. Still today a significant percentage of best-practice treatments are plant-based. The problem is that those treatments were discovered over centuries, millennia even, of human practice. Finding a new solution today is extremely rare. I would have considered my career successful to find one such treatment in a lifetime. Many have spent lifetimes and found nothing."

She scanned the faces in the room before returning to Decker. "I'm still not convinced we ever left Earth. But, for the sake of discussion, let's say we have. The opportunities would be tremendous. So many new plants and animals. Each packed with proteins, enzymes, and other complex molecules we've never seen before. But it's still a matter of years, decades even, of cataloging, analyzing, testing—and that to find one useful molecule. We need not just a useful molecule, but a molecule with a particular use—one that counteracts this particular infection. That's not a needle-in-a-haystack problem. It's more akin to finding a needle lost somewhere in the Sahara Desert. In a matter of days."

"If not hours," Tornquist amended.

Culpepper nodded. "The first step is to isolate the infection. Then I can run it against the things I've already cataloged. And maybe identifying the infecting agent will help narrow the search. Still, it's beyond a long shot."

Decker fought the urge to look down at Zindell, unconscious on the medical bed in the middle of their gathering. Everyone knew what was at stake here. No reason to remind them.

He turned instead to Steadman. "How's the search going?"

"The drones are covering, and recovering, a lot of territory, but they haven't found anything."

"Why?"

Steadman started to answer, but Swenson stepped up again. "It's possible he just kept running and is beyond the ten-mile radius we've covered so far."

Steadman started to interrupt, but Swenson raised a hand to dissuade him. "With that said, I share Commander Steadman's belief that he's likely much closer but managing to elude our search."

"How?" Decker asked.

Swenson shook his head. "I don't know. The heuristics incorporated into the image analysis algorithms are designed to detect things in plain sight. They're not designed to find something actively hiding. Dr. Sakhr and I are reviewing some of the video to see if we can pick up on anything the automated algorithms miss, but we can only review a small percentage of the total data collected."

Decker looked back at Steadman, who glanced over at Swenson, who seemed not to notice. Steadman said, "I still recommend we be patient. We're just two days in. Time is on our side. He'll eventually make a mistake."

The reflex to look at Zindell took him before he could override it. Time wasn't on *his* side. But Steadman was right. The two issues weren't connected.

He turned to Swenson. "Okay, Rusty, make your case. Let's hear it."

Swenson's eyebrows scrunched together, then his eyes lit up and he stepped forward. "There's a trade-off

271

between the time we spend up front doing technical studies to figure out whether a particular … Two … food … is safe or not, and the time we have on the backend after someone actually starts eating it to see whether there are any problems. The more we delay on the front, the less time we have to evaluate the results."

"So what do you propose?"

"Drs. Tornquist and Culpepper have already fully characterized a handful of foods. I should start controlled tests eating those foods."

Tornquist raised both hands. "Just to be clear, 'fully characterized' means we've identified everything that's in it, not that we know those things are safe to eat."

"Granted," Swenson said, "but it also means there's nothing more you can do to answer that final question. You know all you're going to know before someone actually eats it. Any more delay is wasted time."

Decker looked at Tornquist.

She clinched her jaw. "It's a valid point. The counterargument is that with more time we'll be able to characterize more potential food sources. We may be able to identify options with a lower risk profile than the things on our current list. Or maybe the portal will come back online."

Decker turned back to Swenson. "Why you?"

"Because this whole strategy is predicated on my assertion of compatibility between life here on this planet and life on Earth. I have zero proof. It's just something I believe. And I have to admit I could be wrong. I can't ask anyone else to take the risk based solely on my unsubstantiated theory."

Decker looked at the team. "Any other input?"

Sakhr stepped forward. "I think Mr. Swenson is right, but I think I should be the one to take the risk."

Decker raised an eyebrow. "Why?"

Sakhr glanced over at Swenson. "I agree with Rusty that it's low risk, but it's not zero risk. In the current situation, I'm more expendable."

Decker raised both eyebrows and drew his head back. "How do you figure?"

"This is no longer about the mission. It's about survival. You, Mr. Steadman, Mr. Guerrero—your survival skills and training will be essential to keeping everyone alive. Dr. Tornquist, Dr. Culpepper, even Dr. Zindell—their technical expertise is also critical to finding the resources to keep everyone alive. Mr. Swenson—his engineering expertise, his problem-solving skills, his ability to maintain and manipulate the equipment—is also critical. My field is geology. Rocks and dirt. Of some value to the original mission, but hardly likely to make a difference in our ability to survive here without support from Earth."

Decker looked around at the rest of the team, inviting further input. He looked at Swenson. "Okay. You've made your case."

Swenson grinned. Sakhr frowned.

Decker nodded to Sakhr. "As have you."

Swenson and Sakhr both furrowed their brows.

He turned to Tornquist and Culpepper. "I need the two of you to put together a plan. Which foods. When. How much. What to monitor. How long. When can we be ready to start?"

Tornquist looked at Culpepper. "Lunchtime?"

Culpepper nodded.

Decker stood up. "Dr. Culpepper, when you have the list of foods, take Mr. Guerrero and go shopping. We'll meet back here for lunch."

Tornquist stepped forward. "Just to be clear, who's going to be eating?" She looked at Swenson and Sakhr.

Decker turned to walk out the door. "I am."

Day 9, 0845 Hours

"Skipper, you can't be serious!" Steadman said as he caught up with Decker outside the medical lab.

Decker kept walking. "Oh? Why not?"

"*Why?* You're in command. You're the team leader. You're the only thing holding this bunch together. If we lose you, the mission falls apart. You have two volunteers. Three. Count me in too. I understand it isn't easy to ask other people to take risks, but that's part of being in command."

Decker's face went rigid as he abruptly stopped and turned to face Steadman. "Yes, I'm in command. Yes, I'm the leader. No, I'm not the only thing holding this bunch together. Yes, I have volunteers. More than three, if I read my people right. And yes, sometimes being in *command* means you have to order people to do things you know might lead to their deaths. But being the *leader* means something too. Sometimes it means you have to lead. You have to get up in front of your troops and show them what it looks like to face death with the courage of your convictions. That you believe death is not inevitable. That you believe this battle is winnable."

Decker resumed course, Steadman falling in on his wing. "Swenson is right. We're wasting valuable time. Sakhr is also right, at least partly. Survival without a prompt restoration of the connection to Earth will require a team effort. But not all of us are equally critical to survival. I think he underestimates his value to the team. Right now it's about food and water, and he feels useless. But if this situation persists, we'll need his knowledge of geology and mineralogy. I, on the other hand, offer nothing that isn't duplicated elsewhere on the team. In most cases by a superior capability. You're more than capable of taking the leadership mantle if it comes to that. I've had survival training, but nothing like what you and Guerrero have been through. I know nothing about science or engineering. I'm the only logical choice."

"And if Swenson is wrong?"

Decker looked back at Steadman. "He isn't."

THIRTY-TWO

Day 9, 1200 Hours

Decker walked into the medical lab and found the whole team waiting there. He'd been expecting just Tornquist and Culpepper. And Zindell, of course.

"So, where do we start?"

Culpepper slid a tray of nuts across the table toward him.

Decker picked one up. "It looks like an almond." He looked at Culpepper.

She nodded and gestured for him to eat.

Decker touched it to his tongue. It didn't seem to have much flavor.

He bit the seed in half, taking part into his mouth and rolling it around.

He started slowly chewing.

He swallowed. "It tastes like an almond."

Culpepper nodded.

"I don't understand," Decker said. "I'm supposed to be trying something native to this planet. 'Two-food,' as Mr. Swenson called it."

Culpepper gestured toward the half of a nut still in Decker's hand. "That is. It's also an almond. At least as far as you can prove by me. The DNA profile is an exact match—at least within the range of normal variation within the population of almond trees—for an Earth almond. So far the only exception we've found to the 'almost but not quite' principle. But a notable exception. Or, proof that we're still on Earth."

Tornquist shook her head. She turned to Decker. "We looked at all the potential food sources we've identified so far and applied a weighted filter. Things with recognizable nutritional value would float to the top of the list. Things with known toxins would be pushed to the bottom. Things with unknowns or other risk factors would also be pushed down. This came up at the top of the list. Like Earth almonds, it has trace amounts of arsenic in it, but well below the level to be a problem. Like Earth almonds, it's loaded with nutrients. Identical in every way we can measure."

Decker popped the rest of the seed into his mouth. "So, can we all live on almonds?"

"No." Tornquist glanced at Culpepper. "It'll be enough to stretch our Earth rations significantly, but eventually we'll need to find other things we can tolerate."

"So what's next?" He scooped up half the remaining seeds and shoveled them into his mouth.

"I'd really like to give this a day before we move on to anything else. Just to be safe."

Decker looked at Swenson, who shook his head. "I agree that would be safer, but I don't think it's prudent."

"Explain." He scooped up the rest of the almonds and shoveled them into his mouth.

"Same argument as this morning. Nothing has changed. We have several identified candidates that we're not going to learn anything more about until someone tries them."

Culpepper's face pinched up. "What *has* changed is that Commander Decker has now tried one of the local foods. We need to bide our time to see if he has any reaction to it before moving on."

Swenson pointedly looked at the unconscious Dr. Zindell on the other side of the lab. "A wise man recently told me, if it looks like a duck, and walks like a duck, and quacks like a duck, it's a duck. There's nothing magical about this planet. Physics and chemistry are the same here as on Earth. I have absolutely no doubt about the clinical competence and professionalism of Dr. Tornquist and Dr. Culpepper, so I have no doubt that those are chemically and biologically indistinguishable from Earth almonds. The outcome will be no different than if you'd eaten a package from our own supplies."

Decker swallowed the last of the almonds as he tipped his head to Tornquist. "What's next on your list?"

Swenson interrupted. "If I may … I think I understand the rationale behind the weighted filter, but that may not be the most efficient way to structure the problem."

Culpepper's face reddened. She opened her mouth to retort, but Decker held up a hand as he looked at Swenson. "What do you mean?"

"Correct me if I'm wrong, but the idea behind the weighted filter was to pick the foods that represented the lowest risk to our health and safety but also offered the best nutritional values."

Tornquist nodded.

Culpepper stood with her arms crossed and her jaw clenched.

"You asked a relevant question a few minutes ago. 'Can we all live on almonds?' That's the real question. What does it take to survive? If we just work our way down the filtered list, we may end up with a whole lot of safe, nutritious foods. With a lot of nutritional overlap, and with a lot of nutritional gaps."

"And you have a better idea?" Culpepper spat.

"I'd start with a prioritized list of nutritional requirements. Carbohydrates. Protein. Sugar. Vitamins. Minerals. What is the minimal set required to keep us alive, and what components are most urgent given our available supplies? Then I'd modify Dr. Culpepper's existing filter to search for the best candidates for each of those nutrients, in priority order. And if we find that we have high-priority requirements without any as-yet-identified source with acceptably low risk, that gives us something we need to treat with urgency."

Decker turned to Culpepper. "What do you think?"

She dropped her arms with an audible huff. "Fine. Who's going to tell me what we need?"

Decker looked to Tornquist. "What's at the top of your nutritional priority list?"

She rubbed the back of her neck. "I'd put carbohydrates at the top of the list, mostly because that's where our existing supply is thinnest. The fruits on Dr. Culpepper's list all look to be good sources. After that will come proteins. The almonds are a source, but the proteins in nuts are incomplete. Eventually we'll need to identify a source of meat."

Decker grinned at Steadman and Guerrero. "Feel like doing a little hunting?"

Steadman perked up. "You point. I'll shoot."

Decker turned to the other side of the lab, where their zoologist was still unconscious.

Sakhr cleared his throat. "I can't address that with Dr. Zindell's expertise, but the drone we've had spiraling outward from camp to map the surrounding area has found herds of several different types of animals in the grasslands to the southeast of us. We haven't taken a close look, but they're probably grazers. Swenson's design pattern theory would suggest that's a good place to start."

Decker turned back to Culpepper. "What's in your fruit basket?"

Culpepper pressed her lips together in a grimace. She shook her head and crossed the lab to a refrigerated cabinet. She pulled out a sealed container, removed the lid, and slid it across the table to Decker.

"It looks like a pear. Except it's red."

Culpepper nodded at Decker then turned to look at Swenson. "It isn't."

She turned back to face Decker. "But it's very similar. Same shape and physical structure. High water content. It shares a lot of proteins and enzymes with pears, but it also has many that are different. Some of those are found in other Earth fruits and vegetables. Some we've never seen. Nothing we regard as high risk, but there *is* risk nevertheless." She glared at Swenson.

Decker held it up to his nose and sniffed it. "It smells … sweet." He took a tentative bite and rolled it around in his mouth. The flavor was delightful, but he kept his expression neutral as he shifted his head around making a show of savoring the morsel before he swallowed.

Sakhr leaned forward. "Well?"

Decker licked his lips. "I'm not sure." He took another small bite and repeated the performance.

Tornquist stepped closer. "Any burning sensation? Bitterness? What does it taste like?"

Decker swallowed. He slowly shook his head. He took another bite—a big one this time.

Tornquist snatched the rest of the fruit from his hand. "That's enough for now. Tell me what it tastes like!" She put it back in the container and handed it to Culpepper to put away.

Decker kept chewing. Slowly. Keeping his expression neutral.

Swenson shook his head and laughed.

Tornquist shot Swenson with an evil glare before turning her attention back on Decker. "Now, mister! Before I confine you to sickbay for the duration of the mission."

Decker grinned at her. He finished chewing and swallowed.

He gestured at Culpepper. "She's right. It has the texture and consistency of a pear. But the flavor is quite different." He worked his tongue around in his mouth, still tasting the fruit. "The closest thing I can think of is a strawberry. It's really quite good."

Tornquist held a finger in his face. "I want you in here for evaluation every three hours. Earlier, if you feel anything out of the ordinary."

Sakhr took a step forward. "What about the almonds? Since they seem to be identical to Earth almonds, would anyone object to the rest of us—on a voluntary basis—adding those to our rations?"

Tornquist shook her head. "The good captain here just ate all the almonds we have. We should collect more, but I'd like to give it twenty-four hours before anyone else eats any. We're not in that big a rush."

Sakhr looked dejected as he stepped back. His stomach chose just that moment to growl loud enough that everyone heard it.

Tornquist simpered. "You'll live."

Culpepper stepped up to the middle of the room. "One caveat that everyone needs to know about. There are two types of almond trees on Earth, differentiated by

282

a single gene. One type produces what are referred to as sweet almonds, which these are." She looked down at the bowl. "Were. The other type are called bitter. The gene for bitter almonds is recessive, so most trees won't have it, but some might. Don't eat any almonds until I've verified the source is okay."

Sakhr rubbed his hand over his mid-section. "Right now I don't think I care whether it's bitter or sweet. I'd just like a little something extra in my stomach."

Culpepper almost smiled. "It's a little more complicated than that. What makes almonds bitter is a dramatically higher arsenic content. One won't kill you. A handful will significantly incapacitate you, and might even kill a small child."

Decker rubbed his hands together. "Okay. Everyone get some lunch. Then I want two teams out in the field. Dr. Sakhr, Mr. Steadman, you're foraging for nuts. Dr. Culpepper will show you what to look for and how to do it. Dr. Culpepper, Mr. Guerrero, after you get them started, continue the search for candidate foods. Dr. Tornquist will update you if she identifies any gaps in our list."

Everyone filed out of the medical lab except Tornquist and Decker—and her lone patient.

Decker nodded toward Zindell. "How's he doing?"

Tornquist frowned. She leaned her head back and took a deep breath, slowly letting it out. "Not good. All I can do is try to keep his body temperature below one hundred and five and keep him full of fluids and glucose.

283

Supplies of both of which are dwindling fast. When we planned medical stocks, we didn't count on an extended period of isolation from our supply line. At this rate, we'll be out of glucose tomorrow afternoon; saline tomorrow night. If he lasts that long, he won't last more than a few hours once those run out."

Day 9, 1330 Hours

Culpepper and Guerrero parked the four-wheeler at the edge of a grove and hiked across the hillside to get a better look at the flora. Most of the trees were roughly twenty-five feet tall with broad leaves that mixed two distinct shades of green and sported jade-colored fruits of various sizes. Culpepper collected a few of these from low-hanging branches, but her intuition was that they weren't ripe. She stopped short when she came upon a tree with the same green globes with a few red ones in the very top.

"I don't suppose you brought a ladder?"

Guerrero followed her gaze. He leaned his rifle against a nearby trunk and set his pack on the ground. "Who uses a ladder to climb a tree?"

He jumped up to catch the first branch about eight feet off the ground, pulled himself up into the tree and started climbing.

"I don't think that's a good idea. Some of those branches don't look strong enough."

"It's not about the tree. It's about the climber." Guerrero looked down from the tree and grinned. "You must be one with the force, Padawan."

Culpepper mumbled, "You're about to be one with the ground."

Guerrero chuckled. He was getting close to the red fruit now, but the branches were getting smaller.

"The reason those are still up there is that those branches are too small even for Mikey. You're twice her weight."

Guerrero looked down at her and huffed. "Please!" He stretched out to reach one of the fruits. "I'm three times her weight if I'm half."

In that instant, Culpepper heard something crack. The world seemed to shift into slow motion. She saw the branch under his right foot give way. Rather than pull himself back against the trunk to distribute his weight, he stretched out with his right hand just another half inch to grasp the fruit. His right foot skidded down the side of the trunk, shearing off the small branch that had been supporting it. As his weight shifted, the limb under his left foot gave way too, and then his left arm, wrapped around the trunk, lost its grip.

With all the grace of a ballerina in a tornado, Guerrero spun his body around in free fall and reached out to grab at a passing branch with his left hand. He caught the limb and arrested his fall, but an instant later another loud crack announced its demise.

285

Now falling feet-first, Guerrero spotted two bigger branches below him and tried to get one foot on each. He succeeded, but the limb under his right foot gave way too, sending him cartwheeling out of the tree.

He reflexively tucked into a ball and hit the ground hard, shoulder-first and rolling, ending up sprawled flat on his back.

Culpepper rushed over to Guerrero's motionless form. "Alex! Are you okay?"

Guerrero didn't respond. She grabbed his left wrist and felt for a pulse as she leaned down with her cheek in front of his face to check if he was breathing.

"Is this what you're looking for?" Guerrero said.

Culpepper jumped back and glared at him.

Guerrero, still lying on his back on the ground, held up the red fruit still clutched in his right hand. His smug grin just made her madder.

She took one step forward and then swung through with the other with a powerful thrust at his shoulder, just at the last instant regaining enough self-control to pull the kick. It still connected pretty hard.

"Ow! What was that for?"

"For nearly getting yourself killed!" Culpepper tried to walk away, but as soon as she put weight on her right foot, she nearly collapsed.

Guerrero sat up. "Getting myself killed was never in the cards. Worst case was a cracked rib." He gestured toward the tree with his right hand, still holding the fruit. "This ain't my first tree."

Culpepper was hobbling around in a circle, trying to walk off her twisted ankle. She bent down and grabbed a handful of what was available and hurled it at his head. The fistful of leaves and twigs was no match for the intervening air and fluttered to the ground short of her target.

Guerrero let out a mirthful snort. He got up and walked over to where Culpepper was circling.

"I'm sorry." He held out the fruit as a peace offering.

She grabbed it out of his hand with a huff and limped away to where she had set her own pack.

Guerrero picked up one of the broken tree branches, pulled a multi-tool out of his vest and folded out a wood saw. He made quick work of trimming away twigs and the ragged broken end, then cut it to length and offered it to Culpepper.

Culpepper stared at the cane, then glared at Guerrero. "How is it that you're the one who just fell out of a twenty-five-foot tree, which I told you not to climb, but I'm the one who's limping?"

Guerrero smiled and offered the cane again.

She grabbed it out of his hand and quickly pulled it back over her shoulder like a bat, ready to swing for the bleachers.

He ducked his head and held up one arm to block the blow, but it never came.

She pulled it back down and limped over to pick up her pack, muttering under her breath, "Probably bounce off your head and the ricochet would come back and knock me out."

Guerrero offered to take Culpepper's pack, at least until she could work the pain out of her twisted ankle. She refused, insisting she could carry her own load. It didn't take long for her to regret it—limping across the uneven ground with a cane and carrying a heavy pack—but she wasn't about to admit it.

The next time they stopped to look at something, Guerrero picked it up without asking. Culpepper consoled herself with the thought that he deserved to have to carry both packs after the stunt he'd pulled.

Her ankle improved quickly, and before long her limp disappeared. She found herself using the stick more to poke and prod at vegetation than to help her walk.

She couldn't help thinking how magnificent this place was. Here within just a few square miles were groves of at least a dozen different types of fruit and nut trees. Grass and other groundcovers grew where the trees were thin enough to let some light through. Wildflowers. Mushrooms. She even found a couple of patches of plants that looked like onions and something like a potato.

"It just doesn't make sense," she mumbled to herself.

"I beg your pardon?" Guerrero said.

"What? Oh. I was just saying that it doesn't make sense."

He shook his head. "You're going to have to be more specific. I'm not sure I can point to a single thing on this mission that *did* make sense."

"Yeah. Well, I was referring to the trees and plants here in these hills. At least a dozen different kinds of trees within a few square miles, none of them particularly dominant. A typical wooded area will usually have one— maybe two or three—type of tree, depending on the soil and climate. One variety performs better in that circumstance and chokes the others out."

She motioned to the grass around them. "Even the groundcover. One type should dominate. Maybe two or three, depending on how much shade a particular area gets. But between grasses, vines, flowers, roots, mushrooms … there are at least dozens here in this one region. That isn't natural."

"So you think someone planted all this here? Who? Why?"

"Whoever's running this experiment. But that doesn't make sense either. The ground cover and vegetables could have been planted weeks or months ago, but the trees … some of these trees have to be decades old. It couldn't realistically have been done solely for the purpose of this research project. Maybe they're using an existing managed nature preserve somewhere. But it still doesn't make sense. When you plant something like this, you line the trees up in rows. Put this type here, that type there. Organize it. But here there's no discernible pattern. It doesn't make sense."

Culpepper knelt down beside a patch of greens and gently inspected them. She held her hand up to Guerrero. "Give me the little shovel."

Guerrero knelt down beside her. "Let me do that. I'm starting to feel pretty useless around here."

You are pretty useless, flashed through her mind, but she clamped her mouth shut before it came out. *Be nice.*

She stood and let Guerrero work. As she looked around at the rest of the orchard, she caught motion out of the corner of her eye. Her head followed the motion— and she almost screamed.

THIRTY-THREE

Day 9, 1430 Hours

Guerrero pulled up a batch of greens with what looked like carrots dangling underneath as Culpepper crouched beside him. He held them up, waiting for her to take them.

When she didn't, he looked up from the dirt and saw her staring wide-eyed into the distance, holding her breath. He dropped the shovel and reached for his sidearm as his head pivoted to follow her gaze.

"Mikey!" He released the grip on his gun without drawing it.

Mikey sat in the middle of a patch of groundcover and seemed to be eating. Or grooming. He couldn't tell which.

He rose and started slowly walking toward the chimp. "Hey, little buddy. How've you been?"

Mikey jerked around in his direction at the sound. She started to get up, but when she saw Guerrero she sat and went back to what she'd been doing.

Guerrero sat down beside her. He noticed she had a pretty big gash on her left arm, probably a gunshot wound from Solansky's escape. It had just grazed her, but it wasn't likely to heal properly without treatment.

Mikey wrapped her long arms around Guerrero's neck and gave him a hug before she let him go and went back to her task.

Culpepper watched with wide eyes, her mouth hanging open. Mikey would scoop up a handful of leaves—something that looked like clover—and chew on them for a minute. Then she'd spit them into her right hand and rub it into the open wound on her left arm.

Culpepper knelt beside the chimp, who looked up at her. She reached her hand out to gently touch the gash, but Mikey jerked the arm away and glared at her.

Culpepper sat back. She pulled up a handful of clover and rubbed it between her fingers. Her eyes welled up with tears. "This is it!" she yelled.

Mikey jumped into Guerrero's lap, wrapping her arms around his neck.

Culpepper dropped her pack and unzipped the top. She pulled up all the clover she could get her hands on, stuffing it into the bag until it was packed full. She zipped the backpack, slung it over her shoulder, and turned to run toward camp. "Bring Mikey as fast as you can. We have to get back. Now!"

Day 9, 1441 Hours

Guerrero stood and shifted Mikey around to ride on his shoulders, then took off after Culpepper. He considered going back for the four-wheeler, but it was in the opposite direction and she had a sizable head start.

Guerrero activated his comm as he ran. "Dr. Tornquist, we're headed back to camp on foot and in a hurry. Meet us at the campfire."

Guerrero caught up to Culpepper and kept pace with her, concerned about the pace she had set on a bum ankle. If the ankle gave out it would slow them a great deal more dramatically than just setting a more conservative pace.

Mikey, on the other hand, had other ideas. She seemed to think this was a race, and one she wanted her team to win. The chimp bounced on Guerrero's shoulders, trying to spur him on. When he wouldn't overtake Culpepper, she began slapping him on the back. Finally, she started banging on his head.

The chimp finally got to him just before they reached camp. Guerrero surged forward and arrived at the campfire a few steps ahead of Culpepper.

Mikey jumped down and raised her hands over her head in the universal celebration of victory, dancing around in front of Decker and Tornquist.

Culpepper collapsed to her knees, breathing so hard she couldn't talk.

Tornquist rushed over to her side. "What's going on?"

293

Culpepper opened her mouth but no words came out. She stripped off her pack and pointed to Guerrero.

He opened it and showed the contents to Tornquist. "What I think she's trying to say is this may be the cure for Dr. Zindell's infection."

Day 9, 1452 Hours

Tornquist took the pack and raced into the science lab.

Decker and Guerrero helped Culpepper up and half carried her into the lab as she recovered her breath. They set her down in a chair.

"We found … Mikey … in the orchard …. She was … chewing this clover … into a mash … and rubbing it … into the wound … on her arm."

Tornquist looked over at Mikey, who had followed them into the lab. She started toward the chimp just a little too fast and Mikey turned toward the door. Tornquist stopped in her tracks.

"It's okay, Mikey. I'm not going to hurt you. I just want to look at your arm. I promise I won't touch." Still looking at Mikey, she said, "Alex, can you give us a hand?"

Guerrero knelt down and held his arms out to Mikey, who came over and wrapped her arms around his neck. He lifted her up and carried her over to Tornquist.

"The bad news is, we're going to need to put a few stitches in that. And it does look infected. I can't tell without some blood work whether it's the same infection.

If it is, it isn't having the same effect on her it's having on Dr. Zindell."

Culpepper was finally getting her breath back. "She's been treating it with oil from the clover. She extracts it by crushing the leaves, then rubs it into the wound."

Tornquist pulled a Petri dish out of an incubator on the counter and slid it under a microscope. "It's possible. But I don't want to get anyone's hopes up. There could be a million other reasons why she's not being affected as strongly."

"But it's possible?" Decker asked.

"Yes," Tornquist said as she crushed a clover leaf and dropped it onto the Petri dish.

"What can I do to help?" he asked.

"Coffee," said Tornquist.

"Water," said Culpepper.

THIRTY-FOUR

Decker walked into the medical lab for his morning checkup. He was early, but he figured he'd get this out of the way before breakfast. Maybe Tornquist would have results from his morning blood tests in time for the morning status meeting.

Tornquist and Culpepper were both there keeping an eye on Dr. Zindell. He noticed two sleeping pallets pushed back against the wall and realized they'd both spent the night here.

"Good morning," he said. "How's Dr. Zindell doing?"

Tornquist looked up from her microscope. She looked like she hadn't slept in a week, but he knew better than to say that.

She motioned him to a chair as she got up from hers, collecting a syringe as she walked over to him. "He's better. Not a lot, but at least turned in the right direction."

She wrapped a band around his upper arm and proceeded to draw blood from a vein in his forearm.

296

"How are you feeling?" She asked. "Anything I need to know about?"

"I feel fine. Hungry, but no more than everyone else. Ready for the next round."

Tornquist set the blood sample aside and flashed a light in Decker's eyes.

"How are you doing?" Decker asked.

"Tired." Tornquist attached a blood pressure cuff and watched the machine make its measurements.

"Dr. Culpepper has been keeping an eye on him to give me short periods of rest, but it's been touch-and-go for several hours. No sooner do I fall asleep than she has to wake me to address something that's changed."

"But the clover seems to be the cure?"

Tornquist looked back over to Zindell's still form on the bed. "I'm not ready to call it a cure. It seems to counteract the infection, but it isn't clear that it will completely eradicate it. If we stopped administering serum now, I'm sure the infection would quickly overwhelm him. We also don't know what damage has already been done to his body's organs, and we don't know what damage the serum itself might be doing to him."

"When will you know?"

"When he wakes up. *If* he wakes up."

Decker nodded toward Mikey, who was sitting on the foot of Zindell's bed. "What's with Mikey?"

Mikey gently rocked back and forth, transfixed on Zindell's face. She had a white bandage wrapped around her upper arm where the bullet had grazed her.

"Who knows?" She shrugged. "That would be a good question for our zoologist. She hasn't strayed far from his side since Guerrero brought her in. Maybe she feels some connection because they were both shot by Solansky. Maybe she understands that we're using her clover to fight his infection. Maybe she just appreciates all the snacks that Guerrero and Culpepper keep bringing her." She inserted part of the blood sample into another instrument. "I thought about running her out. Wild animals are generally not welcome in sterile medical facilities. But after Guerrero convinced her to let me clean and stitch her arm, she's been very cooperative with blood samples and other poking and prodding. She's been enormously helpful in developing the regimen we're using to treat Henry."

Culpepper interrupted their conversation. "Dr. Tornquist, you need to see this." Culpepper pushed herself away from the microscope to make room for Tornquist.

She looked through the instrument. "This looks like the organism infecting Dr. Zindell. I thought you were analyzing water samples from the stream."

Culpepper nodded, her lips pursed. "I am. That is."

Day 10, 0830 Hours

"We have a new problem." Decker addressed the team assembled in the medical lab. "Dr. Culpepper found the same bacteria that infected Dr. Zindell in the water from the stream. Until further notice, everyone is to stay clear of the stream and waterfall, and any other sources of water you might come across."

Sakhr leaned forward. "The still is almost ready to test. Shouldn't that eliminate the bacteria?"

Tornquist shook her head. "Probably, but not necessarily. If the boiling point of water is hot enough to kill the bacteria, it should be effective. If the bacteria can survive that heat, it will just migrate through the apparatus and reintegrate into the distilled water. It's one of several questions we need to answer. It just takes time. Meanwhile, we need everyone to conserve what drinking water we have. If the still doesn't work to produce drinkable water, we'll have a big problem very quickly."

"What about Mikey?" Guerrero asked.

Steadman glared at him.

Decker shook his head. "I'm sorry, Chief, but I can't justify allocating part of our water supply for Mikey."

Guerrero waved dismissively. "No. That's not what I meant. I've seen Mikey drinking water from that stream. I've seen her wading in the water and scooping it up with her hand."

Tornquist looked thoughtful. "She probably has some kind of natural immunity. It's something else to look at."

299

Guerrero shook his head. "No, she doesn't. You saw yourself that she became infected too, but only after she was grazed by the bullet from Solansky's gun."

Decker looked at Tornquist, who was staring into space with her hand to her mouth. "What are you thinking?"

She shook her head. "It's possible. They both had open wounds. Maybe the bacteria is airborne but requires an open wound to infect."

Steadman rolled up his sleeves. "I don't think so." He held out his arms. "I've had numerous minor cuts and scrapes since we got here. For some of them, I used antibacterial ointment from a first aid kit. Others I didn't. But if it was that easy to knock out, I'm sure the steps Dr. Tornquist took post-surgery to prevent infection would've been adequate."

"You said you found it in the water," Guerrero said. "Maybe Mikey contracted it when she went into the stream after being shot?"

"That's certainly possible," Tornquist said. "But we know Dr. Zindell went nowhere near the water after he was shot. He was carried from his quarters straight here."

Decker saw Steadman's eyes light up. "Chris?"

Steadman looked at Tornquist. "Supposing this is waterborne, could it survive out of water for any length of time?"

Tornquist drew her head back. "I'll need to run more tests to say for sure, but it's quite common for bacteria to survive, sometimes for extended periods, in dry environments. Why?"

Steadman looked at Decker. "Two days before Dr. Zindell was shot ... the day we had the altercation with Yogi. Before that, we spent some time studying the pool at the waterfall. The rocks around the edge were slick with moss. Dr. Zindell lost his footing and slipped into the water. He didn't fall, but his pants were soaked up to about the knee." He turned to Tornquist. "I'm guessing the bullet carried fibers of his pants, and maybe his socks, into the wound."

Tornquist nodded. "Yes. There were cloth fibers, probably from his clothes, in the wound." She looked around at the rest of the team. "It's feasible, but it's still just conjecture. Until Dr. Culpepper and I have time to prove the limitations of transmission, local water is off-limits. Don't touch. Don't even go near."

Sakhr raised a hand. "I know this is getting ahead of where we are, but what about filtering as an alternative, or supplement, to distillation?"

Tornquist shook her head. "We don't have any filtration systems. All of our water was intended to be supplied from Earth through the portal. And I wouldn't begin to know how to construct one from scratch."

"I might," Sakhr said. "My occupation put me in parts of the world where clean water is still a luxury. I'm not an expert, but I've learned a lot about the process. The first thing usually tried as a filter is activated carbon, derived from either coal or charcoal. It doesn't get everything but

301

gets most things. As you said, we'd just have to try it and see if it works. If I can find any coal deposits nearby, it should be easy to rig an apparatus. If not, we can create charcoal—though that will take a bit more work."

Decker nodded. "See what you can do. Let me know if you need help."

"Oh, I'll need help," Sakhr said. "The most likely place to find coal around here—without several months of digging—is inside caves. Deep inside caves."

Day 10, 0850 Hours

"I might be able to help you with that," Swenson said to Sakhr as they walked out of the medical lab.

Decker overheard and fell in behind them. The trio walked across the compound to Swenson's workstation in the men's quarters.

Swenson pulled a small case out from under the desk. "This came in the last shipment we received from Earth. With all that's happened since then, I had forgotten about it."

He opened the case and pulled out a small sphere about the size of a softball. He switched his comm to a different frequency and said, "Activate," and tossed it to Sakhr.

It was a slow lob, but directly toward Sakhr's head. Sakhr wasn't expecting it and reflexively batted at it to knock it away as he ducked his head.

And completely missed.

When he turned his head back, the object was hovering inches in front of his face.

Sakhr reached up to grab it, but when he did the object swerved to the right and evaded his grasp. After several more vain attempts to catch it, Sakhr stopped trying. "Okay. What is it?"

Swenson tapped his comm again. "Map."

The object immediately began moving slowly through the room and then into the hallway in the center of the building. Where it found an open door, it went into the room. After a few seconds, it came back out and continued, finally returning to the common area where they were gathered.

Swenson tapped his comm again. "Return." The object took up a position over his right shoulder. He held out his hand, and the device landed softly.

"After Yogi destroyed our first reconnaissance drone, the guys back home took it personally. Knowing there were caves nearby that we'd want to explore, and knowing there were bears nearby, and knowing bears don't generally like intruders in their caves, they thought we might need some help. This is a prototype. They wanted us to give this a try before they spun up any more of them."

Sakhr nodded thoughtfully. "What can it do?"

Swenson set it back in its case. "The idea is to send it into a cave—or cave system—and let it map everything. It records audio and video, visible and infrared, with illumination to work in dark places. Right now the mapping algorithm should be able to do an exhaustive map of any cave system. It also has, as you've seen, the ability to execute evasive maneuvers if anything tries to attack it."

"Can it find coal?"

Swenson shook his head. "Not inherently. Right now it just records audio, video, and location. If you can look at the video and identify coal, we can find our way back to it. If you can tell me what to look for, we might be able to train it to detect a particular signature. For now, we'll have to rely on a manual review of the data. Of course, we'll also be looking for bears—or any other critters we might want to know about before venturing in."

Decker picked the device up and looked it over. "When we were trying to track down missing comm signals you said that we would likely lose communication deep inside the caves. How will that impact this?"

"They thought about that. If it loses comm, it just records everything for eventual upload. It also has a configurable check-in interval. Even if it hasn't finished the mapping operation, it will work its way back out until it can reestablish communication, upload, and check for new instructions before going back in to finish the process."

Decker tossed it back and forth between his hands. "Can it dodge a bullet?"

Day 10, 1200 Hours

Decker looked at the plate in front of him. "So, what's this?"

Culpepper pursed her lips. "A baked potato." She tilted her head. "I think."

Decker looked at her. "You think? And you're asking me to eat it?"

She nodded. "You're the one who insisted on being the guinea pig. As to what it is? It grows like a potato—in the dirt. It looks like a potato—more or less. DNA looks similar to a potato—sort of. And it bakes like a potato—or microwaves, in this case. And it should be a good source of carbohydrates."

Culpepper had already cut the vegetable in half. It was a little more yellow than Decker thought a potato should be.

He scooped out a spoonful. The texture seemed about right.

He sniffed it. No discernible smell, but his nose had never been that good. He'd always considered that an asset, having chosen to spend most of his adult life living in a long, thin tube submerged underwater in close quarters with a gang of malodorous men.

He put it in his mouth. He chewed it for a few seconds and then swallowed. "It tastes like a potato. Which is to say it doesn't have much flavor." He looked at Culpepper. "You have any plans for butter, sour cream, bacon, chives?"

Culpepper made a rude gesture. "Eat, Mr. Smarty Pants. One spoonful isn't going to kill you. We need you to eat the whole thing."

Decker chuckled. This was progress.

He proceeded to eat, asking between mouthfuls, "How's Dr. Zindell doing?"

Tornquist frowned and shook her head. "Not good, I'm afraid." She walked over to his bedside. "This morning I was beginning to believe we had turned a corner, but it looks like it was too little, too late."

Decker swallowed. "The clover isn't working?"

"Oh, it's working." She closed her eyes. "But his body has run out of resources, and he still has a long fight ahead of him before the infection is purged. We ran out of glucose to give his body energy to sustain the fight this morning. He's on the last IV of saline solution to keep him hydrated now. His blood sugar level is already dangerously low, and I'm out of ideas for how to prop it back up."

Decker swallowed the last of the potato. "It's a shame you can't stuff a couple of those pear-thingies you gave me yesterday down that tube. That'd perk him up."

Tornquist spun around and looked at Culpepper. Culpepper raced out the door shouting, "I'll meet you in the kitchen!"

Day 10, 1215 Hours

Decker followed Tornquist as she rushed into the kitchen. She swabbed the countertop with sterile wipes, then disassembled the blender and started cleaning it.

"What's going on?" Decker asked.

"We can't 'stuff a couple of those pear-thingies' down his IV, but we can puree a couple of them and pour them down a feeding tube into his stomach. The sugars and liquids should have the same effect. Not as quickly as an IV, but better than nothing."

Culpepper raced in carrying two of the strawberry-pears. "Whole?" she asked.

Tornquist sterilized a knife and handed it to Culpepper. "Peeled and seeded."

Culpepper started preparing the fruit while Tornquist reassembled the blender.

Tornquist asked Decker, "When you ate the fruit yesterday, did you experience any gastrointestinal symptoms? Gas, upset, reflux, diarrhea, anything?"

"No. Nothing."

Culpepper dropped the carved fruit into the blender.

Day 10, 1521 Hours

Swenson's computer beeped. "Fresh data from the bat probe."

He pulled his chair back up to the console. "It looks like a larger cave this time. The probe didn't finish the survey in the fifteen-minute interval and is just reporting partial data. Let's look at what we have."

Sakhr pulled up alongside Swenson as they reviewed the video uploaded by the probe.

"Limestone," Sakhr said. "Like the others. No surprise there."

"No bats, though. I wonder why that is."

"They're in there," Sakhr said. "Probably in much larger numbers than the smaller caves we've seen. They'll be farther back where it's darker and quieter."

They both watched in silence as the video replayed the journey of the probe through the cave.

Something caught Sakhr's eye. "Wait. Go back. What was that?"

Swenson rewound the video and froze it.

Sakhr closed his eyes and shook his head. "You have to be kidding me. Can you zoom in on that?"

Swenson expanded the image, clearly showing a candy bar wrapper lying on the cave floor.

THIRTY-FIVE

Dr. Sakhr found an empty chair by the morning campfire and sat with his breakfast on a tray on his lap. Swenson and Decker were on one side of the fire engaged in conversation, apparently having already finished their breakfasts. Guerrero and Culpepper were opposite, talking intermittently as they finished theirs.

Sakhr looked at his plate and said a silent prayer of thanks. It had become a routine act for him to say such a prayer before eating, but it struck him this morning how truly grateful he was for what was before him.

Half of the meager portion on his plate was emergency rations from the mission supplies. Not particularly palatable, but nutritionally vital. The other half was a handful of nuts. Almonds. Two-food, as Swenson liked to call it.

Hope.

It seemed nothing was going according to plan. This was supposed to have been a three-month field trip. He had done many of these before, often away from home

309

for much longer stints. But now their supply line was lost, along with their way home.

One dead. Another clinging desperately to life. A third, a murderer on the run—and possibly still gunning for the rest of them.

The mission no longer about geology, but about survival.

He picked up one of the almonds and looked at it. A simple shape. Packed full of molecules so complex that even the most advanced science known to humanity still couldn't synthesize them.

Alien molecules, essential for life. Identical in every way to those on Earth.

Surely a sign from God. We were meant to be here. We will survive.

Day 11, 0830 Hours

"How was breakfast this morning?" Decker asked as the last of the team filed into the medical lab.

Sakhr smiled. "I don't remember ever eating almonds that tasted so good."

Decker nodded. "Let's get started. Dr. Tornquist, update on Dr. Zindell?"

Everyone turned to look at the side of the lab where Zindell was still unconscious in bed. Someone had pulled a chair up beside the bed and Mikey was sitting in it. She turned to face them—appearing to listen in on their conversation—but had one hand turned back over her shoulder gripping the railing on the bed.

"He's improving. Significantly. But I still can't tell you when, or if, he'll regain consciousness."

"Mr. Swenson, have you made any progress decrypting Solansky's communications?"

"No. I've isolated the files I think were used to couch encrypted messages. It looks like he was sending a status report every night, and receiving instructions every morning. But I don't have the skills to crack the encryption. Even if I did, it would take a lot more computational horsepower than we have available here. Unless we can get Solansky to turn over the encryption key, I don't see us learning anything more before we reestablish the connection with Earth."

"What about the portal?"

"No change, and I'm out of things to try from this end. We're waiting on Earth."

Sakhr leaned forward. "Suppose something was wrong with our end and Earth was trying, but unable, to connect. What would they do?"

"First, they'd try sending a comm system through to the space-based portal still in orbit around the planet. Assuming they were able to connect, it would start broadcasting, and we'd have picked it up."

"Wait." Sakhr sat upright. "There's a second portal here?"

Swenson nodded. "Yes. Sort of. The technology works two ways. In theory, you only need a portal on one end. But the accuracy of targeting on the open end is sensitive. We're fifty-seven light-years from Earth. At this distance,

311

we couldn't realistically put something within a hundred miles of the intended location. That's one part in sixty trillion, which is really incredible accuracy, but obviously not good enough if you're going to send people to the planet's surface. So they sent an empty transport chamber, space-based, slightly larger than this one, into the solar system near the planet. When it arrived, it got its bearings and maneuvered itself into a stable orbit. With a chamber on this end, they could get a precise target lock. They sent our portal through to the orbital relay, which then forwarded it to the planet's surface. Over the much shorter distance, accuracy wasn't a problem for placing the portal on the planet's surface."

"So if something was wrong with our portal, Earth should still be able to relay shipments to us through the space-based portal?" asked Sakhr.

"Yes. Which is another reason to believe the problem is on their end. But if they also can't connect to that portal, they'd try sending a probe satellite into the solar system using the open-ended technique. As soon as it got here, it would start broadcasting and simultaneously maneuvering toward the planet. And we'd have heard from it by now."

"So something has happened on Earth that prevents them from even making an effort?" Sakhr asked.

Swenson started to answer, but Decker cut him off. "It looks that way, but we don't have enough information to know for sure. Rather than worry about what we don't know, and can't do anything about, we need to stay focused on what we do know and can do. Dr. Culpepper, what's the status of the search for food?"

Culpepper looked back and forth between Sakhr and Swenson. She opened her mouth to speak, but nothing came out. She finally looked at Decker. "We now have almonds, strawberry-pears, and potatoes tentatively qualified for consumption. We have several other fruits and vegetables in the pipeline that look promising. One key gap is a source of vitamin C, but yesterday Mr. Guerrero found a grove with some kind of citrus that may help fill that gap. Nutritional analysis is ongoing. If that's all we have, it's enough to extend us indefinitely—ignoring that changing seasons may limit availability. I think it would be prudent to try planting a garden, but we'd need to construct some sort of greenhouse."

Swenson grimaced. "Why do we need a greenhouse?"

Culpepper clinched her teeth. "Because the plants available to us won't grow in the cold of winter. I can't be sure until it happens, but from the condition of the trees and seed-bearing plants around here, I think we're about the middle of autumn. The food sources we've identified won't produce much during the winter. Or well into spring, for that matter."

Swenson smirked. "You're assuming that this planet even has seasons. We don't know that yet."

Culpepper glared at Swenson. "*I* do. The fruit trees are clearly adapted to seasons. Their cycles of growth—putting on leaves, flowering, putting on fruit, shedding leaves, going dormant—are all synchronized. Every tree

313

in the region is within a few weeks of the same point in the cycle. Consistent with mid-autumn. The soil conditions are also consistent with periodic cycles of the deposition of a new layer of dead leaves followed by an extended interval of decomposition."

Swenson smirked again at Culpepper. "The best I remember, it was early spring when we left Earth."

Culpepper glared red-faced at Swenson. "In the northern hemisphere. In the southern hemisphere, it was early fall."

Swenson nodded. "Fair enough. It means at the very least that we transported several thousand miles in an instant."

Sakhr shook his head. "Except that we're not in the southern hemisphere. If you've been watching the path of the sun through the days, it rises south of east and sets south of west. And it's never directly overhead. Always a few degrees to the south. Which means we're in the northern hemisphere; consistent with where they told us we would make planetfall."

Now Culpepper glared at Sakhr.

Decker cut in. "What can we do about it ... the coming winter?"

Culpepper looked back to Decker. "About the fruit and nuts, not much. We need to collect as much as we can as it ripens and store it. We'll need to convert the supply building to cold storage. Most of the fruits will probably last a few weeks if kept cool, but we'll need to freeze most of it to have it remain edible through the winter. Taste and texture will suffer, but the bulk of the nutritional value should remain intact. Many of the smaller, faster-growing plants I think we can grow in a greenhouse. If we start soon, we might expect to see fresh produce by mid-winter. There are a lot of assumptions rolled up into that. The biggest one being that the growing cycles of these plants are similar to those on Earth."

Swenson started to say something, but an abrupt hand gesture from Decker shut him down.

Decker turned to Steadman. "Mr. Steadman, the search for Solansky?"

"We went out last night after dark to check out Dr. Sakhr's cave."

He pulled a plastic bag out of a pocket in his vest. The empty wrapper of a protein bar was wadded up inside. "He was definitely there, but probably several days ago, and it doesn't look like he stayed more than one night. I would guess that's where he holed up his first night on the run."

"We're stepping up the focus on caves," Sakhr said. "We have the drones paying special attention to the areas around cave openings looking for any signs of a trail, and we've implemented a systematic process to survey and document every cave we find."

Decker was about to dismiss the meeting when Sakhr raised his hand. "If I may?"

Decker nodded.

Sakhr turned to Steadman. "Commander, I noticed when you were unpacking shipments from Earth that many of the pallets were wrapped in plastic. Do we still have any of that?"

"Yeah. It's all rolled up in the back of the storage room."

"How large are the pieces?"

"The first few crates we cut the plastic off. Those are probably eight to ten feet long and two feet wide. After that we started unrolling them—Guerrero thought we might find a use for the plastic. Those are two feet wide and anywhere from twenty to a hundred feet long. Why?"

Sakhr smiled. "I think Chief Guerrero's foresight just gave us what we need to build Dr. Culpepper's greenhouse."

THIRTY-SIX

Day 11, 0915 Hours

Commander Steadman entered the common area of the men's quarters to find Swenson and Sakhr sitting at the computer console watching drone surveillance video on separate monitors.

"Mind if I join you?"

"Not at all," Swenson said, rubbing his eyes. "Maybe you'll see what we're missing. He has to be out there somewhere."

As Steadman pulled up a chair, Sakhr said, "Maybe not. Maybe his reliance on caves got him tangled up with a bear. Maybe there's nothing left but a few teeth and a shinbone lost somewhere in a cave."

Steadman sat in front of another monitor. "He should be so lucky. If Guerrero finds him, he's likely to end up *missing* a few teeth and a shinbone, and still be alive."

Sakhr stared wide-eyed at Steadman.

Steadman focused on the monitor. "Tell me what I'm looking at."

Swenson paused his feed and rolled his chair over beside Steadman. He pointed at the screen. "This text in the corner tells you this was shot by drone six today a few minutes after seven a.m. This overlay in the other corner shows you where this image fits in a larger map of the area. You can click here and zoom this out to help get your bearings. These are the controls to pause and play; these will change the speed, both forward and backward. If you want to look at other video, maybe a specific location or time, let me know and I'll show you how to find it."

"What's this?" Steadman asked, pointing at a symbol on the screen.

"That's where the pattern recognition algorithm noticed something that changed in that location from the same area on the previous day. Anything that changes is fed to another algorithm that tries to determine whether the change might be significant. That one isn't, or we would've been alerted."

"So you're looking for things that change from one pass to the next?"

"Well, one day to the next. The search pattern repeats multiple times a day, but the lighting changes from pass to pass. Differences in shadows as a function of time of day cause too many false indications, so we compare new data against the same run on the previous day."

"So the search pattern repeats? Same time of day. Same search path."

"Yeah. Not ideal, but we have to work with what we have. If we still had a connection to Earth, we could have modified image-processing algorithms within hours. Unfortunately, that's beyond my skill set."

Sakhr looked at Steadman. "So you think he's figured out the pattern? He knows when the drones are coming. And when they're not. He only comes out when they're not."

Swenson lurched back to his console and started typing.

Steadman rose from his chair. "Not yet, Rusty. Get it ready, but don't change anything until after dark. Then keep the three search drones flying the exact same pattern. Bring in the mapping drone and have it start probing the gaps. Be random. Be stealthy. Be unpredictable."

Day 12, 1047 Hours

Where would I hide?

Steadman studied the console in front of him. Swenson had built a three-dimensional simulation of the surrounding terrain from a composite of drone surveillance data.

The caves would provide decent cover, day or night.

Sakhr, sitting at another console to Steadman's right, rubbed his eyes as he continued to watch a live stream from one of the drones. Swenson, sitting on the other side of Sakhr, took another shot of coffee as he watched the feed from a different drone.

What's he doing about water? Food? Steadman wondered. *He has to come out sometime.*

He thought he caught a glimpse of motion in one corner of the screen. A fraction of a second later his console started squawking.

The drone automatically adjusted course, bringing the motion to center-screen and tracking a figure running away from the camera. It was moving fast through the trees, only visible intermittently.

He must have seen the drone!

Sakhr jumped up from his workstation to look over Steadman's shoulder.

Swenson was typing feverishly. "Retasking drones one, two, and three. Converging on your location. We'll have backup in fifteen seconds. Full coverage in two minutes."

Steadman activated his comm. He pushed down the adrenaline rush to steady his voice. "Tango is up. Alex, get ready to go airborne."

As he bolted from the room, he called over his shoulder, "Route the video to Blue and send coordinates. Keep me posted."

THIRTY-SEVEN

Day 12, 1058 Hours

Guerrero nimbly whipped the blue four-wheeler along a jagged path between the treetops. He kept low enough to stay in cover but high enough that there was room between the trees. Decker had overridden the altitude limitation, and now Guerrero and Steadman were rapidly climbing high into a mountain pass in pursuit of Solansky.

And that was what occupied Guerrero's thoughts. How should it go? Take the kill shot to make sure he went down? Or make sure he saw it coming ... make sure he'd have plenty of time to know he was about to die before it happened? Or make sure he felt it ... long and painful?

Swenson had reported that Solansky had disappeared into a cave. One drone had followed him in, but it couldn't go very far before its communication signal became too weak to continue. Swenson was in the process of recalling the caving drone, but it was already out of touch in another cave and wasn't expected to be available for another fifteen minutes.

TWO

Steadman pointed to a spot on the display set into the dashboard. Guerrero maneuvered the vehicle to Steadman's spot. It was a small clearing a short distance upslope from the cave entrance. Out of sight of Solansky if he was waiting for them inside. Or so they hoped.

Both men bailed out of the vehicle, Steadman leading the way downhill into the woods. They made their way to an outcropping of rock that overlooked the cave entrance.

Steadman whispered into his comm. "ETA for the caving drone?"

"Twelve minutes."

Guerrero tapped Steadman on the shoulder and pointed out two pathways, one on either side of the cave entrance.

Decker's voice came over the comm. "Hold tight. He's not going anywhere."

Guerrero edged forward and whispered in Steadman's ear. "What's the plan, boss?"

Steadman keyed his mic. "Roger that. Redeploying to a better position."

Steadman motioned Guerrero to the left, then took off to the right. As Guerrero made his way around, he kept low and looked for the best compromise between proximity and concealment.

He was about ten feet from the cave entrance when he decided he was as close as he could get without losing cover. He looked across to the other side and saw Steadman taking up a position opposite him.

Steadman held up three fingers. Guerrero nodded. Both men pulled their night-vision goggles into place.

Steadman held up a closed fist. Then raised one finger. Two. Three.

Day 12, 1105 Hours

What part of "hold tight" was unclear?

Decker watched the reconnaissance video as Steadman and Guerrero assaulted the cave. He felt Swenson and Sakhr looking at him.

Decker tapped Swenson on the shoulder. "Follow them in with a drone. Dark. Night vision only. Keep it as high as you can so we don't run into anyone accidentally."

Swenson started typing. The video feed on his monitor shifted and then swooped rapidly toward the cave entrance. As the drone passed from light into darkness, the image switched suddenly from color to black. A small patch of floor near the cave entrance glowed a faint green, the artificial color of a night-vision camera, where sunlight had warmed the opening. The rest of the scene was completely black.

After a moment the contrast adjusted and faint contours of cave walls could be seen. The drone scanned until it found an opening in one wall. It moved quickly toward it, the camera looking down a tunnel. Two bright green figures were running away down the length of the passage.

"Follow them," Decker said.

The drone chased the two apparitions down the tunnel.

"We've already lost comm signals with Steadman and Guerrero," Swenson said. "We'll lose the drone too before it gets very far."

"Can you have the drone follow them even after it loses contact with us?"

The engineer tapped a few quick commands. The video went dark. "Done. Confirmed the commands were received before we lost the connection. I didn't have time for anything sophisticated. If it loses them, which it could, it'll just park itself. Then it'll be up to us to find and recover it."

"ETA for the caving drone?"

Dr. Sakhr rechecked his console. "Still eight minutes before we expect it to check in, three more before we can have it on-station."

"We have another problem, though," Swenson said. "We haven't mapped this particular cave yet. And we have no idea where they are inside. So we can't just have it race in to meet up with them. All we can do is tell it to search and then wait to see what it finds."

"Could there be other exits from this cave?"

"It's possible," Sakhr said. "Most of the caves we've looked at have been small with a single opening. We've only found two larger cave systems. This might be a third. It clearly connects to something beyond the outer cavity."

"Have you located other openings nearby that haven't been mapped yet?"

Sakhr pulled up a map on his console. "Depending on how you define 'nearby,' anywhere from two to ... well, depending on how far the cave system reaches, there could be any number of other openings."

Decker tapped Swenson on the shoulder again. "Bring in every drone you have. I want one watching every cave opening you can find that might be connected to this one. Prioritize by distance from ground zero."

Day 12, 1115 Hours

Swenson sprang forward in his seat. "Sir! Drone Three just came back online."

Decker rushed over to Swenson's side. "Where? Give me video."

The video switched back to color and showed the outside of another cave entrance. Steadman and Guerrero were both visible, circling around the entrance and looking at the ground.

Swenson checked the location of the drone. "They're almost a mile west of the other entrance. A few hundred feet downslope."

Decker keyed his comm. "Status?"

Decker counted to eight before Steadman responded. "We saw him running away through a tunnel when we entered the cave. We followed him in this direction but lost him. The tunnel eventually led to this entrance, but if he came out here he didn't leave a trail."

"Roger that." Decker turned to Sakhr. "ETA on the caving drone?"

"It's en route now. Should be there in three minutes."

Decker keyed his comm again. "The caving drone should be on station in three minutes. Find a secure location and stand by."

THIRTY-EIGHT

Decker came out of the medical lab to see the team beginning to form up around the campfire. He tapped Steadman on the shoulder as he walked past him toward the science lab. Steadman followed, closing the door as they entered.

Decker looked at him. "Explain your thinking."

"We were hot on his trail. He was on the run. It was our advantage, and we needed to press it."

"You were on his turf. It was clear he knew exactly where he was going when he ran into that cave. He could have been leading you into an ambush."

Steadman clinched his teeth.

"Chris, you're the one who recommended this strategy. Wait him out. If we go after him, we're playing into his strength. Be patient. Leverage our strength, our technology. Those are all your words, and it was a sound strategy. What changed?"

Steadman raised his chin. "With all due respect, sir, I made a command decision based on my assessment of

327

the facts on the ground. I'm not accustomed to having my judgment in the field questioned."

Decker took a step forward, getting into Steadman's personal space. "Nor am I mine."

Steadman stared at the wall over Decker's shoulder.

Decker stepped back and leaned against a table. "Chris, this isn't a black op on some backwater island in the South Pacific. We're isolated on a planet fifty-seven light-years from Earth, responsible for the lives of five civilians, with an agent of a hostile foreign power on the loose and gunning for us. I think I understand why you want to get him. I do too. But we have to do it without getting anyone else killed. You're not replaceable. Guerrero isn't replaceable. We could have lost both of you today. Then it would have been me and Mr. Swenson trying to take Solansky down."

Decker looked directly at Steadman. "Do you really think that would have worked?"

Steadman closed his eyes and exhaled. "I'm sorry, sir. I see your point. It won't happen again."

"Just to be clear, Chris, our first priority is to not get anyone else killed. And 'anyone' includes you and Alex. Our second priority is to get Solansky. And our third priority is to get him alive. We still don't know if he could hold the key to getting us back to Earth."

Day 12, 1930 Hours

The temperature had already dropped a few degrees just since sunset, and a stiff breeze from the south added to the chill. It looked like Culpepper was finally right about something.

Guerrero added more wood to the fire as everyone huddled in close. "I don't get why there are no humans here. If aliens brought all this here from Earth, why didn't they bring humans too? If God created it and went to so much trouble to create every detail so much like Earth, why leave out the people? If all this evolved independently, why didn't something like us evolve too?"

"That may be the best argument we've seen here for evolution." Culpepper took a sip of coffee. "Evolution doesn't require that any particular form of life come to exist. It merely allows it as one possible outcome from a random process. It may also be that we just got here too early. Evolution moves slowly, requiring at least millions of years. Maybe there hasn't been enough time yet for something as complex as humans to develop."

Swenson shook his head. "I won't rehash the arguments against evolution, but at least as far as the 'alien' and 'God' hypotheses go, it's a fair question. First, I think we have to allow that it's still possible they're here but we just haven't found them yet. Maybe there aren't that many, and they're on a different part of the planet, well away from here. But the odds are pretty low. We already have a complete satellite map of the planet with pretty good detail. Not so much as a campfire. No cultivated fields. No organized villages."

Culpepper shrugged. "Maybe they're just not into building things. Or burning things. Or digging things up."

329

Swenson chuckled. "Yeah, but that's pretty much what we humans do. Tame the earth. Work the garden. If they're not doing those things, it's hard to argue they're an analogue to human. As for the 'alien' hypothesis, we can only guess at their motivation. Maybe they did, but the humans didn't survive. Maybe they didn't want another intelligent species running loose in their garden. Remember, I'm not a fan of that theory, so I may not be the best person to guess why they did what they supposedly did. As for the 'God' hypothesis, again we can only guess at what he was thinking. Both the Christian and Jewish philosophies hold that humanity is unique in creation. Man is not just another animal, but something more. The *only* thing 'created in the image of God.'"

Dr. Sakhr nodded thoughtfully. "Islam teaches the same thing. And it also teaches that God created life elsewhere in the universe."

Swenson tipped his head toward Sakhr. "What isn't clear is whether man is unique only among life on Earth, or in *all* of creation—the whole universe."

Guerrero shook his head. "But why go to all the trouble of creating life here if he's not going to create men here to take care of it?"

Culpepper rolled her eyes. "Like this place needs men. It seems to me it's done just fine here all by itself."

Swenson laughed. "Point taken. In fact, why create the rest of the universe if it's ultimately all about Man? Create a sun, a planet, a few people, and you're done. Why *did* God create all those galaxies filled with all those stars surrounded by all those planets? The question 'why create men?' in the first place is a great deal more difficult to answer. But 'why create them on Earth and not here?' or 'why create them only on Earth?' If that proves to be the case, one viable explanation is that God intended from the beginning that humanity should spread to the stars. Which was, incidentally, one of the postulates that led Dr. Kreitzman to his theory."

Day 13, 1205 Hours

Guerrero walked through the door to find Tornquist sitting at a computer console, Zindell unconscious in bed, and Mikey sitting in her bedside chair. Just like yesterday.

Mikey perked up when she saw him. He said, "Hey, partner," and tossed a strawberry-pear to her. She snatched it out of the air and took a bite before offering a gentle hoot, a bit of fruit hanging from her teeth.

Guerrero laughed. "Didn't your mom teach you not to talk with your mouth full?"

Tornquist looked up from her console. "Good afternoon, Alex." She nodded toward Zindell. "He's doing much better. He still hasn't regained consciousness, but his fever has broken. That's a good sign."

He walked over to Zindell's bed beside Mikey and patted her on the head as he looked at Zindell's silent form. *Another failure.* His whole reason for being here was to protect these people, and all he had done so far was to fail. First Pam. Now Zindell.

And Solansky was still out there. Somewhere.

But that would change. He wouldn't fail again. He couldn't. He owed that to the rest of the team.

Tornquist joined him at Zindell's bedside. "I'm curious how your dad got you off the hook after the Chuck incident."

It took a moment for the statement to register and for his mind to shift gears, but he couldn't help laughing. "I'm not sure I know the whole story on that one. The next day my dad got a call from the head coach, off the record, saying he'd heard the mayor was pressuring the district attorney to have me charged with battery."

"Pam said your dad was a Texas Ranger."

"Yeah. Was and is. And before that, he was a Green Beret. He's the one who taught me and my brothers how to fight. And how to not fight. And how to know when to do which. Dad was law and order personified. At work and at home. There were rules, and the rules would be obeyed. But he also taught us that there were reasons for the rules. That the rules teach us to live in community with other people, to strive together instead of against, to respect each other."

"So what did your dad do?"

"First he called the district attorney and suggested that he should call the mayor and say that, in view of his personal relationship with the family of the accused, he felt it best to recuse himself from the matter and refer it to state authorities. Then he called the mayor's assistant and asked him to schedule a meeting with the mayor for the next afternoon, but just list it as 'a Texas Ranger with a personal matter to discuss.'"

"And?"

"And when he and I showed up at the mayor's office the next day we were ushered right in. The expression on the mayor's face said that he'd been expecting a Texas Ranger to discuss a matter that was personal to him, the mayor, not a matter that was personal to him, the Texas Ranger. But he charged right in. Told us he had medical records and affidavits from doctors showing the damage I'd caused, and he was going to see to it that justice was served. And then he'd come after us with a civil case for medical expenses and psychological harm."

"It sounds like the apple didn't fall far from the tree."

"You got that right."

"How did your dad respond?"

"He said he thought that was a great idea. Teach the boy a lesson. Get everything out in an open courtroom in front of the public so there wouldn't be any whispers about backroom deals with corrupt politicians or law enforcement. Then he asked the mayor if he'd interviewed any of the witnesses yet, or if he'd had a chance to review the security camera footage from the stadium parking lot. 'Well, no matter,' he said. 'Those things will all come out in court.' The mayor turned a pale shade of white; told us the meeting was over and to get out of his office."

"So what happened after that?"

"Nothing. At least not from the mayor or Chuck. On the drive home, dad said he was proud of how I'd handled the situation—though he suggested the dislocated shoulder might have been a bit excessive. 'I could argue that either way,' he said. I think mostly he was glad I didn't break his neck."

Guerrero cringed, the words escaping his mouth before the imagery registered.

Tornquist put a hand on Guerrero's forearm. "You didn't do this, Alex."

Guerrero clinched his fists. "No, Solansky did."

"Yes, Solansky did. But there's more at stake here than just avenging Pam's murder. How would your dad tell you to deal with him?"

The question caught Guerrero completely off guard. He'd spent the past five days plotting vengeance against Solansky. How he could catch him. What he'd do when he did.

But he didn't have to wonder about what his dad would say. He knew.

Day 13, 1525 Hours

Grace Tornquist nursed a cup of lukewarm coffee as she sat by the burnt-out campfire. The chill of the morning was long gone, replaced by a beautiful sunny afternoon.

She looked at the mountains in the distance. It was times like this she really wished she had Culpepper's job. Or Zindell's. Any excuse to spend all day out exploring all this splendor. It was a welcome consolation to know she would have plenty of opportunities. Whatever happened with the portal now, she knew she could never go home.

But thinking of Zindell reminded her that her job was inside. She needed to get back in there.

Like it will do any good.

She was about to get up when Culpepper walked up beside her.

"Warm up your coffee?" Culpepper had brought the pot with her.

Tornquist held out her cup with a smile as Culpepper topped it off.

She sat down beside her and took a sip from her own cup. "You look worried. Afraid he's not going to make it?"

Tornquist looked at her coffee. Part of her job was to stay optimistic. Keep up the morale of the team. Even when she didn't feel it.

"His fever broke more than eight hours ago. His blood shows to be clear of the infection. I've weaned him off most of the meds, including the painkillers. I can't find any clinical reason why he's not waking up. The pain in his leg alone should make it impossible for him to sleep." Tornquist took another sip of coffee. "These are the reasons why it's against the rules to practice medicine this way."

Culpepper put a hand on Tornquist's arm. "You had no choice, Grace. If you played by the rules, he'd be dead already. Because of you, he's not. As long as he's alive, there's a chance he'll make a full recovery. There's still hope."

Tornquist put her hand over Culpepper's and smiled at her. "Thanks. Sometimes it just helps to have someone you can unload on."

"I know we didn't start out on the best of terms, and that's all on me. But you've been there for me, and I'll be —"

Culpepper's words were drowned out by a deafening howl coming from the medical lab.

Minutes earlier

Day 13, 1531 Hours

Zindell felt for a moment like he was floating in space. As his mind surveyed his surroundings, he gradually became aware of the reality around him. He realized he was waking up.

His leg hurt. Badly. Like someone had run a drill through it. With a dull bit.

He was lying in a bed. He tried to shift his legs, but they wouldn't move. Tied down? No, it felt more like a heavy weight resting on them. Maybe they were just that weak. The rest of him sure didn't feel very strong. What was wrong with him?

He opened his eyes. Blackness.

That's not good.

As he blinked he could feel his eyelashes dragging against something. He drew his hand to his face.

The arm works. That's something.

His hand found something covering his eyes. He pulled it up and was relieved to see light.

A sleep mask. Whew!

He looked around the room. It took a moment for the unfamiliar surroundings to register with him.

The medical lab. On Two. It wasn't a dream.

He tried to move his legs again, but they wouldn't budge. With effort, he lifted his head to look down at his knees.

A shot of adrenaline coursed through his veins as he saw a shaggy brown pile of something on his legs. His whole body jerked in an effort to dislodge the ... what was it?

The sudden movement brought it to life. It uncurled itself and stared at him. Big eyes. Bigger teeth.

They watched each other, Zindell on the verge of panic, his brain still in a fog. Something was familiar, but ... what? This was a chimpanzee. A wild animal. A predator. Sometimes vicious. What was it doing here?

The animal hooted. It picked itself up and crawled up over his body toward his head, planting one hand on either side.

The chimp leaned its face down toward his.

A memory clicked.

"Mikey!"

She planted a sloppy kiss on his forehead, then hopped down from the bed and scooted over to the door. She leaned out through the door and let out a loud howl.

TWO

"Dr. Zindell. It's good to see you've decided to quit sleeping on the job. I have a good mind to dock your pay."

Culpepper's jaw dropped.

Tornquist gave Decker a stern look.

Zindell laughed. "If what these two tell me is true, I'm going to need every penny of it just to pay my hospital bill. Five days?"

"Give or take. But the outcome was never in question. You've been in good hands."

Decker looked at Culpepper. "On the subject of which, Dr. Culpepper, I want to congratulate you on the achievement of a lifetime. I'm sure this will be just the first of a career filled with new discoveries, but this will always be the one people remember. The beacon that signals the breadth of opportunities that await us."

Culpepper took a step back and drew her hand up to her chest. "Me? But—" She gestured to Tornquist. "Grace—"

Tornquist held up her hands, palms out, then pointed back to Culpepper.

"But … Guerrero … Mikey … the clover …"

Tornquist smiled. "Surely you're not going to try to credit a meathead and a monkey with this discovery?"

Culpepper sat down heavily.

Meanwhile, Zindell inspected a sample of the plant that Culpepper had given him. "This isn't ordinary clover."

Culpepper looked up. "What? Well, it's not an exact match for any variant of clover on Earth, but it's enough like them to still be considered clover, at least in a broad sense."

He hesitated. "I don't mean this as a criticism, Dr. Culpepper. You saved my life—you and Dr. Tornquist—and I can't tell you how grateful I am for that. But have you ever been accused of not seeing the forest for the trees?"

Her face contorted. "What?"

"You've been so busy studying the cells, the oil, the enzymes, the DNA." He held it up to her. "Did you ever look at the shape?"

"Yeah. Roundish green leaves, about half a centimeter in diameter. Clover."

"Did you count them?"

She took the sprig from his hand. "Well, I'll be …" Her eyes grew wide as she leaned back against the table for support. "It's a four-leaf clover."

Zindell smiled. "A whole planet covered with it."

Tornquist grinned. "Who says God has no sense of humor?"

THIRTY-NINE

Sakhr woke with a start when his console started beeping. He sat up straight, trying to clear the fog from his head. He picked up his coffee mug and looked into the bottom. Empty.

He looked at the console.

Why is it beeping?

Equipment failure. One of the perimeter sensors had gone offline.

What would cause that?

He heard doors opening behind him. Turning to look over his shoulder, he saw first Steadman, then Guerrero, coming out of their quarters. More doors.

They'll want answers.

He turned back to the console, the fog finally beginning to clear. "One of the perimeter sensors has gone offline. I'm checking its history. Someone wake Swenson."

"Already here." Swenson dropped into his own chair at the adjacent console.

"Cause?" Decker asked.

Sakhr pulled up the video from the problem sensor and started running it backward. "Solansky!"

"What?" Decker said.

Sakhr pushed the video to the big screen and froze it. The moonlit face of Jacob Solansky was clearly visible in front of the sensor. He held in both hands a big stick with a bigger rock tied to the end. A homemade sledgehammer, the instrument of the sensor's demise, wielded like a baseball bat. The frozen image captured in mid-swing.

"I'm getting no signal from that pod." Swenson studied his console. "Logs indicate that he approached at a dead run, perpendicular to the line of sensor pods. No other pods picked him up on the way in or out, so he probably left along the same path."

"Could he have continued straight into the compound?"

"No. The perimeter array is two concentric circles, with the individual sensors in each circle offset from each other. So there's still an inner circle with all the sensors intact. He would have been picked up by at least one of them if he'd continued toward the camp."

"Get every drone you have up in a search pattern on that side of the perimeter. Night vision. See if you can find him."

Swenson typed a few commands. "Done."

Steadman leaned back against the wall. "We have him now."

Decker shook his head. "Let's not count our chickens just yet. Wait and see if the drones pick up his trail."

"Oh, I doubt they will. He's had a five-minute head start, and he's figured out how to hide from our night-vision capabilities. But he's playing our game now, on our turf. He's telegraphed a strategy, and we can use that against him."

Decker looked up at Steadman. "How so?"

"He's coming after us, but the sensor array is a big problem. He can't get to us without us having several minutes of warning. Once he gets here, we have him outnumbered and outgunned. So he's going to try to degrade the array. He knows we can't replace what he destroys. If he can punch enough holes, he'll have multiple opportunities to attack without losing the benefit of surprise."

"So, how does that help us catch him?"

Swenson ran a hand through his hair. "I have an idea."

Day 14, 1430 Hours

Decker entered the common area of the men's quarters. "How's it going?"

Dr. Sakhr's attention was focused tightly on his console. "Get ready to break left ... wait for it ... break left, break left!"

Guerrero shifted the mouse and attacked the keyboard. "Coming around. He's nimble, this one."

"He's headed up the hill. There's a fork in the trail up ahead. Let's see if we can get in front and herd him down the right fork."

"Roger that," Guerrero said.

Decker looked over their shoulders at the video console. "Is that a panther?"

"Some kind of big cat," Sakhr said. "I'll ask Zindell about it later ... and ... Now!"

Guerrero slid the caving drone out from behind a rock and directly into the path of the cat, causing it to turn down the other fork. Wasting no time, Guerrero steered the drone to follow after it. He was hot on its tail when it suddenly darted left into a crevasse.

Sakhr cringed. "Didn't see that coming."

Guerrero pulled the drone back into a hover.

Decker patted him on the shoulder. "Looks like you're getting the hang of it."

"Getting the hang of it?" Guerrero chortled. "By tonight I'll be hanging Christmas lights with it."

Sakhr shook his head. "It'll be a lot harder if we have to do this at night, which seems likely. Even with the high-gain cameras, it'll be hard to see much. We're fortunate there's so much moonlight."

Decker nodded. "The flip side is that it'll be a lot easier to follow him without being seen at night. Speaking of which, chasing the cat is good training for speed and maneuvering. Have you thought about how to train for stealth?"

"That's what we're doing now," Guerrero said.

Decker drew his head back. "That was stealth?"

Guerrero laughed. "No. *This* is stealth."

He had maneuvered the probe to a position about fifty feet away and behind several trees. The color video feed Guerrero had been using to navigate showed mostly foliage, but a hint of the cat could be seen between the branches and leaves. It had hunkered down between two rocks, but its head was up—presumably looking for the probe that had been chasing it.

"It wouldn't really tell us anything if we'd just followed him for a while," Guerrero said. "He might see the probe but dismiss it as a bird and pay it no mind. But Solansky wouldn't make that mistake. So first we had to teach our cat that he needed to worry about the probe. Now, if he sees it, he'll react and we'll know. If he doesn't, we'll know we're getting good at this."

Decker shook his head. "Something tells me I don't want to know how you taught him to worry about the probe."

Guerrero grinned. "No animals were harmed in the making of this motion picture. At least not physically."

Decker put a hand on Sakhr's shoulder. "How are you doing at riding shotgun?"

"I'm getting the hang of it. The biggest challenge has been to learn to communicate succinctly so we can coordinate in real time. He says I'm too loquacious."

Decker patted Sakhr's shoulder. "I'd be willing to bet he doesn't even know what that means."

"Hey!" Guerrero said, not looking up from his console. "I resemble that remark."

Decker chuckled.

When Swenson proposed the idea, Guerrero thought he could handle the caving drone by himself. The idea was to use it to track Solansky next time he popped up. Solansky was on the lookout for the big drones, but he didn't know about the smaller one. It would be easier to follow him without his knowledge.

At least in theory.

But the presumption was that when they caught up to him he'd be running, probably through dense woods. The drone would have to keep up with him, which meant moving fast while being flown remotely; without being seen, which meant keeping terrain and foliage between the drone and Solansky; without being heard, which meant not crashing into anything while moving fast among the trees and rocks; without losing sight of Solansky, which meant looking in one direction to keep an eye on Solansky and simultaneously in another direction to keep from crashing into anything.

So it became a two-man job. Guerrero's piloting and concealment skills to maneuver the drone, and Sakhr to track Solansky and keep an eye on the broader terrain. Steadman had wanted to manage the tracking, but Decker needed his strategic mind free to watch the big picture.

Where was Solansky going? What was he after?

TWO

Steadman heard the door open behind him. Decker came in with a pot of coffee and several cups. Steadman took one and held it for Decker to fill. "Thanks, Skipper."

"Any changes?" Decker asked as he filled a mug for Swenson.

Steadman raised an eyebrow. "Since you left here five minutes ago? No. Feels like Christmas Eve."

Swenson looked up with a furrowed brow. Decker said, "'Not a creature was stirring, not even a mouse.'"

Swenson turned back to his console. "Thanks for the coffee. Not sure how we'll survive once this runs out."

Decker tilted his head. "I'll make sure Dr. Tornquist and Dr. Culpepper have caffeine on their list of nutrients essential for survival."

"It's been more than thirty hours since his last strike," Swenson said. "What's he waiting for?"

"Hard to say." Steadman took a sip of coffee. "He's clearly very patient. And very well trained. He knows if he moves too quickly, gets too sloppy, he'll get caught. But he also knows time isn't on his side."

Decker set the coffee pot on the table. "His patience also tells us he's not desperate. He's found food and water. And if he's trying to sync up with someone else's timetable, that isn't happening soon."

"Someone else?" Swenson looked up at Decker. "You mean like the Russians are coming?"

346

Decker nodded. "It's a theory. We don't know, one way or the other. That's why I still want Solansky alive."

An alarm sounded on the console. Swenson checked the source. "Speak of the devil. He's inbound. Northeast quadrant. Bearing forty-three. Launching the bat probe. He'll reach the sensor pod in five seconds."

Decker pounded on the door to Guerrero and Sakhr's quarters.

Steadman watched over Swenson's shoulder as he flew the caving drone in the direction of the perimeter sensor probe that was about to be attacked. Video from the condemned probe was streaming on a side monitor and showed Solansky's approach. *He waited for dawn. Why did he wait for dawn?*

As Solansky destroyed the perimeter probe with his makeshift sledgehammer, Guerrero and Sakhr raced into the room and took their seats. Guerrero said, "I've got the stick."

"You've got the stick," Swenson replied.

"Recommend a path around the right side of the hill," Sakhr said. "You'll have cover from a grove as you approach from that direction."

Guerrero swung the drone around. "Roger."

"Why did he wait until sunrise?" asked Decker.

Steadman shook his head. "I've been wondering that myself. I think he realized darkness was to our advantage. We have night vision. He doesn't. Maybe he figures daylight will level the playing field."

Swenson's head popped up. "Our drones are certainly easier to see in the daytime."

"Yes!" Steadman tapped the table with a fist. "Mr. Swenson, get several of the regular drones up. Put them in a search pattern, but keep them away from Solansky. Close enough that he can see them in the sky, but far enough that he'll think they haven't spotted him."

Swenson moved to an open console.

Decker looked at Steadman. "Decoy? Give him what he's expecting so he'll be less likely to notice the caving drone?"

"Exactly. If he doesn't see a drone response, he'll have to wonder why. Better to let him think he's evaded us so he'll be less guarded."

"We're approaching the sensor pod location," Sakhr said. "Recommend a path to the left until we find him."

"Drifting left," said Guerrero.

"We just passed the damaged probe. He should be coming up on the right."

Steadman knelt down beside Swenson and spoke softly. "He's using daylight so he can see the drones coming. Maybe we can use the sun to hide one. Can you have a drone track him and automatically maintain its position so it stays directly between him and the sun?"

Swenson looked up from his console. "Yes … maybe … it will take a while. There's a lot of math involved. Time of day, time of year, orbit around the sun, rotation of the planet, location on the planet. It's not something I can set up right now."

Sakhr interrupted. "I might have seen him … motion ahead about one thousand feet … bearing fifty-one."

Guerrero said, "Adjusting."

"Confirmed! I've got him," Sakhr said. "He's in a dead run. Straight ahead, bearing forty-nine."

"Coming to a parallel path, setting up behind and to his left."

Steadman patted Swenson on the shoulder. "May not be needed. Let's see how this pans out."

Steadman stood and watched the video as Guerrero and Sakhr tracked Solansky through a grove. A side monitor had a static map of the area with an overlay of the positions of Solansky and the probe.

"He's coming to the edge of the grove," Steadman said. "Expect him to turn toward you to stay inside the tree line."

"Noted," said Guerrero. "Pulling back a bit."

"Freeze!" Sakhr said. "I think he stopped, but I lost sight of him. He may have ducked under cover."

All eyes were on Sakhr's monitor, looking for some sign of Solansky.

Guerrero said, "Orbiting right around his last known location."

Swenson went back to his console and started typing feverishly.

"There!" Guerrero and Sakhr said in unison. The probe motion stopped, just the top of Solansky's cap visible over a rise in the terrain.

"Keep moving," said Steadman. "We need to see more than just a cap. It could be a decoy."

The probe resumed motion to the right, climbing to see over the rise. Steadman's heart sank when he saw the stick holding the hat up.

"Pull up and back," Steadman said. "Give me a wider view."

"If I do," Guerrero said, "I'll be in open sky."

Swenson interrupted. "Belay that. New video coming up. I've got him. On the move. Doubling back into the grove. Take up heading two-seventy and stay in the trees. I'll guide you in."

Guerrero's probe raced into the trees, swerving left and right as it headed in the general direction Swenson had given.

"I have him again," Sakhr said. "Recommend a position to his rear and right. He's moving slower now but still running. Lost his hat somewhere."

Steadman patted Swenson on the shoulder. "Good work, Rusty. I thought you said that would take a while."

"It was your idea. I just realized that with a simple geometry trick I could eliminate the math. Or at least most of it."

Decker looked at Steadman. "Explain."

"Mr. Swenson took one of the standard drones and positioned it directly between Solansky and the sun. If Solansky looks in that direction, all he'll see is the blinding light of the sun. It gives us a second set of eyes.

When the caving drone lost the trail, Mr. Swenson was able to find it."

Sakhr interrupted again. "He's coming up on the river."

Steadman looked at the terrain overview map. "He's probably holed up in a cave in the mountains. He'll have to cross the water somewhere."

"Why not cross the land bridge to the south?" asked Decker.

"He certainly could, but he ran in the wrong direction. From where he is now he'd have to hike more than ten miles to circle the camp and cross to the south."

Swenson shook his head. "The caving drone will be exposed if it follows across the river."

"We'll cross that bridge when we come to it," Steadman said. "He'll be easy to track with your solar drone while he's in the river. That should give us a couple of minutes to swing Guerrero's bat probe around to cross far enough away that he can't see it. For now, just make sure you're not spotted if he turns up- or down-stream before crossing."

Decker looked at Steadman and pointed on the terrain map to a narrow spot along the river about half a mile downstream from Solansky's current location.

"Maybe," Steadman said. "That would certainly be the easiest and fastest spot to cross. But that also makes it a location we'd be likely to be watching."

"Anywhere he crosses the river, he's exposed."

"True. Even at night. In that cold water, his body heat would light up a night-vision camera like a full moon against a clear night sky."

"He's stopped," Sakhr said. "Or at least he's not running anymore."

Everyone turned to look at Sakhr's monitor. Solansky was looking up into the trees.

Decker put a hand on Guerrero's shoulder. "Careful, Mr. Guerrero. No motion if he looks in your direction."

Guerrero was already hiding behind a tree, but when Solansky turned to look in the opposite direction, Guerrero took the opportunity to back the probe up and put a second tree in between.

Sakhr overlaid thermal imaging on the color video so they could see Solansky's silhouette more clearly.

Solansky walked over to a nearby tree and pulled a fruit off a low-hanging branch. He ate the fruit, then threw the core into the nearby river. He started pulling more fruit from the tree, loading himself up with as much as he could carry.

"Breakfast," Decker said. "But is he near his base, or just taking a break? He can't carry that much very far."

"It's more than he could eat at one sitting," Guerrero said. "He's planning to hole up somewhere nearby. Maybe for the rest of the day, then cross the river at night."

"It's also possible he doesn't have a base," Steadman said. "A base makes it easier to survive, but it also makes it easier to get caught. If he has the skills, he's better off staying on the move."

Decker leaned against the wall. "But it looks like, at least for the next few hours, he may be settling in."

Steadman was studying the terrain map of the area. "Yeah. His first tactical error. Mr. Swenson, do you think you can take over the drone piloting from Mr. Guerrero?" He put a hand on Guerrero's shoulder. "Saddle up."

FORTY

Alex Guerrero navigated the blue four-wheeler between the hills, keeping it as low in the valley as he could.

Whoever picked the colors for these things wasn't thinking about tactical missions.

He was on mission now, and any thoughts of any actions other than following orders were not part of the flow.

No one else gets killed.

Take Solansky.

Take Solansky alive.

Still, as he tried to anticipate what might happen in the next few minutes, he couldn't help considering what Solansky might do that would force the alternative. And if it came to that, he knew he wouldn't hesitate.

Steadman was riding shotgun and studying the terrain around where Solansky had taken refuge. He was just a stone's throw, or at least an apple core's throw, away from the river. The area was thick with large fruit trees providing effective cover from drones searching the area.

If they didn't already know precisely where he was, he would have been very difficult to spot.

Even from the ground, he wouldn't be seen until they were within a few feet of him. He'd found a wash that fed into the river where the lay of the land covered him on three sides, and fallen trees provided an effective wall toward the river.

They approached the grove from the east, opposite the river. Guerrero maneuvered far enough into the trees to provide some degree of cover in case Solansky started exploring back in this direction. They would have to do the final approach on foot if they hoped to get close enough to catch him without spooking him first.

Guerrero parked and they both got out. Mikey jumped out of the back of the four-wheeler to join them. She had climbed in as soon as they started loading equipment back at the compound.

"I have a bad feeling about having her along," said Steadman.

"I'm not keen on it either, but I'm not sure what we could have done to stop her from following us. She's more likely to cooperate and keep quiet if she thinks she's part of the team than if she thinks we're trying to leave her out of something."

Guerrero knelt beside Mikey, who hooted softly at him. He put a finger to his mouth and shushed her. He pointed at Mikey and then up into the trees. She climbed up into the nearest tree and looked down at Guerrero. He gave her a thumbs-up before turning to walk in the direction of Solansky's hide. Steadman headed out too, taking a path slightly north of Guerrero.

They had about half a mile to hike to set the trap. The idea was to bracket Solansky in a triangle, with the river to his west, Steadman to the northeast, and Guerrero to the southeast. Decker was waiting upstream in the white four-wheeler. Once they sprang the trap, Decker would sweep downstream to close off that escape.

As Guerrero and Steadman moved toward their respective staging positions, Mikey would jump down out of her tree, move forward, and climb another tree. She stayed between the two and would look forward in the direction they were traveling when she got up into a tree.

Guerrero reached his spot and flattened himself against the ground looking over a rise toward Solansky's location. The location looked right, but he couldn't see Solansky. He keyed his comm. "Bravo set. No joy."

Steadman responded. "Alpha set. Eyes on target. He wouldn't be visible from your position."

Decker chimed in. "Delta is set. Alpha, you have the ball."

At that moment Guerrero heard a ruckus as Mikey bailed out of her tree and raced at a full gallop due north.

Swenson's voice came over the comm. "Cover! He heard something. He's looking around."

Guerrero tried to press himself deeper into the ground, but it wasn't giving. He knew the top of his head was visible if Solansky knew where to look, but he was more likely to be seen if he moved than if he just stayed still. He held his breath and kept his binoculars pointed toward Solansky's location.

She must've seen Solansky from the tree. Probably remembered being shot by him, so she ran away.

"I'm pretty sure he saw the chimp," Swenson said. "No way to know whether he recognized her or not. But it looks like it made him nervous. He's hunkered down and looking around."

Steadman said, "I need access to the video from the two drones."

"It's on your tablet," Swenson said.

Guerrero kept his eyes on Solansky's position. He could occasionally see just the top of his head pop up over the edge of the wash.

Why did she run north? Camp is southeast of here.

"Let's wait him out," Steadman said. "If everything stays quiet for a while, he might decide it was just wildlife. Guerrero, next time he turns away from your location, I need you to back down the slope. Wait for my cue."

Guerrero remained motionless as he continued to peer over the embankment.

"Go!"

Guerrero quickly and quietly inched his way back until he was sure his head was below the sightline from Solansky's position.

Steadman said, "You're clear."

No longer able to observe Solansky's position directly, Guerrero rolled over onto his back and pulled out his tablet. He was about to ask Swenson to link him into the video when he saw it was already there.

Solansky was doing exactly what Guerrero had been doing moments earlier—remaining very still and keeping his eyes open. The differences being that Solansky didn't know where to look, and didn't have access to binoculars or surveillance drones.

Guerrero looked at his rifle. This would be over already if they didn't care about taking Solansky alive. The trees would be a problem, but he had already identified several vantage points on higher ground where he was confident he could get an angle for a clear shot.

Guerrero activated his comm. "Is Zindell on the line?"

After a brief silence, Sakhr said, "I'll call over to the med lab and get him."

"Get Culpepper and Tornquist on the line too."

"What are you thinking?" asked Decker.

"I'm thinking I remember seeing a tranquilizer gun in the manifest for his equipment."

"Problem," Steadman said. "A tranquilizer gun is not a sniper rifle. I don't see a vantage point close enough to get a clean shot."

"What? There aren't any trees on your side of the forest?"

Day 15, 0830 Hours

Guerrero met Culpepper about a quarter mile due east of his perch. Tornquist and Zindell had worked out a suitable load for the tranquilizer darts. Culpepper volunteered to bring the rifle and darts out to meet him. She'd taken the remaining four-wheeler and parked near Guerrero's vehicle, then hiked here.

Guerrero took the gun and darts. "Thanks."

As he turned to leave, Culpepper asked, "What else can I do to help?"

Before Guerrero could answer, Swenson interrupted on the comm. "We may have a problem here."

* * * * *

Back at camp, Decker's voice came over the radio. "What's up?"

Swenson said, "It looks like Mikey got tangled up with Yogi. Yogi is giving chase, and Mikey is heading in Solansky's direction."

Tornquist and Zindell had joined Swenson and Sakhr to monitor the mission. Tornquist said, "This is why you don't let your dog off-leash in the woods. He'll chase the bear for a while until the bear gets tired of the game and turns around to chase the dog. Then the dog will come running back to you, and bring the bear with it."

Zindell's eyes were glued to the video feed. "No. Well, yes. That's true. But I don't think that's what's happening here."

As they watched the video, they saw the bear had stopped giving chase. Mikey had gotten too far out front.

Decker, in his four-wheeler, couldn't see what had their attention. "Speak, Doctor."

Mikey stopped and turned back toward Yogi, hooting and hollering at him. As the bear started lumbering

359

toward Mikey again, the chimp grabbed a tree branch and pulled it back.

Tornquist nudged Zindell. "What? Oh. Mikey isn't running from the bear."

When the bear got close enough, Mikey let go and the branch struck Yogi in the face.

Yogi let out a roar and resumed the chase.

"She's taunting him. Leading him."

"Leading him where?" asked Decker.

"Hard to say exactly," Swenson said. "They're not moving in a straight line. Definitely in the direction of our stakeout, but not clear whether she's headed toward Guerrero and Steadman, toward Solansky, or just away from the bear."

* * * * *

Steadman watched the video feeds on his tablet. They were coming in his direction. Whether Mikey had a plan or not was academic. Steadman needed to get out of the way. The difficulty was that there were too many constraints on where he could go. Northeast was the only egress that wouldn't expose him to Solansky's sightlines.

Since Yogi was coming in from the north, he'd have to move quickly to get far enough east to be clear before they ran into each other.

He keyed his comm. "I'm moving northeast. Keep eyes on Tango."

* * * * *

Guerrero crawled back into his position but kept his head down below the embankment. He pulled his tablet out to get a fresh view of the tactical situation. He could see Steadman's escape route, but if the bear broke in the wrong direction at the wrong time, he'd be right on top of Steadman.

Guerrero laid down the tranquilizer gun and picked up his sniper rifle. He started looking around for a place where he could get enough elevation to provide cover for Steadman without becoming visible to Solansky.

He didn't see good options.

No one else gets killed. That was at the top of the list.

He picked out the best tree to put him in a position to cover Steadman and started to climb.

* * * * *

Jacob Solansky peered over the embankment again. He estimated it had been more than twenty minutes since he'd seen the chimp jump out of the tree and race off to the north. Maybe it was nothing.

Maybe it wasn't even the same chimp. If it was Guerrero's pet, it would've gone south toward their encampment.

Maybe it was chasing food. Or maybe it saw something that scared it. Maybe it had seen him from the tree and *he'd* scared it.

Or maybe they'd managed to track him and were out there waiting to pounce.

He'd picked this spot because it offered good cover against aerial searches and because it was defensible. What it lacked were good escape routes. In hindsight, he wished he'd prioritized that higher.

361

Hindsight's always twenty/twenty.

He scanned the horizon one more time. He was about to dismiss the whole idea when he caught a glimpse of motion.

He looked back to the southeast and saw it again. Something climbing a tree. Whatever it was was mostly obscured by the trunk, and all the branches and leaves between them, but something big was definitely in that tree.

It stopped about halfway up. When he saw a rifle extending out, his heart skipped a beat. He drew his handgun and braced it against the top of the embankment.

Why wasn't the rifle pointed at him? It looked to be aiming at something off to the north.

Well, no matter. He wasn't going to pass up an opportunity to take out one of their lethal weapons. He sighted in on the figure.

Unfortunately, the target's body was almost completely obscured behind the trunk. At this distance with a pistol, the odds were against him hitting even an exposed arm or hand. Even if he did, the shot wouldn't be fatal. And the sound of the gunshot would emphatically answer any questions they might still have about his whereabouts.

Wait for the shot. Be patient.

The adversary pulled his rifle back without firing a shot.

What's he up to?

The climber started down, still keeping himself on the back side of the tree where Solansky couldn't get a clean shot.

He was about to lose the opportunity. He was debating whether to take whatever shot he could get at the edge of the tree and hope for the best when he heard a commotion behind him.

He spun around to see the chimp racing over the opposite edge of the wash and directly toward him. The animal was waving its arms wildly and emitting an earsplitting scream.

Solansky raised his gun to fire at it, but before he could get off a shot his attention was seized by a bigger threat.

A bear came racing over the edge of the wash and sliding down the embankment directly toward Solansky. Reflex and muscle memory pointed the handgun at the center of the bear's mass and fired three quick rounds into its chest before it reached the bottom of the slope.

Solansky turned toward the water, expecting the bear to fall into a crumpled heap. He needed to make his escape quickly before Steadman or Guerrero homed in on the gunshots.

But as he was turning, he caught sight of continued motion from the bear. It picked itself up with a thunderous roar and charged straight at him. It took him only a fraction of a second to bring the gun back around. But in that fraction of a second, the bear closed most of the intervening distance.

TWO

Solansky managed to get two more shots into the bear's chest as he tried to raise the gun for a head shot, but the bear was too fast. It crashed into him, knocking him to the ground, then fell on top of him, pinning his arms.

Solansky couldn't point the gun but fired two more shots in the vain hope that they'd hit something.

The bear pushed himself up and opened his jaws. The motion freed Solansky's arms enough that he could point the gun into the bear's belly.

As the bear's jaws came down around Solansky's throat, he fired the rest of the clip as quickly as he could, certain beyond doubt that it would be too little, too late.

Day 15, 0845 Hours

By the time Guerrero got to the wash, it was over. As he slid down the embankment, he saw Steadman coming down the other side to join him. Yogi was still moving, though just barely. When he saw Guerrero and Steadman approach, he tried to pick himself up, managing only to roll off Solansky and collapse again to the ground. He let out a low growl and stopped breathing.

There was no question from the condition of Solansky's body that he also was dead.

Guerrero heard a soft hoot and looked up to see Mikey staring over the edge of the embankment at him. Mikey came down beside them and hooted again.

She held out a fist to Guerrero.

Guerrero picked her up. As she wrapped her arms around his neck, he said, "This isn't something we celebrate."

FORTY-ONE

Decker hiked down the hillside toward camp, the trail going dim in the twilight. The memorial service for Weaver would be tomorrow morning, and he'd needed time to collect his thoughts.

He could see the team beginning to collect around the campfire in the distance. It had become a ritual for them over the past three weeks.

Family time.

He was proud of what they'd accomplished together. They were quickly becoming quite a team. Crises often do that. They bring out either the best in people or the worst. And sometimes both.

It seemed that almost nothing had gone according to plan on this mission. But in his experience, things rarely did. Helmuth von Moltke once said, "No plan survives first contact with the enemy." Contact with the enemy had certainly derailed things here. But they had come together when it counted. Stood with courage. Learned to leverage each other's strengths.

Dr. Culpepper had perhaps come the furthest. She and Swenson still argued about whether God was behind all this or it was just nature, but the arguments now were less personal and more intellectual. She had finally grudgingly admitted that they were most likely really on another planet.

She and Sakhr were making good progress on a garden and greenhouse on the south end of the camp, Culpepper doing most of the gardening and Sakhr building the greenhouse with help from Guerrero.

Dr. Sakhr was another success story. He was finally getting to put some effort into mineral and geological surveys, but his biggest contributions had risen from his willingness to step in wherever he was needed and do whatever it took. He'd taken shifts monitoring surveillance drones, volunteered to be Guerrero's spotter when they were using the caving drone to track Solansky, built Swenson's still, and was now building Culpepper's greenhouse. His resourcefulness and out-of-box thinking made a big difference.

Dr. Zindell was still recovering from his gunshot wound but didn't let that be an excuse to not get his job done. He was working well with Dr. Culpepper, despite the two having gotten off on the wrong foot, and despite still disagreeing strongly about the interpretation of their research.

Between Tornquist, Culpepper, and Zindell, they had closed most of the nutritional gaps and were already eating mostly local food. Culpepper had even found a source for caffeine, which was what would be in everyone's mug tonight. It was more akin to tea than coffee, but so long as it had caffeine, no one was complaining. Swenson wanted to call it "twofee," but the others were desperately searching for a different name. Decker was afraid if they didn't come up with something soon, the name would stick.

Zindell had finally gotten his steak-and-potato dinner last night thanks to Guerrero's marksmanship, Steadman's skill with a grill, and Zindell's own study of the indigenous animals.

He was proud of Guerrero too. His idea to use the tranquilizer gun to try to capture Solansky alive was more than just good tactical thinking. It showed the emotional maturity to be able to set aside his thirst for vengeance for the good of the team. It was most unfortunate that circumstances prevented the execution of that plan. Their last hope of learning what might be happening on Earth was gone.

As Decker neared the campfire he could tell the conversation was already in full swing, but as he joined the circle everyone stopped talking.

"Don't stop on account of me. I might get the idea you're all here planning a mutiny."

Culpepper, never one to avoid conflict, spoke. "We were just comparing theories about what's happening on Earth. Care to share your thoughts?"

Decker looked off to his right toward the silent portal. He looked back at the team. "I really don't know any more than you, but you have a right to an honest assessment. You all know Earth is less than unified. Over the last twenty years, the Republic has done a lot to advance the causes of peace and prosperity around the world, but the reality is that not everyone wants peace, and not everyone wants prosperity. At least, not everyone wants everyone else to be prosperous. The Republic wields a lot of power in the world today. Most of it economic. We have a formidable defense capability, but it's no secret we don't have the preeminent military on the planet."

"You think war has broken out?" Sakhr asked.

"No. It's possible, but I think a full-scale war is unlikely. If word has gotten out about this transport technology, which seems likely, given Solansky's presence on the project, it would certainly be cause for concern. This is a major technological leap ahead of every other nation on the planet. Even without knowing any details of how it works, they'll assume the military applications are similarly daunting, and they'll feel threatened. But the reality is that each of the major military powers fears the others more than it fears us. If one stands against us, the other two are more likely to come to our aid than to celebrate our demise."

"So, what do you think happened?" asked Culpepper.

"My best guess is a small-scale targeted attack. Probably sabotage by a sleeper cell. We now know they penetrated the program. Solansky would have been able to give them the location of Kreitzman's facility where

369

the portal work was being done. That's all they'd need to hit to put us in this predicament."

Sakhr looked into his cup. "And if Kreitzman was killed in the attack?"

Decker looked at Swenson.

Swenson grimaced. "I don't know for sure, but it was my impression that Kreitzman was very careful to make sure no one else knew enough to replicate his work. If he's lost, so is our way home."

Culpepper rolled her eyes. "That sounds pretty arrogant, keeping it all to himself. He put our lives in jeopardy with no backup plan."

"Maybe," Swenson said. "In his mind, it was stewardship. He felt he'd been given a powerful gift and with it a responsibility to ensure it wasn't misused. He hasn't kept the benefits of that gift from the world, only the secrets behind it."

Tornquist asked, "Do you think he might have archived the information somewhere, set to be released if anything happened to him?"

"No, I don't think he would have done that. First, it creates a weak link. All someone has to do is hack the archive. Second, just because something happened to him is no reason to unleash terror on the rest of the planet. He would have no control over who might get access to the archive after his passing. In his mind, our being stranded here is a small price to pay for the safety of Earth. I think he would also argue that the theory itself will always be archived with the original source. And that source is the only one who has the right to decide to whom it should be disclosed."

Tornquist raised her eyebrows. "The original source?"

Swenson looked at Culpepper and pursed his lips. "God. Dr. Kreitzman never took credit for his theory. He always said he believed the insights he had were given to him by God."

Culpepper rolled her eyes and shook her head. She opened her mouth to speak, but Decker cut her off.

"I think it's important for us to remember that we don't know that Dr. Kreitzman isn't alive and well, and working feverishly to come after us. But it may take time. Especially if international politics is giving them bigger problems to deal with. What we have to do today, and what we have to do tomorrow, doesn't depend on what's happening on Earth or when the portal will reopen. If the portal connects tomorrow, our mission isn't yet complete. We still owe Earth a more comprehensive study of the life on this planet. If the portal never connects, our survival depends on a more comprehensive study of life on this planet. We have the skills. Over the last three weeks, you've proven that."

Decker gestured to the hills and mountains surrounding them. "These hills overflow with all the resources we need. The question for us is not whether or not we'll survive. The question is whether we choose to just survive or to thrive. I don't know what the future holds, but I know what we have to do tomorrow. That's our focus."

371

TWO

Day 21, 0900 Hours

Decker led the single-file procession as they hiked the half mile to the top of the hill. Steadman and Zindell were waiting at the summit, but everyone else had chosen to walk. Zindell wanted to walk too, but Tornquist insisted hiking half a mile uphill over rugged terrain on crutches wasn't an option.

As he approached the top of the hill, he saw two groomed mounds of fresh dirt, and a third hole not yet filled.

He'd spent most of two days walking the surrounding hills looking for this location. He settled on this spot because it overlooked the valley where they'd made landfall. If she were here, she could look out over them as they worked. She would be able to see the garden and the greenhouse. The surrounding hills with their groves of fruit trees. And in the distance, the mountains.

But not the waterfall. As much as Pam had loved the spectacular view of the water cascading over the cliffs, it just didn't seem appropriate. Not the waterfall.

Steadman and Guerrero had taken care of burying Solansky yesterday. There was no memorial service. No one begrudged Solansky the dignity of a decent burial, but no one felt any need to pay respects.

They'd also buried Yogi. Zindell had come up for that. And Mikey.

No one thought Mikey really understood what was going on. She had bonded with both Guerrero and

372

Zindell, so when they both loaded up in the four-wheeler, she tagged along.

Still, it seemed fitting somehow.

As for why Zindell went, he'd spent three days studying Yogi's remains and collecting tissue samples. He'd probably developed something of an emotional connection over that time.

He wanted to keep the carcass for further study. Steadman too had argued that the hide might prove valuable if they had to tough out a harsh winter.

But Decker insisted on burying Yogi between Weaver and Solansky. He wanted the grave to serve as a reminder. Their actions here had consequences.

As Decker reached the site, the rest of the group circled around the grave. Mikey sat on the ground between Zindell and Guerrero. She kept looking up, first at one, then the other, as if trying to understand what was happening.

Steadman and Guerrero had come earlier in the morning and lowered the makeshift casket, built from shipping crates joined together, into the ground.

Decker remained silent for several minutes, giving everyone time to reflect on what they would remember about Pam and the impact she'd had on their life.

He remembered when he first met her, just before this mission began. The infectious smile she couldn't suppress, no matter how hard she tried. The thorough professionalism with which she performed her duties. The courage she showed in overcoming her fear of Mikey to offer her a snack. Only to scream like a schoolgirl the next day when Mikey sneaked up behind her and stole her cap. Her enthusiastic participation in campfire debates.

Decker cleared his throat. "She wanted to name this planet Benignitas. It's a Latin word with three different meanings. The first is kindness, benevolence, friendliness, or courtesy. I think she sensed all of that in this place. Or, perhaps, she only saw a reflection of herself. She was certainly all those things."

Tornquist wiped a tear from her eye.

"The second is liberality, bounty, or favor. Certainly an apt description of the world that now surrounds us. And I think those who knew her would say it describes her as well. The third is leniency, forgiveness, or mercy. And while I think it's hard to see any of those in this circumstance, I think it's important to remember that it was not this world that showed her no mercy. That came from another place, and we brought it here with us. That transgression cost us our dearest treasure. But we've found all of that here. Forgiveness. Mercy. Benevolence. Bounty. And we will always remember Pam's sacrifice that opened this planet to us and to everyone who follows."

Decker paused, struggling to maintain his composure.

"May your spirit dwell forever in the house of the Lord Most High."

FORTY-TWO

The man behind the desk reread the report.

There's definitely been an industrial accident of some sort at one of Dr. Kreitzman's facilities. Best guess is about ten days ago. Everything about it has been classified under national defense criteria, so details are sketchy and hard to get. What we can piece together is that a large explosion took out the facility but was contained within the structure. Several (no exact count available) confirmed fatalities and a larger number of serious injuries. Location and purpose of the facility are not known, nor is the cause of the explosion. There have been no civilian observations consistent with such an industrial accident, so it is presumed to have occurred at a secret facility outside populated areas.

It appears Dr. Kreitzman's activities are beginning to extend beyond energy and into national defense. Recommend strongly that we redouble efforts to place assets inside his organization.

Insubordinate dolt. It's not your job to make recommendations. It's your job to observe and report.

It was good information, though. It called into question the proposition that they were on another planet. The bomb was set to go off well after the scheduled cargo transfer. If the explosion occurred here, the purported transfer never happened.

It would be interesting to see if and when any of the project team popped back up. Were they all in the facility where the explosion was contained or were they elsewhere?

Solansky's handler, the conduit for his reports, had been caught and interrogated. His trail led back to Russia. Not ideal, but it could have been worse.

I still have another man in there. This isn't over yet.

AFTERWORD

Since at least the beginning of recorded history, mankind has looked at the stars with wonder. Not all civilizations have had the same understanding of what the lights in the night sky represent, but they've all pondered them with awe. It's as if somewhere deep in our souls some part of us knows that we were meant to be out there.

But how do we get there? And what will we find?

As science has expanded our understanding of the nature of the universe through the centuries, our imaginations have led the way. This is the domain of science fiction: to imagine how things might be, in the absence of certain knowledge.

This is also the beginning of science. We call it a theory, an idea about how things might work. It's a fancy word for a guess. The scientific process involves making observations about the way things happen, imagining why they might happen that way, and then finding ways to test whether our idea about how things work is correct.

A theory is not a fact. It is a possible explanation for a fact. Newtonian physics is a theory. General relativity is a theory. Darwinian evolution is a theory. None of these are themselves facts, and for all three of these, we can point to hard physical observations that prove them to be incorrect.

Despite these contradictions, we continue to use these theories to describe our universe. We do this either because they're the best theories we have and they work for most things (Newtonian Physics and General Relativity), or because we don't have another theory that doesn't make us extremely uncomfortable (arguably the reason Darwinian Evolution still holds sway, despite its gaping holes).

So why this book?

I hope you've been entertained by this story. More than that, I hope that you've found something in it that inspires you. And maybe you've learned something too.

As I said before, science fiction is about imagining what might be. Over the centuries, as our collective understanding of what *is* has evolved, science fiction has evolved with it.

Obviously part of the science in this story is fictional. This is, after all, science fiction. But most of the science presented is real. Every branch of science, when you get past the popular misrepresentations, points to design in the universe.

What if the universe *is* a created, designed thing? What if there *is* a God out there who designed it? If it's true, what impact does that have on how we answer the questions asked earlier: "How do we get there?" "What will we find?"

I hope this book will inspire you to think about those questions.

If the idea that science and faith can complement—rather than contradict—each other is new to you, I hope this story will encourage you to dig deeper.

If you come to this story already established in faith, I hope you'll recognize that *real* science can't help but tell us about the God who created the world we study. I also hope you understand there's a lot of junk science out there; we live in a world full of people invested in the premise that there is no God who will try to twist reality to support their position.

The apostle Paul told us to "Test everything. Hold on to what is good."

So think. And don't ever stop.

BY THE AUTHOR

Alex Guerrero and Teri Culpepper had nothing in common.

He was an elite warrior, trained to be a leader in Earth's premier fighting force.

She was an academic, a professor of botanical sciences, struggling to keep enough grants coming in to support her meager research.

But now circumstances have forced them together, the lives of eight people hanging on the success of their daring mission into unexplored territory on an unknown planet.

Can they work together to find the secret to survival on this alien world, or will their rivalry doom the entire expedition?

Also watch your favorite bookseller for **ONE**, the upcoming midquel to **TWO**.

ACKNOWLEDGMENTS

With any creative effort, the creation is a reflection of its creator. So just as we learn about God when we study his creation, you'll learn a lot about me when you read this book.

Who I am, and thus what this book has come to be, is the product of a lifetime of interactions with people who have influenced me. It would take another lifetime to recount them all, so I'll just mention a few here.

I'd like to thank the folks at the Rockwall Christian Writer's Group for their valuable support, critique, and coaching. Without you, this project would likely never have come together.

My beta readers provided valuable feedback that substantively improved the final product. In particular, I'd like to thank author Luke Scott, author LM Hinton, and Greg Eastman for taking the time to read this book in its raw form and for their insightful comments.

Several non-fiction books have influenced my thinking regarding the reconciliation of faith and science. These include: I Don't Have Enough Faith to be an Atheist, by Norman Geisler and Frank Turek; Signs of Intelligence:

Understanding Intelligent Design, edited by William A. Dembski; Darwin's Black Box: The Biochemical Challenge to Evolution, by Michael J. Behe; and Intelligent Design: The Bridge Between Science and Theology, by William A. Dembski.

I'd also like to thank John Langford, my middle school Sunday School teacher, who taught me that real men trust in God;

Eddie Keilberg, my high school physics and chemistry teacher, who taught me that true science doesn't contradict the real God;

My mom and dad, who raised me in a home where I knew I was safe and loved, and who both worked hard and made personal sacrifices to make sure my brothers and I had every opportunity to become everything God created us to be;

My wife, Christy, and our son, Ben, whose endless faith in me made this project possible;

And most of all, the God who chose me to play this small part in his story.

ABOUT THE AUTHOR

Steve Swaringen is a husband and father living in Rockwall, Texas. He earned a Bachelor of Science degree in Electrical Engineering from Texas A&M University, College Station.

He believes passionately that if our faith is true—that God created this world—real science cannot help but point the way to its Creator.

To learn more, visit SteveSwaringen.com.

www.ingramcontent.com/pod-product-compliance
Lightning Source LLC
Chambersburg PA
CBHW070629180626
46817CB00006B/2082